Sacred sacre

TRUST ME I AM A PRIEST

LEO CAVANAGH

THREESCORE PUBLISHING LIMITED

Published by 3SCORE PUBLISHING
Sothams Farmhouse   Pond Hill
STONESFIELD 0X29 8PZ

www.3scorepublishing.co.uk

info@3scorepublishing.co.uk
01993 891956

©2010 Leo Cavanagh
World copyright reserved

ISBN 978-0-9564029-2-9

The right of Leo Cavanagh to be identified as the author of this work has been asserted by him in accordance with the Copyright, Designs and Patents Act 1988.

All rights reserved. No part of this publication may be reproduced, stored in a retrieval system, or transmitted in any form or by any means electronic, mechanical, photocopying, recording or otherwise, without the prior permission of the publishers.

3SCORE PUBLISHING is a writers' cooperative for publishing books by or about older people.

1

Abuse, hypocrisy, cover-up, anger at the betrayal of the innocent by those with a vocation to holiness.

Do you remember your feelings of surprise and anger about these things in the cold winter and spring of 2010? In March, in the aftermath of over nine years of investigation and two official government reports, the Roman Catholic hierarchy in Ireland finally received a blistering public rebuke in the form of a letter from Pope Benedict XVI.

But in that atmosphere of distrust there were allegations that this same Pope, Joseph Ratzinger, had himself reassigned a chaplain priest known to be an abuser to another position giving access to children, when he was the Archbishop of Munich back in 1980. Then, when he reached Rome Cardinal Ratzinger had headed the Congregation for the Doctrine of the Faith under Pope John-Paul II, and the CDF had been slow to handle cases of abuse like that by Father Murphy of deaf and dumb students in the USA.

Why should you care about this? Maybe my own anger will show you why. I was not abused – or maybe it was abuse? – but in the months following March 2010 I heard from someone who was definitely abused, and I have learnt to share his outrage.

Maybe you will sense a deep anticlericalism in me. I won't try to hide it. Why am I so outraged? Because of the callous cruelty but even more because of the cover-ups that made the abuse all the more cruel.

You may shrug and say 'Let the Roman Church get on with it'. But I am not happy unless the guilty are named, blamed and punished. I had suspected that some crazy mind-set of the clerics was the reason for all this evil. Circumstances taught me that it was true. I learnt just what that mindset was.

So, back in the spring of 2010 I read about it all and wondered, like you, how it had happened.

Early in 2010 the real stories for most of us were not the clerical sexual scandals but election fever, the fear of a double-dip recession, and general Afghanistan gloom. I was moping after a sad bit of history with a special female member of the Roman church which I will tell you about later, when suddenly I found myself thrown into investigating one particular clerical criminal incident, with a mandate to pin the blame for it squarely where it belonged.

It was on an April morning that I got a call from Bill, who was an editor with *Sunday Seven*, with the hint of some investigative journalism work. Still affected by the failure of my marriage to Sarah Louise, I had not yet recovered my normal high-powered steam as I nursed a sense of hurt and unwillingness to go out and see friends. My reputation was based on articles which were deeply researched, often around an interview with people who put themselves gently on my dangled hook. The fun was in watching them wriggle, and my sense of justification came from the fact that I knew they deserved exposure. That sort of journalism needs a network of newspaper editors and commissioning editors for TV willing to make promises to be interested in the outcome, so every idea needs to be sold before you go out and do the hard work. I am good at getting the facts and analysing them, so in my recent fallow period I had kept the wolf from the door by writing briefings and reports for a business-to-business market research agency: but in terms of career, I was fearful that I had lost my way. If not having the courage to run with a new idea is the same as being depressed, maybe I was depressed. I didn't want to talk to anyone unless I had to.

I call myself an investigative journalist. I am not one of those intrepid souls bearding fraudsters in their hideaways, but a more reflective investigator looking to interview those dodgy high-placed folk who deny or are unaware that they have anything to be ashamed of, and who are willing to speak to me. I had been lucky to get where I was, depending on a nice balance of reputation and obscurity. I was not notorious enough to be on the *'no interview'* lists of the public relations departments, but well enough known to have my articles accepted by British newspapers of every variety. Two books had helped to get me started, one the near-spoof *Pre-eminent Victorians*, the other a short documentary of army life from the viewpoint of the military wives, in their own words. That had made

3

me a feminist and wiped out most of what was left of my naivety: but not all of it by any means. After all, I met Sarah Louise after the army book.

Bill sent me two attachments. The first was an incomprehensible piece of legal talk, seemingly to do with two clerics, Monsignor Peter Mobile, the British Ordinary of *Pietas* and Bishop Marcus Andrews of the Langdon Diocese. I knew of the first through personal experience, but nothing at all about the bishop. The second was a photograph, which had been scanned and didn't reproduce that well.

I ran my eyes over it. There was a circular archery target on the left side of the picture, set up on a lawn. It was obviously a warm summer day and there was a sense of spaciousness about the composition. On the right there were seven naked boys, all between eight and ten years old at a guess, each holding an extended bow in their hands. Each boy had an arrow in his bow, and was pulling the string back tautly. It was a fine piece of stylish bowmanship I guessed, but the beauty and fascination of the picture went beyond that. Each boy's legs were bent, one leg almost making a right angle with the ground, while the other stretched behind. It was a beautiful photo, no doubt, but it was also really intriguing.

I called back Bill. We went back a long way, in fact we were at school and university together, and we had both started out working for the university media. Bill was a mover and shaker, so ambitious but so successful – at what? Downmarket journalism – he sniffed at my relative poverty, I sneered at his dumbing down, but then, he had never de-dumb-dumbed, had he?

"It's Greek, this photo", I said to him, taking in the stance of male athletes showing their genitals with cocky nonchalance. "In feel, I mean." These were unselfconscious boys, I thought, innocent of any self-display.

"We've not traced it", said Bill, "But we think it comes from a brochure of a nudist camp. Nothing recent though. Originally black and white, with a relatively long exposure time."

"That could account for the quality and contrast, and maybe some of the concentration on the boys' faces. But what has it got to do with the first document?" I asked. "I can't see either of the priests taking a holiday in a naturist colony."

"We're going to find out. There's a whistle-blower here who is frightened to speak his name, and we're sure that someone like you should be able to get through to him. You don't have to have a by-line unless you want it. Alexis Lecce will be the second string for whoever takes this on. You know her?"

"Not really. I think Sarah Louise may have mentioned that name, but I never met her. She belonged to *Pietas*, I'd pretty sure. You want to make a show of balance, I suppose. Can I use the research for other articles?"

"It's not closed down, absolutely not, if you want to write an exposé of *Pietas* for example. You know why I thought of you, don't you?"

"You mean Sarah Louise being a member, of course, and all the business of the annulment."

"Yes. I felt that you would have something to drive your research."

"Like hatred?" I asked. "You're not in luck. Even though you might think there is some grudge factor in what I target, it's not true. I can't afford to get away from objectivity, facts and more facts and even giving the counter-case an airing. I don't have a legal department, after all. Not like your eminent journal. But hold on – what are you proposing to do with the dirt about these clerics? Are you spoiling someone else's career or just targeting the Church in general?"

"Oh come on Mike! I just thought that with Sarah Louise being a *Pietas* member you would have an edge, maybe a better insight into what a Christian sect can do to your life."

"They're not a sect, Bill. Yes, I do have an insight. I know their rock hard stubbornness of belief, how narrow-minded they are, and their eagerness to follow the Vatican line and impose it on the lives of everyone else. I call their mind-set fascist. But I don't hate them, just respect them."

It was a lie of course.

"I'll forget you said that" Bill replied. "Meet us for lunch."

I switched into my business mode. The only thing my father had ever taught me was the fear of being poor.

"What are you going to pay?"

"Send a proposal for five days research and an article, whether published or not we'll pay you. Pitch your rate for a national paper with a bigger circulation than those things you usually write for."

"Means how much exactly?" I asked. He told me, adding "We'll pay expenses as well."

"Do I get to Rome?" The Icelandic volcano's closedown of flights over Europe was just ending, and I fancied a visit to Italy.

"Not without authorisation. And not unless you have to. I don't think you should expect it – it's an English job. The first thing is to get the hunches together, this week. Do you know how to get started on it?"

"Could I have the cuttings on the two clerics?"

"Who have you been working for? – *The Times*? Well, of course you have. I'm afraid we don't work like that. No Mike, you'll need to do this yourself. Maybe Google will have something. But Alexis will have some ideas. She brought us this story, in fact" Bill concluded.

"I appreciate that I haven't got the job yet", I replied "but can you tell me if there is in fact some specific dirt at issue? I'm not a spiteful person, I swear, even if Pietas destroyed Sarah Louise's and my marriage. But if there is some child abuse or that sort of thing it will give a direction and even a feeling that I'm doing something worthwhile."

"It must be, but it's a bit tenuous at the moment. I'm sure you'll find people out there who know. See you."

I felt pretty sure that abuse was at the back of all this: it was a big story just then, as I have explained. The Irish Church had recently been shown to have concealed tens of cases of abuse over more than a quarter of a century, and only all the force of government had got the facts out into the light. Just a month before, in March 2010, there was that protest in Rome on behalf of two hundred deaf boys abused in the USA by Father Murphy, a priest never brought to justice. The protesters didn't hesitate to call for Pope Benedict's resignation, and His Holiness was going to be in England in the autumn of the same year, 2010.

An hour and a half later I was waiting inside Alighieri, an Italian restaurant close to Sloane Square. When you went in and left the street behind you it was like the muffled shutting of a Daimler's door. The walls were as white as the sharply folded linen and there was a tang of durum bread and starch. This is warm, welcome urban employment, I thought, rather than the slog of suburban scratching at a living and the loneliness of my latest life. I was alliterating in relief. No doubt I should phone Bill before having a drink, but using a mobile would be disrespectful to the style of the users of a rich holy space like this.

I ordered a Campari soda, less to bolster my status as an intellectual than to calm my nerves, and continued to compose myself as I slowly sipped it. I was unusually jittery: how could I succeed in teasing secrets from people whose lives were devoted to doing good and at the worst at least looking as if they were good? The fact that the briefest earnest eye contact with a religious person was enough to trigger strong feelings of repugnance, intellectual snobbery and condescension in me and my friends did not change the assurance of the pious that they were good people in a world of swivel-eyed sinners and cynics. I had once given them the benefit of the doubt, but something had tipped me into despising the whole clerical caste.

Bill came through the door with Alexis Lecce. Alexis was twenty-seven, Mediterranean in colour, small and narrow-waisted, and dressed in a black trouser suit with a white blouse. She had large brown eyes, calm and not yet beset by wrinkles. Those eyes could be neglected in an audit of her facial beauty because her mouth was always expressive, now showing her white teeth as she smiled towards me, showing a brief delight in having me as a colleague she believed could do the business.

All this was before we spoke. I saw that the way she held her head was graceful, enquiring and upright, and those large clear eyes had met mine with every atom of those qualities. She looked quite a bit aggressive, as well. Bill led us to a table and our conference began.

"Alexis reminded me about what you could bring to the story", Bill said. "Authority and an established and growing reputation as an investigative journalist and writer of polemics."

"He wants to tempt me with the prospect of uncovering more dirt", I said to Alexis.

"What are you working on at the moment?" Bill asked me. "This guy has always been a ticking bomb, Alexis" he explained. "Even when we were working on *Cherwell,* the university paper, he would upstage me by writing big exposés once a term while I was slogging away at the bread and butter."

"It's nothing I can tell you about" I said, "You'll have to ply me with alcohol to prise it out."

Bill switched to his other guest. "Alexis is newly on board with us, but has a background in research."

"For TV documentaries, mainly", she explained. "Did you see the recent one on the gang-masters? I arranged the covert filming and got most of the story together."

"Alexis, we know you're good" Bill said.

"It was remarkable stuff", I said. "I don't think anyone got better viewing ratings for a documentary than that one. I can't say I saw your name, but you never can without speed-reading. I thought it was researched by a lawyer?"

"Alexis didn't appear in it" Bill explained, exchanging a glance with her, "and that's why we can use her again for the current work." Was there something they weren't telling me, I wondered. I didn't learn the full story of Alexis' place in the investigation until later, and that fact still rankles. But I was there to get some really well-paid work, so what the hell?

"Blimey", I said, "We're not trying to entrap clerics are we? I'm sure you could do that, Alexis. I know they're not all homosexuals."

"No, it's different", Bill explained. "And any more bigotry like that and you won't get the project, I'm sorry Mike, but that is your last chance. Anticlericalism? – button it! Alexis suspects that we have a really *good* priest behind this curious whistle-blowing. Yes, Alexis wants to help because she is in fact a Catholic. It's fair to call you a devout Catholic isn't it, Alexis?"

"Maybe that's going too far."

"But you go to Sunday Mass?" I asked. Going to Mass every week defines a devout Catholic.

"I try not to miss it" she said.

"What is Alexis supposed to be doing?" I asked. "Provide balance versus an agnostic sceptic?"

"Yes" Bill answered. "Something like that."

"Somewhat different from your reputation Bill", I said, "printing dire stories that ruin careers and have a tiny correction in an obscure corner if they should later turn out to be untrue."

"You'd better choose what you want to eat, Mike", Bill said, "because there's no such thing as a free lunch."

We ate extremely well. Our lunchtime planning session began with a toast.

"*Pietas!*" said Bill.

"May it prove worthy of its name" said Alexis.

"May it have a mystery that can be illuminated" I added. We drank.

We decided to concentrate on *Pietas* rather than the Bishop at the start of our research. Despite the deepened distrust of the Church in the current clerical abuse scandals, Bill thought I would have no trouble in getting an interview with Monsignor Peter Mobile, their 'Ordinary' or chief.

"Just show your usual diplomacy, Mike."

"I'll get an interview with *Pietas*" I promised.

Alexis chipped in.

"I'm already a viator – that's what they call us – with *Pietas*" she explained. "So I can almost certainly get us an interview with Peter Mobile."

"Actually I think I've got the best entrée" I said, "because of my ex- wife Sarah Louise's membership."

"I've told Alexis about that" said Bill.

"I hope you told her the truth. Fact was, we were never married properly at all. Anyway, *Pietas* was involved quite a lot, and a weasel lie to get in there is not against my mores. But isn't telling lies against your creed?" I asked her.

"If I was as literal as that I would never have been a sleuth", Alexis said.

"A sleuth - I haven't heard that word for years. Do you smoke and drink whisky?"

"I don't mind the whisky. But you're lucky to have me, Mike, don't doubt it. You must be aware that to outsiders *Pietas* is more secretive than a Masonic Lodge."

"It sounds as if you are not as enamoured of *Pietas* as you used to be, Alexis", I said. "Have you decided to shop them?"

She blew out her rather attractive lips and said "Ish."

"Ish - that's about as brief an answer as you could give. What made you decide to go on a sleuthing track?" I asked.

"It's a bit of a story" she replied. "But I promise you'll find out."

"Alexis tells me she actually knew Sarah Louise" Bill said.

"Yes, I did. But the news value has to be in connection with clerical abuse, doesn't it Bill? Surely, with all these awful revelations just now? Have you read about the Boston diocese investigations in the *Guardian* today?"

"Oh of course. There is an anti-Church bias around the media in Britain, and we're part of it too" Bill admitted. "But don't you think Pope Benedict is a bit much, Alex? – all holier than thou, but with such a lot to account for?"

13

"Well, Bill, His Holiness, as Cardinal Ratzinger, was the Prefect of the Congregation for the Doctrine of the Faith for over twenty years, and so he was responsible for handling accusations of abuse against the clergy, worldwide. Maybe he does."

"He's the Pope, what do you expect?" Alex laughed. "Though I must admit that he looks to me like a schoolboy who is always thinking 'Am I the brightest in the class?' and then deciding that he *is* top of the class – at least until bedtime."

No love lost there, I thought. We really must both be on the same side, after all.

"You know, it might be better if you made the approach to Peter Mobile, Alexis" I said. I was getting cold feet about losing face if Monsignor Peter Mobile turned me down. A female always has more success in getting an interview with a difficult male prospect because men still like to please the ladies, even in the 21st century. That could be true for the Monsignor, even though women have a low place in the *Pietas* world. But I knew I was fooling myself, even as I spoke, so reluctantly I told them about my real reason for caution.

"Given Bill's awful warning about keeping my anti-clericalism to myself, I need to fess up to a little history with Peter Mobile" I told them. "I do know him. Actually, quite well."

That put the two in a sympathetic posture, I hoped. What I had to tell made me wince, even now.

14

"It was when Sarah Louise and I were being counselled about our marriage – all six weeks of it as it turned out. Peter Mobile himself was our counsellor. You'll find this hard to believe, but I actually flirted with the idea of joining *Pietas*." In fact this was a slightly doctored version of what actually happened, but it seemed appropriate for them at the time.

"Oh, oh!" Bill said. "So you can go back, surely, and say that you want to go on with conversion, can't you?"

"You're an insensitive cynic Bill" Alexis said. "You've not got a hack who wants to bribe a criminal to tell their story to *Sunday Seven*, you know, no matter what your guys normally do."

I thanked Alexis. "Actually, if push came to shove I could do exactly that, except – except I did something that will surprise you – I actually wrestled with Peter Mobile. Yes, wrestling, like they used to have it on television."

"Wrestled?" Bill asked in amazement. "In the buff?"

"No, it was quite innocent, even if odd. That's what he does with lots of men. All right, young men."

"I've heard that" said Alexis. "Dodgy if you want to point the finger, but otherwise?"

"I don't like him" I admitted, "but what I want to say is – we have been as close as that."

"Are you coming out as gay, Mike, is that it?"

"I don't think so. No, there's something unfinished about Peter Mobile in my life. I think the project will

15

give me some closure. I've told you about it because I want to keep everything out in the open."

"And because you'd be mortified if we heard about it later from someone else" Bill said triumphantly. "Thanks for telling us, Mike. I'm sure you can do this job."

2

It only took two days to get through the door at *Pietas*.

The first reason was that *Pietas* had decided that a flight from the media – refusing interviews with journalists – was a poor strategy in the after-abuse-scandals world. The movement had no scandals and no schools in Britain, plus none of the long-term history that set most clerical abuse back in the decades before 2000. Importantly, unlike the Legionaries of Christ or some older-established orders and societies it had no seminaries and no seminarians bringing stories of abuse to the public arena.

The second reason was that the British public were still intrigued to know whether other Roman Catholic institutions resembled *Opus Dei* as depicted in *The Da Vinci Code*. The real *Opus Dei* organisation had used the interest in that book to correct its many slanderers and reach a wider public. It had spoken up for the Pope too, defending his record on clerical abuse. Most other Roman Catholic institutions were not that keen to meet the press, but *Pietas* – whether justified or not – seemed to feel they would now get sympathetic treatment rather than a fictional blackwash.

Of course *Pietas* is not *Opus Dei* – it is beyond it in its popularity with the Vatican, untainted with any links with fascism in Spain and very much smaller. It is still young, growing and absolutely at one with Vatican teaching.

17

I waited for Alexis outside the Roman Catholic church that was the centre of the *Pietas* parish in London – the only parish they possessed in the whole of England, though there was another one in Scotland. It was quite an impressive neo-Gothic Victorian structure, and there were elegant buildings behind which there was a school and the *Pietas* headquarters. Monsignor Peter Mobile, the cleric in the leaked email, was both the parish priest here and the English Ordinary – the head – of *Pietas*.

I had visited this place three or four times before and after Sarah Louise and I went through the ceremony of marriage, but though I had actually been in Peter Mobile's personal flat, as well as the official rooms below, I had never been to the office which was his main place of work outside the church itself.

Alexis appeared around the corner. "We're going to visit the school and then go on to see the Monsignor at 10.30 for coffee", she told me. Today she was in a white skirt, her arms were covered and she looked pure-distant-virginal-demure.

"Good disguise, sleuth" I said.

"Remind me to show you how to say sleuth with the proper respect", she replied. "I can't say that your garments are that great for someone who is published by *The Times*."

"You don't know the dress code of journalists, do you? I never wear a suit, for heaven's sakes."

18

"Or iron your trousers, obviously."

I took stock of her remark. I needed to get myself up to scratch, clearly. Being the son of a soldier had always meant that appearances had got to be kept right, and absolute tidiness was essential for all kit. I would get out the iron tonight. Catching sight of the rest of my clothes, I knew Alexis was wrong. I looked into the mirror at the reception area and saw a straight-backed medium-height young man with a good button-down shirt, a sweater around his shoulders, big glasses, a dark but clean-shaven face, and a bald-shaved head. I should be recognisable anywhere as a professional in casual gear. Shamefully, the trousers were baggy, but she would see, she would see.

We went in to see the Head Teacher, and were taken into two classes of eight and nine year olds to observe the lessons.

I noticed that one of the classes was almost entirely made up of white children while the other had a standard London ethnic mix – that was odd.

We met the Headteacher, and I asked her some questions. Yes, this was a Catholic school, and fee-paying, so it was run on the lines laid down by *Pietas*.

She dodged my question about the lack of an ethnic mix in one class. "There's nothing sinister about it", she said. "Monsignor Peter chooses which children go into which class himself – that's based on what he knows about the parents."

"Are you operating a two-tier system then?" I asked.

"Ask him. *Pietas* is not afraid of rankings and hierarchies and differences and streaming and the rich way that different skills are spread around. But it may have more to do with religious practice – why don't you ask him?"

"You're not egalitarian?" Alexis asked.

"So right!" the Head replied. She stood up behind her huge well-ordered desk and joked – "and the Head has more important people to see just now."

"Not a Bangladeshi mother looking for reassurance", I thought to myself.

We walked across the playground to the tall presbytery, which I recalled from my pre-marriage visits with Sarah Louise. The corridor from the arched front door was wide and painted white, and there were large offices on either side where the reception rooms of a Victorian family house had once been. We passed by the St Pius room, which had particularly painful memories for me.

We walked upstairs towards a small room on a mezzanine floor two flights up at the back of the property. "Just take a look at the rooms here as you go past" she said. "It's a students' hostel and a youth club, you know."

I knew. The smell of good carpeting had faded a bit over the past two years, but there was still that stuffiness in the air despite the high ceilings. The big sash windows were all closed on this spring morning, and there was a quiet air conditioning hum.

20

Alexis knocked on the door of the Ordinary's office. I had never set foot in this part of the premises before. There was a shout and we went in.

You might have a mental picture of Peter Mobile as Italian, thin, wearing a cassock and a smug self assured simper, with the pomposity, primness and wisdom of 'Dignity'. But he wasn't like that at all. I saw again a short, stocky man in his fifties, with white frizzy hair and piercing blue eyes. I felt a need to control my lips as I recalled with distaste my past infatuation with Peter Mobile, not as a person to be loved but as a teacher who would release me from the fears and obsessions that tainted my life.

As always, Peter looked quizzical and little inclined to make serious statements: the face of a naughty boy or a stand-up comedian with a wicked sense of humour. That was what his face promised, but what it always delivered was a message, a message of hope to those who could embrace an almost impossible standard of behaviour in their private and public lives.

That was the facial language from this cleric. But I could not be charmed by this man, could I, not again?

His body language was as restrained as ever, despite wearing a bright white tracksuit. He had squeaky clean new trainers which my later internet research identified as expensive and top of the range. But as he moved forward to crush my hand in his strong wide-nailed fingers I noticed that his slight limp had got even more detectable. Maybe he needed orthopaedic correction for those tiny feet?

He spoke to me first, though Alexis had arranged the interview.

"Old friend", he said, to which I did not reply. "Alexis, how nice to see you" he added. "Though I wonder should I thank you though for bringing in such a notorious big gun as Mike Claver to write about *Pietas*. I hope you'll be more objective than some of your journalistic colleagues, Mike. You do know more about us than most of them."

"Of course, all those things about *Opus Dei*", I replied. "*Opus Dei* claim that the problem with writers about them is that they have just got it plain wrong."

"I think *Opus Dei* have a good case there."

"Are you sympathetic to *Opus Dei*?"

"I'd be lying if I said I wasn't. But we are a different body, with our own special niche in the Church. Shouldn't I give you a journalist's briefing about the Catholic Church before we talk about *Pietas*, *The Noble Way*?"

"Peter", I answered, "you know that I attended the prenuptial course here, I was even thinking of becoming a Catholic for heaven's sakes. Besides other things. We don't need that."

I dreaded sitting listening to preaching which always sent me off hunting hatreds around the furniture and flooring as my tormented ears searched for a signal that the message was coming to an end. I refused to look any propagandist in the eye.

22

I went on. "Though I'm not a Catholic I *have* had quite an acquaintance with one not so long ago." I hoped he was picking up a little menace in my tone.

"Of course, of course, I've not forgotten Sarah Louise. Let me say how sorry I am that it didn't work out. But I hope that *Pietas* made a good impression on you."

"The care and attention of the members was truly impressive."

That was true. As for its general outlook, I couldn't say how strangely I felt about it, so I let Alexis jump in. Even then she had sensed that I was a loose cannon and liable to reveal my anger by some rude gibe at any time. She was right of course.

"How much time do you have, Peter? I think we need to get to the meat."

"You've turned down the meat which was the Church. So I'll give you the gravy, which is *Pietas*. We have an hour."

"Well I can ask a question about that connection" I said. "I understand that *Pietas* has evangelical Protestant members, and that it even has a Muslim cell. That sounds as if Roman Catholicism isn't that important."

"Slow down!" the cleric said. He mimed burning his fingers, with an 'infectious' grin. When I write 'infectious' I really mean that was the jolly impression he wanted to create. It was far from making me smile, and in fact it made me wince. My reaction was quite a

23

bit different from when I had first seen him use that gesture, I admit.

He said "We have identified an urge that is common to all religions – beyond worshipping the same God, I mean – for a practice of their religion which is worthy of the dignity of man as we understand it in the 21st century. In a simple way, how could a good Buddhist or a good Muslim or a good Jew or Protestant or Catholic Christian – how could each one live a life which is fully engaged with the world and live out the highest aspirations of their religion?"

"And the answer is?" I prompted. "You don't mind if I take notes, do you?" I asked. "*Ear tufts, let grow as balance versus vanity?*" I wrote. "*Very still, no fidgets.*"

Peter Mobile replied "The answer is that all religious people are involved in exactly the same quest to live well and achieve good in their lives."

Alexis chipped in "But when people say that the fundamentalists of all religions resemble each other, they are not usually paying them compliments."

"Yo yo!" I added. "Yes, they resemble each other in their mulish adherence to absolute conformity, their intolerance, bigotry and lack of any intellectual rigour. So how on earth can people so devoted to what makes them especially distinct ever join together in some body like *Pietas*?"

"You've got it off your chest, have you?" Peter Mobile teased. His good teeth flashed white against his sun-tanned face.

He went on. "What you say is true of so many fundamentalists, but they aren't the ones who join the way of piety. We attract those who wish to avoid the dangers of Phariseeism – I trust you know that word for un-self-critical zealots?" - I nodded – "but hang on to the sense of the absolute claim of God on their worship."

"In practice, do you have members of different faiths, and do they worship together?"

"Yes, we do have members like that. No, they don't worship together."

"Could I have your numbers, please – of each, including the Roman Catholics, of course?"

"It's too early to quantify yet. You know that the Church only started with twelve apostles: we don't get discouraged by small numbers."

"But isn't this a smokescreen?" Alexis asked. "Surely it's the RCs that are your backbone. That's what it is all about, isn't it? Carrying out the will of Christ manifest in the teaching of the Church?"

"Yes", he said, nodding sagely. I felt renewed irritation at his 'man of wisdom' mask. Nothing winds me up as much as the 'humble seeker of truth' posture.

"You don't like me telling the truth as I see it, do you Mike" he challenged. "You'd rather have a ding-dong."

"Well it makes for better journalism" I conceded.

"Listen", he said. "I'll give you the *Pietas* pitch, which I give to everyone. When you take it in, you've got the full Monty. May I?"

"I've heard it before, surely?"

"Not exactly like this." He turned a still somewhat impish face towards us and spoke.

"We are all just nothings, specks of sand. But we are not troubled because we have learnt that a loving, powerful but pitifully weak God wants to talk to us and walk with us. The word of God, one of the names of Christ, talks to us, plays with us, eats with us, walks with us. Talks to us as we are, and says 'You matter'.'

'Which means that everyone and anyone else matters too – they all matter. You must talk to them too, for God has spoken to you.'

'Amazingly, God addresses you as his equal in individuality and ability to share joy, saying 'Have my same love for those around you'. Recompose your face to smile and look to the eyes of your neighbour. Widen and widen the numbers of people you think are worthy of your care. Listen to them! Argue with them! The Word of God says be open to God and to others.'

'Even as you hear this message, you are achieving it. For you feel you are nothing, but you have been invited to a banquet as an extra guest and now you find you have been taken to the top table. Because the Word of God says – you are important.'

'And you find when you accept the invitation that you have to extend it to others. Now you are going to have to smile at people you wanted to ignore. Now you are going to have to speak to people you fear will snub you.'

'Risk it! As a writer your vocation is to the truth, but it is also to speaking and spreading that truth by the skill of your words.'

'Join those who are full of love, love found by practice. Listen to the Word of God and risk this belief – that you can change. Not on your own, but in talking and listening to the word as preached by *Pietas* within the Catholic Church."

So that was his sermon, with its personal message to me. He sat recollected as his blue eyes appraised us.

I haven't done justice to it, but he was good at his pitch. His implicit assumption was that I was still unhappy, unsure about how to live, and troubled by my own cynicism and anger. Spot on.

Then, as I turned away to renew my search of the floor for shreds of nonsense on which to hang my evasions of his bright eyes, I was surprised and delighted to suddenly see a copy of the picture of the boys with the bows and arrows on the wall almost behind me. That same picture that had been emailed to me was beautifully framed here, hung in a position which I now realised was significant to the person working at the other side of the desk: Monsignor Peter Mobile, no less.

As soon as I could I turned the conversation to the picture.

"Peter – what's with this picture? Isn't it a bit odd for a celibate priest to have such a picture on show?"

"Ah, you've seen it. Alexis is a candidate wayfarer of our society – could you explain it Alexis?"

"It's absolutely new to me" she said. "I think you'll need to do that."

"I'm surprised you didn't see it during your marriage course, Mike. Well, this is called 'The Arrows of Innocence' – that's what we call it in the movement, anyway. It represents mankind's highest spiritual aspirations."

"Not!" I said. I had no sense that scepticism would rattle Peter Mobile in any way – it never had done in the past. "I bet you haven't had anyone with the guts to tell you that this looks like the sick fantasy of a homosexual paedophile, have you?"

"I'm not rising to that. It is called 'Innocence' you know, and there's nothing else but innocence there. You are bringing a nasty – yes, nasty, Mike – prurience to something simple and good."

"With a spiritual message? Are we supposed to be reminded of a muscular Saint Stephen bristling with arrows and blood, when it looks like slim Cupids tilting at unclothed pagan gods? It's a 21st century equivalent of the erotic paintings of a Renaissance Pope. It's ludicrous", I laughed.

He stood up. "There's no point in continuing like this", he said. "You are here in an incredibly aggressive frame of mind and there's nothing I can say to you that will change that."

Alexis gave me a look of exasperation – I had messed up right at the start.

"I'm sorry – I judged that you could engage at that level of ..."

"Insult?"

"Vigorous discussion."

"You're absolutely right, but I'm talking as the representative of *Pietas*."

Alexis interposed "Mike wanted to know if the fact that one of your classes seems to have no ethnic minorities at all was part of a policy."

"That's another aggressive line of questioning I hadn't expected. Christians believe in the absolute equality of all men before God."

"Sure", I said. "But is that being practised?"

"Another time, another time. It's been good to see you two: if you have any more questions, put them on an email and I'll look at it for you."

He was pushing us towards the door, and a moment later we were outside his room, with the door shut behind us.

"You idiot!" Alexis shouted as we walked across the yard from the front door. "What was the matter with you?"

"I'll put it right", I said. "I don't know why everything suddenly went wrong there. Peter Mobile and I have history, and it seems to be stronger than I'd expected. I thought his pitch was quite reasonable."

"No doubt you now have achieved the legendary fairness of one of your interview put-downs" Alexis said sarcastically. "Well I've heard all that *Pietas* stuff before, and I can tell you that the message gets weaker and weaker with repetition. If it was so wonderful, why did you have to be so rude?"

"I don't know. It just came out. I didn't think he would be so upset. He has that mixture of lightness and sincerity" I said. "Humour and aspiration together. But the thought of the reality of the *Pietas* lifestyle - not to mention all the clerics and their closed minds – suddenly flooded back and I couldn't help myself, I'm sorry Alexis."

"You fucking idiot" she said.

3

We went in search of a pub and discussed our next move. I felt drained and incapable of any feeling except distress at my sudden wild ascent into ridiculous anger and sarcasm. I could hardly raise my eyes towards Alexis: I was damaged by my own unwillingness to engage with Peter Mobile.

"You're sulking" Alexis said. "For a professional, you showed no professionalism whatsoever. You've been an arsehole, Mike, and you've messed it up. Come on, what are you going to do about Peter Mobile? Why would he ever talk to you again after that outburst?"

"Well, I suppose my reaction didn't tell him that we knew about this picture, did it? Tell me, Alexis, surely it sounded as if it was a fresh discovery?"

"Mike, that doesn't matter. What he knows is that you associate him in some way with sex abuse, now."

"No, surely, just priests in general."

"You silly twit, what's the difference? You said you had some history with him, wrestling naked, didn't you?"

"I did not! We were wearing trunks."

"Oh were you, in your slips, eh? Could it be that you have let slip your distrust of him, Mike? Or did your slip come off?"

31

"Just lay off the sarcasm, will you? Oh God, what a mess."

But despite her hard eyes, Alexis had softer words to follow.

"There are other things to look at, but maybe he was just flirting with you, Mike. After all he did let you come in to interview him with pleasure, really."

"Yes, yes. I'm not gay, you know, you must know that."

"Yeah, I'll believe you, but why did you wrestle with him, Mike?"

"Lots of people – well, other blokes – did. It was fun, that was the idea, and no fuss. He's an old wrestler. He likes to show you his right ear, you know, it's a bit cauliflowery, from wrestling. Honest, it was wrestling. Mind you, there's more to say about it which I've never said to anyone before. It was after Sarah Louise and I had our marriage problems that we did the wrestling."

"What, was she watching you wrestle?"

"God, no, you make it sound kinky."

"Just you blokes, eh?"

"You've never known, I hope, what it is to reach a state of despair, have you? You'll try anything, you know, anything. I'd heard that people wrestled with Peter, and they seemed happy and sorted. That's what most of the people in *Pietas* are like – sorted. I wasn't, and I thought maybe touching and fighting with this holy guy would cure me, would show me the way out of this maze."

32

"You really were enamoured, weren't you?"

"Oh shut up Alexis, you don't know what you are talking about. I revered him, maybe I was bamboozled, I was taken with him, yes, yes. But it wasn't a crush on him for God's sake. I'm not gay, Alexis, but maybe he thought I was. That's the only good explanation I can give to what happened then."

"Oh?"

I sighed. I had thought I could keep it from Alexis, but I felt I had to explain.

"I managed to get one submission out of him, but he's much too strong to make that credible. He was doing it just to cheer me up."

"So – you can't trust the good intentions of the other guy? Sounds like you, from what I've seen so far." Alexis had a maddening smile.

"Well I'll admit to always looking for a snub behind people's facades. No, as we stood up, he grabbed at my trunks and pulled them out by the waistband and peered down at my penis. Swiftly. We just glanced at each other, and I put on my clothes and went."

"What did you feel, Mike?"

"I felt violated. He had no business doing that, it was abuse, maybe not that much abuse, but it was an invasion of my territory, me."

"Did you tell Sarah Louise?"

"No, no I didn't. I have never told anyone except you."

33

"Did you let it trouble you, did it trouble you afterwards, did you see him again?"

"You know, I wanted to give him the benefit of my faith in him. He was trying to save our marriage, and maybe this was part of the cure? I don't know why, but I felt that he had done that for a good reason, and the good reason was mine and Sarah Louise's marriage."

Alexis had bowed her head a little over her drink, and it was my chance to refresh our glasses and return with some optimism to our professional collaboration.

"So where does that leave us?" I asked her.

Alexis looked surprisingly cheerful for someone whose project had just been destroyed by my savage attack on someone at its very centre.

"Why still so cheerful?" I asked, "I blew it."

"You'll get to him all right – that was just flirtation. He'll see you again if you eat humble pie. Anyway, we're going to get some more material about *Pietas*. I haven't told you, but I've got an invitation to a meeting of the local *Pietas Rifugio* tonight. With you."

"Great! What is the *Rifugio*?"

"It's part of the post-marital training of members of *Pietas*. The married members meet every month in each other's homes, to share prayers and problems. If you are married you get invited to one of their *Rifugio* get-togethers, to meet fellow married pilgrims. That is, if both of you are Catholics."

"I get it – it's a refuge along the way of the pilgrimage. But why would they let us in? We don't match the criteria."

"I'm going to question them about their attitudes to sex in marriage, with you, for a press article."

"Provided that his grace Peter Mobile doesn't stop it" I warned her.

"Look Mike, when I was doing the gang-masters research I learnt that if you don't push on doors you won't find out anything. Let's do it and if there's been a stop to it, too bad."

"I don't know if I can do this" I said. "I think even these people deserve respect. This is sheer gutter journalism – it's lies and shabbiness and –"

"Fun, you twit. Stop posturing. Just shut up, Mike, and let's do it. You know, you may get some unguarded unvarnished truth out of this, Mike, about their true attitudes."

"But won't Peter Mobile be on our case?" I asked. "He doesn't want me sniffing around." To illustrate this I took her hand and smelled it. Her small brown palm had a faint odour of onions. Her hand was removed calmly from mine.

"Cha! He's not omniscient, you know. Even if he hears about this I don't rate that as a complete no for a future interview with him. We'll meet at that pub just by the Broadway at 7.30 tonight and then we'll go along to our *Rifugio* meeting. They do a sandwich supper, by the way."

35

"But it isn't that relevant to the investigation, surely, is it?"

"It's the only way of getting the full Monty", she insisted. "You want to know what that picture means? – maybe they'll tell us. And you've got to do more research on these clerics today, Mike, so don't think that we are mired in any way on this story. Let's go for it."

After an hour of phoning I found a church organisation with a library with old diocesan handbooks in three crammed rooms above a shop in north London. The poker-faced librarian didn't ask me why I wanted to find out about the history of ordinations and first postings of priests. I know I was not the first to come looking for old history there.

"Do you know what diocese they were in?" she asked. "You know, if you gave me the names it would be much easier. Otherwise you will have to go through all these old diocesan yearbooks – there's no central register, you know."

I gave her the names, and she put me in front of a screen, and behold – the databank's search engine took me to some of the basic information I needed. Then I looked at the old diocesan yearbooks.

I made photocopies of the history of their appointments over the whole careers of the two priests, Marcus Andrews and Peter Mobile. I was interested in their fellow priests and in their bishops as they progressed through almost thirty years, and where they were now. They had both begun in the same diocese, and Marcus Andrews had never moved from it. That probably meant they had met at some time. Peter Mobile had moved to another diocese after his second parish. From all the articles I had read about reported clerical abuse, the pattern of concealment of an 'alleged' abuser was to move them around a diocese. Did any of that happen with these two?

I made up a list of the names and phone numbers of the two priests' colleagues from the photocopies. The two differed in their progress upwards. Marcus Andrews seemed to have been made the Bishop's Secretary after only three years as a curate in a city parish. From that position he seemed to have become a bishop quite rapidly, with three years as a parish priest before becoming an auxiliary bishop for another diocese three years before being elevated to the current bishopric of his large diocese.

Peter Mobile had a different progression, through curacies (a junior priest in a parish) at four different places before becoming a parish priest eight years ago at his current parish. It was while he was there that he had been elevated to become a Monsignor – it clearly meant progression.

I started composing a story to tell when I approached these priests' old contacts, and turned over my sheets of photocopies to the information about the Vatican's special representative handling both press relations and internal investigations of abuse allegations, separately from the bishops. He was called the Vatican Questor, and he seemed to have an office comprising himself and a priest secretary. I didn't expect to ever meet him – but I was wrong.

Dialogue that evening at the pub (two extortionately expensive soft drinks) was hectic, as Alexis fed me with things she felt I should know about *Pietas* and what we intended to ask. She warned me that I had to be clear about why I was asking the questions. The *Pietas* members would never want to spill the dirt to hostile interviewers.

"I think we should be straight" I said. "Have they ever come across accusations of abuse, and what do they think the Church should do about the mess it has got itself into?"

"Maybe, how it is that the priests let fellow priests abuse children? What about that for a question? But they'll want to know if they will get tarred as whistle-blowers, you know. It's not beyond imagination that they know of cases of abuse themselves."

"In England?" I asked. "As general as that?"

"You could be surprised. There are several cases, you know that. At the worst, if we find out their attitude to sex, that will be a building block, plus what they think of Peter Mobile. But please don't go at it like a bull at a gate, Mike. Let it just come out, will you? Don't expect too much either."

38

"But don't you think Peter Mobile will be narked when he hears about this?"

"He believes that the movement has the right ideas about sex and celibate priests and all that. Contraception, too."

Alex smirked and went on "Having seen you in action as a professional interviewer, he may count on members just showing you the door too, because of your clumsiness."

"Well thanks for your support, Alexis."

We didn't have far to go to the meeting of the *Rifugio*. The couple hosting the evening, Francis and Marie, lived in an airy house close to a private school, down a suburban avenue. At the front door there was an enormous rack for shoes, and I counted seven pairs for children. I would have guessed they were between five or six and fifteen years old. They appeared from time to time, but seemed to be tucked away behind solid doors, probably doing their homework.

We were introduced to the members of this *Pietas Rifugio*, and I found them as full of curiosity as Alexis had predicted. But beyond that, they were full of charm and – I can't find a better word – sweetness. There didn't seem to be much of a hard edge on these four couples, between the ages of thirty and sixty-five.

Mind you, they did ask me if my views of *Pietas* were coloured by my past acquaintance with it.

39

"Well, Peter Mobile was willing to talk to me" I said, and that seemed to satisfy them.

In fact we talked quite a bit about Peter Mobile before the meeting proper began. "What's he like, the Ordinary of *Pietas*, Peter Mobile?"

"Oh he's great, he's a charismatic person" I was told. "You know how some extrovert people get up other people's noses? He doesn't seem to do that – he's utterly straight, but there's a sort of control about him. It's as if he could really act things up, but he doesn't."

"Well how did he get the movement going – in England, I mean. It's Italian, isn't it? "

"Oh don't give him all the credit. He's just the English Ordinary, harvesting what the first members achieved – who included Francis and Marie. You know, there's nothing to report about struggle or campaigns or any marketing at all."

"It just grew?"

"Yep, sounds like Topsy. No, it's no mystery. Peter Mobile is a great preacher, that's the whole story. He's just pure energy – but it's not aggressive, he respects people like Christ does."

"I suppose no one gets a lot of respect nowadays, particularly if they are in a position of authority."

"True. But folk heard him preach and passed the word on and his parishes grew."

"Any particular age group?" I was looking for connections with children, of course. I acknowledged to myself that I was one of the people lacking respect. But nothing I had heard surprised me – Peter Mobile

40

had always been quietly impressive as far as I was concerned.

"He's been good with young families throughout his career and hung on to the oldies as well" Francis explained. "Teenagers are problematic of course, and he seems to have given up on them personally but not in principle."

"Oh he was more active with the young in the past?" I asked.

"Yes, not the Boy Scout movement but something along the same lines of outdoor activity. You know he's a wrestler, do you? He still wrestles with members, it's a sort of therapy I think. Well, they seem to enjoy it. He used to be quite a cyclist and mountain walker as well."

I was getting close, I thought – no more questions, I didn't want to show my hand.

It was a strange thing that I was doing, hunting around for dirt in a thoroughly dishonest way in order to occupy the high ground. I had nothing but respect for all these people so far, and yet I was playing a cynical game.

Maybe it was the way I worked? Hypocrisy, regret, moral outrage, get the cheque for the exposé? I didn't want to admit to myself that it was exactly like that for me.

This was the first moment that I thought of chucking it in. But now it would mean that I would lose Alexis as a friend. Bill certainly knew what he was doing when he put her on this project.

41

4

We drank tea and ate sandwiches as the meeting proper began with a prayer. Then Francis, the host and the evening's chairperson explained how the *Rifugio* meeting worked, with everyone giving their '*news*' for the last month, and reporting on their 'mutual encounter'. Exceptionally, when the group had visitors from outside, each person would introduce themselves as well. "Mike and Alexis you'll have to do that too."

The couple who started, our hosts, had been married for twenty years and talked about their '*highs*' and '*lows*' over the past month. The events were pretty dull, but the two were warm and full of enthusiasm for the achievements of their children, aged eighteen, sixteen, fourteen and downwards in twos to six years old. Seven in all. It was no part of the evening's work to find out why there was such a large family and how it was supported, but father looked quite laid back while the mother was understandably more than a little bit dark around the eyes.

More '*news*' followed from the other couples, of much the same type. The message was coming over loud and clear: marriage was about having children. But then there was a turn in the discussion which pleased me. It was about contraception, the so-called Catholic litmus test. Was this going to give me the deeper insight into the attitudes to sex of *Pietas* that Alexis had promised me?

Aidan and Marcia had given their brief '*news*' when Marcia went on to talk about a '*low*'.

"It came out of our sit-down", she said. "Mutual encounter", Francis explained for our benefit. "If you belong to a *Rifugio*, you have to have a discussion of where you stand with regard to each other in your love, every month. You need to discuss issues. It's sensible – one sign of a failing marriage is stopping talking to each other."

Marcia's face was turned downwards, and she avoided eye contact with everyone except Aidan, who carefully returned it but without registering either appropriate sympathy or disagreement.

"We have our three children", she said. "I don't want to have any more for lots of good reasons. You know why, and I'll ask Alexis and Mike to take the reasons on trust. So I'm proposing to take the Pill from now on. Or rather I was proposing, but Aidan says no. I want to share it with you…"

"So do I" said Aidan. "This is where your support really matters."

"Should we discuss this with our visitors here?" someone asked.

"Of course we should" said Marie, our hostess. In some ways I wished she had said 'No', because I found the discussion that followed extremely painful. After all, I had received prenuptial instruction from the *Pietas* team before my marriage went belly-up.

43

"This is the practical problem that we all have to face", Marie went on. "Normal fertility leads to large families by today's standards, and not every couple wants that. What should they do?"

"What did *you* do?" asked Marcia.

"We didn't really want seven children when we already had six" she replied. "Nor six when we had five. We love them and are glad we have them. But they came from sexual love whether we wanted them or not. God's will. We practised the safe period for years, and when we had reached number seven we followed the Church's teaching and stopped. You know – having intercourse. We knew it's the only way we could go on in a holy way. Then nature took over, with the menopause."

"I don't know if we are ready for that" said Marcia. "I'd be afraid for our love, whether it could survive that. What you did sounds – unnatural."

"Well, what is natural? It's natural that intercourse produces children. It's natural that not having intercourse does not produce children. Nothing could be more natural."

Francis had no hesitation in looking around the room. "Has any one any doubt about the teaching of Mother Church on this?" He sought out the eyes of the two other male members of the couples, as if only their views were of relevance.

I had expected some shiftiness, some signals of reservations, and some signs of brave support undermined by barely concealed rejection – but there were none. These men and women supported the Roman Catholic teaching that the only efficient and ethical way to control conception was to stop having sex.

Marcia asked Marie the question I couldn't ask.

"You mean that you and Francis live together now like brother and sister?"

Francis answered as Marie signalled her agreement. "We do. Man is made in the image of God, and that has to do with being rational. The rational always takes precedence over the animal. The rational and right thing to do is to use the means God gives to stop having children if you are sure that is his will. Abstinence – not contraception."

My pain was there in the pit of my stomach as they talked, in deadly seriousness – but cheerfully. I wondered if I could tell the joke about 'Tonight's the night!' but I knew it might not go down well.

Well, they could stop having children by stopping sex. The problem Sarah Louise and I had had in our short marriage was that we had never properly *started*.

There was more discussion of the 'safe period' – a time when the likelihood of conception was low. I can't do justice to it, because of my sour musings about my own experience with an RC wife, whose frigidity I now realised was far from being typical of her Catholic women peers.

The *Rifugio* members agreed that the safe period hadn't worked for them. One called it 'Vatican roulette'. I was surprised at their good-natured hilarity about the whole business. Maybe they were so well off that they could afford mistakes? Yes, they were all relatively well off, that was clear.

I was longing to ask if all of them now lived celibate lives together because they didn't want any more children, but would not practise contraception. It was too intimate a question. But it seemed that it was true.

"We are not going to commit sins" was the consensus of the *Rifugio*. "The only good sex is holy sex" one said, seemingly quoting from the words of the Ordinary, Peter Mobile. That seemed to be *no* sex now for some of them. I could barely believe it.

Marcia summed up the meeting's judgements as the discussion reached a pause.

"Thanks to you all for what you have shared with us. Maybe we'll be twitchy when we see you next month."

Alexis whispered to me "If they see them at all."

It reached our turn to introduce ourselves. I spoke first.

"I am not a member of *Pietas* nor even a Roman Catholic or a believer in any God, but I have known your movement through Sarah Louise, who you will possibly know."

There were nods: she was well known.

"Sadly, our marriage has been annulled under Church law and registered as a divorce under civil law. You know that, and I hope you don't mind if I say that

I still find it difficult to talk about it. That's the personal side. On the professional side I'm a writer, and that is the reason I am here. The Church is going through a crisis at present due to the clerical abuse scandal, and I want to find out about the attitude to it among sincere practising Catholics. Naturally when I decided to look at this issue I turned to Monsignor Mobile, whom I had met before – I'm one of the people who have wrestled with him – and he agreed that I might talk to you. Thank you all."

Alexis was known to everyone, as a 'viator' and possible future full member of *Pietas*. She managed to introduce herself without mentioning *Sunday Seven*, to my relief.

"I'm the guilty one in getting Mike here tonight: I was able to clinch the visit through your kindness as well as Peter Mobile's."

No-one asked what her connection was with my research, for which I was grateful.

I took my chance to speak again. "Let me say seriously that I'm not a complete expert on Catholic attitudes to marital sex, for obvious reasons. Everything I've ever heard suggests that Catholics have a lot of guilt around it. You sound a bit mechanical to me – for me it's all about love and joy and happiness as well as children."

"So it is, so it is" said Marie. "Have you seen our picture, the Arrows of Innocence?"

"Yes, as a matter of fact I have, in Monsignor Mobile's office", I said "and I wondered what it is supposed to symbolise. Can you explain its meaning, Marie?"

"It's a picture of some little boys ready to shoot arrows at a target. Now the point about this is that they have a goal for the arrows – it's an innocent sport. Actually they are naked, which underlines the message that sex is not shameful but good."

"So?" Alexis asked. "What's the connection with marriage and sex?"

"The arrows have no point – they do, of course, I mean that they have no purpose except to be shot at a target. That's what the Church teaches – the point of sex is to have children."

Marie chipped in. "And if you're not using it for that, there's no point in the game."

"There's a target in the picture, isn't there?" I asked.

"That's the whole point of using this picture, don't you see?" Marie replied.

"What I meant to say was that if you took away the target there'd be a lot of frustrated little archers."

"That's true if you believe that we are at the mercy of our instincts" Francis said. "But our Church teaches that we can each decide that though we hold the arrow in the bow, we will not send it except to its true target."

His wife Marie seemed to enjoy this as she joined in, but maybe she was being ironic. After all, she did have two teenage sons. She said "So the picture captures the spirit of Catholic sexuality. All ready to go, but not necessarily. Their bows are flexed, but those child archers are static. Look at it, sex for having children is good, but not for anything else."

"I'm bowled over by the challenge", I said. "I thought that Catholics just paid lip service to this teaching."

"Oh they do", Martin said, who hadn't added to this debate so far. "And then most of them deny they have sinned and leave the Church. Have you heard about mortal sin?"

"A little" I admitted. "If you do something very wrong you are liable to burn in hell for ever because of it, isn't that mortal sin?"

"Precisely!" Marie answered. "And shooting without a target is wrong. Gravely wrong."

"Crikey!" I exclaimed, taking care to keep my ankles well away from Alexis' sharp shoes, which might be directing a kick at me. "I thought maybe it meant that condoms would be a good destination for the arrows." This was sheer aggravation on my part, and it worked. As I pulled in my feet towards me and avoided a nether blow from Alex, our genial host looked sternly towards me.

"You've got it entirely wrong, Mike. Shoot arrows at a target or not at all."

"I thought that it was supposed to be fun" I said. "But sorry, I'm only teasing."

"If you can get the target and arrow analogy right, you will understand all of the Church's objection to in vitro fertilisation and hybrid embryos" someone else chipped in.

"Yes, but maybe this is a good point to mention the clerical abuse scandal, isn't it? If I understand you rightly, those abusing priests were not just breaking the law and doing evil things to the children, they were actually ensuring that they are going to burn forever in hell."

"Yes, that's right" said Francis.

"Well how can they do it, then? And if priests are supposed to be holy, how can they continue practising as priests?"

"If we only knew!" Marie exclaimed.

"Do you have personal experience of this sort of thing, Marie?" Alexis asked. Marie's cry had sounded like a real expression of suffering.

"Yes, we have had a problem like this in another parish before we moved here. The priest was connected with the Scouts – he was their chaplain – he went to prison. It had a bad effect on my boys, not that they were involved at all, but they tend to sneer at priests now."

Alexis came in.

"Was there a cover-up, or an attempt at it?"

"I think you could say so, yes. The poor lad who blew the whistle went through the mill as they tried to stop him going to the police."

I chipped in. "That is the puzzle to me. Not how it happened that the priest acted in such an evil way, but why all the other – shall I call them 'holy' men? – behaved like this. To spell it out, tried to cover up what was going on."

"If only we knew!" Marie exclaimed again. "They kept it suppressed for three years, you know, from first hints to the police case."

"Why was it easy to hide?"

"Scandal, reputation, finally detraction, all sins" said Francis. He gave a look around to all of us to signal that was the end of the discussion. But this was my chance, and to hell with Alexis' pussy-footing.

"I'm not asking why it was hidden, I can see that shame would drive the bishops and what do you call them? – hierarchy – towards that. But why was it easy for the parish priests and bishops to convince themselves that the way they hid the crimes was the right thing to do? Why were they told not to report the crimes to the police? Above all, where was their desire for justice to be done to the abused?"

Francis said "Shush. We've had enough about this tonight. Just take this in, please Mike: we are proof that you can practise what Christ teaches."

"Just one more question, Francis. Could I ask Martin, maybe, because I appreciate that you are standing in for *Pietas* in some way? How do *you* feel about this, Martin? If I'm writing about it, I've got to know."

"Utterly utterly betrayed. These are men who hold the body of Christ, his whole divinity in the sacred host in their consecrated hands, and we revere them for their holiness and the dedication of their lives to God." All the members of the *Rifugio* signalled deep disappointment on their solemn faces.

"Do you think the Pope should visit England this autumn?" I asked them. "After all these scandals?"

Francis spoke swiftly and loudly. "Of course he should! He is the biggest fighter against abuse that we have, he has got it out of the closet, and he has said we are all sorry. You see, Mike?"

Everyone signalled agreement.

That was all I could get. At least they hadn't defended the way that the Church had behaved. The meeting seemed to go on forever. There were references to the bible, more prayers, even a meditation thoughtfully led by the sexagenarian husband. I felt a sense of amazement and respect for these people, but also a feeling of pity. It seemed to me that they were losing out. But to achieve a life of perfection? – that really appealed to me, despite everything.

But I didn't lose my chance to talk about the picture again as we were leaving.

"Is that picture, The Arrows of Innocence, specially connected with *Pietas*?" I asked Francis.

"More with Peter Mobile, I think" he replied. "I don't think anyone knows the full story, but it was apparently composed and taken by a youngster who Peter Mobile knew when he was a young curate. The photographer was called Tom, and he died in a climbing accident. The story has it that Peter tried to save him, but he was already dead. Tragic, and very important to Peter."

52

"So all the connection with sex is just accidental?" I asked.

"I think so. He uses it for explaining the Church's teaching, and I think that explains why it is there."

"You don't think it is connected with homosexuality, do you?" I asked.

Francis made a humorous face. "Who knows? It's not an issue, is it? You must have met Peter Mobile. Do you know what I mean?"

I wanted him to explain himself so I answered "No."

"There isn't any question of sin there at all, is there? We are trained to love the sinner and hate the sin. With Peter you love the saint and see no sin. I hope I'm clear, Mike?"

I understood him. I looked at Alexis as we left the meeting. There was nothing in those stern eyes to indicate that she had been impressed by anything at all that had been said during those seemingly endless hours. As we left I got ready for the tirade of rejection of *Pietas* that I felt was going to come.

5

"We've got to talk about it" Alexis insisted, so we went to the Cape of Good Hope pub. Alexis was spoiling for a fight, and began by taking her anger out on the bar staff. The barman was slow and preoccupied with a fiddly order from a group of young men, and as Alex had insisted on buying the drinks, she stood at the bar staring at the barman and repeating again and again "Could you speed it up please?" After ten repetitions, everyone had passed through the stage of staring at her to ignoring this public announcement.

She was prickly, on-speed, ready to fight, patronising, ugly and silly.

"What the hell did you do that for?" I asked her.

"I wanted some service. I'm entitled to ask for it, particularly when the staff seems dead on its feet."

"Can't you see it just winds everybody up? If you were a bloke, someone might have come over and bashed you, and I wouldn't blame them too much." I was quite angry with Alexis and it registered.

She gave me a gimlet-sharp glance, composed herself and took a swig at her bitter. Journalists have good taste in alcohol, and it was a nice drop of real ale: but I couldn't see Alexis impressing her colleagues with another display like that. Was she really that bossy?

"I really need this" Alexis said. "What did you think of them?"

"Oh I thought they were – well, sweet, gentle, and terrifically heroic, despite my prejudice that they are pathetic. Sorry, Alexis, but they did impress me."

She paid no attention to my warmth, and asked "Can you believe it, living like that and still regarding themselves as married?"

"I thought that it was a remarkable stand against present day values" I replied, while managing to keep a straight face.

"It's fiction!" Alexis almost shouted at me. "Utter crap! Remarkable stand against present-day values – do you read the Vatican press-releases, or what?"

"You mean you don't believe they behave like that?" I asked her, not the least fearful of her anger.

"Of course they don't. It's a pack of lies!"

"What, just for our benefit? And why do it?"

"Why? – because they have been taught that that is the way to behave, and any deviation is sinful. So they are in a state where they have to pretend to be good, as they see it in their eyes. Even if they ignore the rules, they pretend that they obey them. It's lies, self-deception. With the possibility of repentance, they can deny wrong-doing, so where's the problem with this game?"

"You're even more cynical than I am, Alexis. I felt a sense of security there, I felt they were all pulling in the same direction and it was a good-hearted one. Listen, I went in there hating them in principle and came out liking them, at least."

"Well you and your 'remarkable stand against present day values'. Stand? – do you think they know what 'stand' means?" Alexis sneered.

I thought of Sarah Louise at once, and her ambivalence about sex. I still couldn't complete a simple thought about my poor wife and her death, because of the pain. My anger against *Pietas* moved inside my chest, but it felt more like confusion now. I had to keep rational. Alexis sneering about virility? – this young virago didn't know what she was talking about.

"You know, anger about them is unnecessary." I was arguing against bigotry, and I found myself defending *Pietas*. "Let me tell you about my dad – the only one in my family alive, by the way. Now if you want to hear someone twisting the truth and loading evil intentions on others, you have to listen to him. Anti-Semitism, all other sorts of racism, anti-religion, anti-government for always! Nasty, vicious with it. Now these people are miles away from that. I don't like them any more than you do, but you have to say they're not hurting anyone else."

Alexis shook her head to signify 'So what?'. I switched topics: the encounter had confused me, and my desire to keep well on the right side of Alexis made me wary of treading on the wrong ground.

"Let's keep it professional, darling" I said "and see where we are. Despite my apparently amazing admiration for these dignified folk, I can see why you smuggled me in to a closer view of how they think and

56

operate. But still, it just wasn't *Sunday Seven* sort of stuff, Alexis. We have just one simple job to do. *We have got to get the dirt on these clerics.* It's all very well having this marvellous background research, but what we need is a story, an act, something wrong that someone has done."

"I agree, I agree" Alexis said, "Sorry to be so rude, I don't know, those creeps get right under my skin."

"Just one last thing about it", I said, "Before we go completely professional. We will talk about it later, I promise. There's a personal mystery about you – why have you come round to detesting *Pietas*, starting from wanting to join them, while I started out hating them but now still find that they have some attractive sides to them? It's got to be a good story – "

" – for later, I agree" Alexis replied. "What do we do next?"

"What happened in the first or second parish that Peter Mobile served has to be the key. He moved out of *St Thomas More's* pretty sharpish. If there was any malarkey it would be down there. I can't think how we can do it."

"Local newspaper search – how about that as a start?"

"Yes, Alexis, could be. Will you do it?"

"No Mike, that's what we are paying for – your investigative ability."

"I'm better at the hypotheses than the field research."

"We need to get to Rome, you know. Now that *would* be field research."

57

"Alexis, you'll have to do some research over here if you want me to include you on a visit to Rome. So – think about it."

"It's such a lot of deception, isn't it? I can't get to talk credibly to a priest on my own as a woman unless I have a moral crisis or plan to get married or something, and you have to pretend to be interested in conversion. It's all so private, and when it comes to getting the dirt no one will want to talk."

"You're probably right." We drank up our beer and set off to our homes. I walked Alexis back to her flat, which was on the way to my bus, overhearing her end of several calls on the mobile phone. All girl friends, I guessed. I was interested in Alexis' love life.

As I left her at her door she leaned up to me and kissed me sweetly, strongly and too briefly.

"Good night Mike" she said, closing her door. "We've had our first tiff."

"*You* think you've got me on toast" I thought.

Sweetly, a toasting fork seemed zanily relevant. Our first tiff, and now I'd had my first stiffy. I walked to the bus stop with a feeling of exhilaration about the evening, the deception, the kindness and steadiness of the married couples, and the smell of Alexis, onions and lipstick and beer. Funny thing about the way she harangued the barman, though. I had no doubt she wasn't perfect.

Just last week there was none of this. I must call Bill and talk to him.

"Bill. Can you spare me a minute?" I asked him on the phone on the following Monday.

"Yo. What have you found out?"

"Nothing much, but I'm off down to the country to search out the newspapers."

I had decided not to mention the picture of the boy archers in Peter Mobile's office, though of course Alexis might mention it. It is good to have something up your sleeve to impress the client when they go cold on a story.

I went on. "Did you ever get any hint from your source about what we are looking for?"

"No Mike, it's where it was, I'm afraid, but I've been thinking about the source. I think our whistleblower is in the Vatican Questor's office somewhere. See if you can find a way to get in there, will you?"

"OK. I rely on Alexis for strategies. We've already seen Peter Mobile you know."

"How did he impress you, Mike? An abuser?"

"Oh no, no, even now that there is a suspicion my perception has changed very little. He was very controlled while looking absolutely capable of anything. Eye contact fantastic. He seemed to be about to reveal something all the time, some big truth I mean, something relevant to us. I feel I could trust him, but I used to feel that about Tony Blair. It may sound corny, but with Peter Mobile I still felt a sense of holiness."

"Wow, you've got it bad Mike. Isn't he gay?"

"Maybe, but so what? It's not an issue with me nor with these sorts of people, I really believe that. You know – celibate, they don't practise any sex because they think it is wrong to do so. Wrong for homosexuals, anyway, and for priests absolutely."

"So you think that Peter Mobile may be the wrong person for a scandal, do you?"

"Bill, I'm determined to find out the truth. We're pretty sure that these two priests must have known each other at the start of their careers, so it could be that one or the other is implicated, or even both. Has Alexis explained about Marcus Andrews being the Bishop's secretary at the same time as Peter Mobile was a curate?"

"Yes. I'm sure you are right – whatever the scandal is, it is *extremely* old, and only worth digging up out of spite and envy. Someone else's, not *Sunday Seven*'s of course."

"Rubbish Bill! Spite and envy is what keeps you going. And if there was abuse it needs revealing because someone has suffered – that's enough for me."

I still feel that of course, and that is why I've written this account. But I've had some problems with my conscience on the way.

Two phone calls established that there was no online database of old stories at the local papers out in the county town where Peter Mobile had been a curate. Was there a microfilm version available? – no, but they held old copies at the County Library.

60

As I took the train down to my country destination late on Monday morning I knew that I was unhappy about the project because I couldn't bring myself to buy the first class ticket that I should be claiming as my right. It was not me, this sort of grubby stuff. I wondered if I could harvest enough from the topic of Roman Catholics for a more intellectual article in a broadsheet paper. I considered the way that Jews and Quakers were both tiny minorities in Britain, but they had made a contribution to the politics, ethos and wealth of the country way beyond their strength of numbers. *"The Roman Catholics punch below their strength";* that sounded aggressive enough to win attention as a quote, whether it was true or not. Suddenly I addressed my own ignorance and why I was unaware of whether MPs who were Roman Catholics voted according to Catholic teaching about abortion and euthanasia.

That got me thinking: maybe there was a way to get to see the Vatican Questor through proposing that I was going to do an article around such a subject? I would need to have a particularly Pope-related angle for that.

I got busy with my lap-top. Using "Bishops call on Catholic MPs" as my entry to the search engine, I soon had a quote from the Media Office of Scotland's RC Church:

> *In his sermon on Thursday, Cardinal O'Brien will also call on Catholic politicians to avoid*

'cooperating in the unspeakable crime of abortion' reminding them of 'the barrier such cooperation erects to receiving Holy Communion'.

Why did he feel it necessary to threaten them, unless they were liable to ignore the strict teaching which forbade abortion under any circumstances? It was relevant to my point.

A little more research brought up the issue of abortion again, this time to do with the removal of RC support to Amnesty, the human rights organisation, because it asserted a rape victim's right to an abortion in countries where that was not allowed.

Back simply to "RC MPs" as a search, and I found *The Scotsman* reported a Vatican drive to influence politicians on ethical issues. Part of the same article about the abortion speech by Scotland's Cardinal was a reference to Jim Devine, a Catholic MP, who said *'...it was 'unacceptable' for the church to try to influence politicians on any issue through making threats over their religious observances.'*

By the time I had reached my destination I had got my approach worked out. I wrote down some key words and looked up the phone number of the Vatican Questor's office. As I stood on the station, I made my phone call.

From past experience I knew that a telephone call was as likely to get me the interview as a letter.

62

I was lucky. The call took me straight to the desk of the Questor's secretary, Father Anthony Mulherin. Could I persuade him to talk to me as well as the Questor? I was sure that any leak to *Sunday Seven* must have happened either despite him or because he was the source.

"Hello. This is Mike Claver. I'm a writer – you may know my *Pre-eminent Victorians* which rehabilitates Cardinal Manning in one of its chapters."

"Yes I *do* know it. We were fed on Lytton Strachey's *Eminent Victorians* at my Catholic alma mater, I think to make history more interesting. So I enjoyed your book enormously when it came out, was it eight years ago?"

"Near enough. I'm flattered you enjoyed it."

The cleric continued "So what can I do for you? You know we're not prepared to talk as yet about the investigative work the Questor is doing about clerical abuse in England. But if it's an issue of digging in to clerical politics in the twenty-first century, maybe we can help you."

"All right. I'm looking at the way that the Roman Church resembles the Anglican in its quite loose grip on the ethical stance of MPs and maybe even lay people who call themselves Catholics."

"That sounds a little – polemical, shall I say?"

"Well, that's what journalism is about. Without veering from the truth, of course."

"I've not been in this job long, but it is the Questor's and my policy to let writers and journalists talk to him.

63

So in principle, yes. I'm not so naive as to think you will let me see and correct your article, but maybe we could talk about it after the interview. I'm trying to think what benefit you would get from thirty minutes with this papal diplomat anyway. He's not English and I don't think he understands what is happening over here in the same depth that I do. Forget I said that, can I trust you Mr Claver?"

"Please call me Mike, and I think you'll have read my stuff and know I'm not going to pull any dirty tricks."

"Right. When? And call me Anthony, please. You're not a left footer are you, Mike?"

"I know a lot about them. What is your title – Monsignor?"

"Just Father Mulherin, a good Irish name, if not quite an Irish family since the 1920s. I'm looking at the diary – how soon? The Questor is going to Rome on Thursday, you know."

"Well, Anthony, I do have deadline problems." My brain was working at lightning speed – could I get a foreign trip out of this project? "It may sound a little urgent, but I wonder if I could carry out the interview in Rome on Friday? Will you be there too?"

"This has to be a first! A journalist hanging on the word of an RC priest! Are you – daft, or what? Or much younger than I thought you were?"

"You know how it is, Anthony. We tootle along ignorant of events until suddenly there is a big change like the death of Pope John Paul or the explosion of the abuse scandal. So there's a very small window indeed for an article on doctrinal fidelity among the RCs. The current interest in the abuse scandal, terrible as it is, will only last until after the Pope's visit you know."

"Well, I'm not convinced about the need for that much speed. These things run along slowly in my experience. You have another motive, I suppose?"

"Yes I do, actually. I think you will know where to dine in Rome, and a post-interview lunch with you, in the best tradition of journalism, is exactly what I need for a broader view."

There was silence on the line. "Let me talk to His Excellency and I'll be back to you" he said. I left him my mobile number and set off for the County Library.

In the taxi I called Alexis. "I may have an interview with the Questor and his secretary on Friday in Rome, Alexis. Can you talk to Bill about it – see if it's on?"

"Jammy bugger" she said. "Why would you need me there?"

"I don't know – but if you can't think of a reason, tough luck! You could carry a hidden microphone, Alexis, why not that? In Italian heat I can't wear a jacket, after all."

"I'll be back to you" she promised.

It took me only half an hour to hit paydirt in the library. Starting a year ahead of Peter Mobile's first move, I ploughed through week after week of local news, looking for anything to do with St Thomas More's, the local Catholic Church.

I found what I sensed was the story in three articles: *TRAGIC ACCIDENT FOR LOCAL ALPINE WALKERS; A DEEP SENSE OF SADNESS*, and *CORONER PRAISES PRIEST YOUTH LEADER IN ALPINE DEATH*

I made photocopies and went out into the street.

6

Outside the library I phoned Bill to tell him what I had found. It was dynamite.

"Listen to this, Bill. Wait till I tell you who was one of the boys in this story." I started to read it. *'TRAGIC ACCIDENT FOR LOCAL ALPINE WALKERS'*

"This is from the local paper back when Peter Mobile had just become a priest. He was twenty-four and the boys mentioned were about fourteen or fifteen. It was August 1979."

I read it in full.

A long distance walk in the Alps by young members of the St Thomas More parish came to a tragic end last week as one of their members fell to his death.

The group of four walkers was led by Father Peter Mobile. Tom Benson, aged fourteen, was reported to have attempted a dangerous slope, on which he slipped and fell to his death.

Father Mobile and the other young holiday makers, Anthony Mulherin and Kenelm Bates returned at once from France.

A Requiem Mass will be held at St Thomas More's next Monday. Besides the inquest in

67

the English coroner's court there will be a hearing in Chamonix, France.

"Wow, there's a lot there, Mike. Who were the boys then?"

"Listen - the secretary to the Vatican Questor is Father Anthony Mulherin. So if he was involved in an incident with Peter Mobile, he might have a motive or maybe just the wherewithal for blowing the whistle."

"That can't be a coincidence. Get on to him at once."

"Bill, do you want the good news or the bad news?"

"Shut up Mike, you're too old for that."

"The good news is I've got an interview with him on Friday. Yes, this very week."

"That's really good. And the bad news?"

"Father Mulherin is off out of the country with the Questor for more than a week. Unless –"

"Don't tell me – you interview him in Rome?"

"I can't surprise you, can I Bill? Can I go?"

"Yes, but I'm not letting you loose without Alexis. You'll have to take her with you. Anyway, I'll get her going to arrange tickets and things, and be sure you have a passport, please. Why don't you come to the bash tonight, Mike?" Bill added, "and show me what you've got?"

It was the first Monday of the month, when our once younger gang of journalists and writers who knew each other as more than colleagues met in a noisy pub near to Waterloo. No, I must insist we are still young. I had dropped out for the past eighteen months, because of the break with Sarah Louise.

"Yes, I'll come" I replied. "You know, we might even get this whole story tied up by Friday night, Bill, to meet your deadline."

"Save it for tonight – I've got to go. See you."

Before I called Alexis I looked at the next two articles again. I scoured the second, entitled *A DEEP SENSE OF SADNESS.* There was nothing there in terms of new names. I read that Father Mobile had delivered a moving tribute to the young member of the congregation.

However, *CORONER PRAISES PRIEST YOUTH LEADER IN ALPINE DEATH* contained more new information.

> *The Coroner praised the action of Father Peter Mobile in trying to pull teenager Tom Benson up from a crevice in which he was wedged in a tragic mountain accident in the French Alps in August this year.*
>
> *"Father Mobile showed no concern for his own safety in scrambling down the rock face to bring the unconscious youth back to safety" the Coroner said. "Sadly, it was already too late to save Tom Benson's life."*

Questions concerning mountain safety training were posed by the Coroner and answered to his satisfaction. A verdict of death by misadventure was recorded.

More information? I judged that the heroic efforts of Peter Mobile to save the young man reinforced his image with me as someone with a lot of courage. Certainly there was nothing shady about this death.

Now what about the other youngster on that walk? – one Kenelm Bates? Was he now another priest, like Anthony Mulherin? Probably not. How could I find him? But why shouldn't I ask Alex to find him? I was on to my phone at once. I told her about the press cuttings and then put on my best charming but bossy voice.

"Alex! How about some research work? I've really hit paydirt in the local press, and I've got an interview with the secretary in the Questor's office, who is obviously our whistle-blower. We're going to Rome!"

"Way hey!" she exclaimed, giving a shriek of excitement. "Bill is just waving at me here, well done. How'd you fix it?"

"He'd read my book which you probably wouldn't be aware of."

"You snob" she riposted, "I can guess what it was. Some of us intellectual Catholics read *Pre-eminent Victorians* at university because it was a Lytton Strachey spoof and kind to Cardinal Manning."

70

My respect for Alexis rose steadily at every meeting. But I mustn't let her evade research.

"Could you have a go at finding this chap, Kenelm Bates, for me? Phone directory, any other ideas you have?"

"Where will he live?"

"I don't know. Try back where the action was in 1979 for a start. Try the lists of professionals, if you've got any, maybe teachers at schools, that sort of thing? He may even have become a priest, who knows?"

"Right, I'm on to it straight away. Bates is so common a name, thank God for Kenelm. I like it."

"Yo, it is quirky" I agreed.

"I've got him", she said. "Phone directory, he's an Architect and Property Improver, and I'm just looking at his website, wow! – he's quite arty in his spare time, too."

"You must be bluffing. I only gave you his name a moment ago."

"Just luck, the best hypothesis was that he hadn't moved from the area. Get your pencil out, here's the phone number."

She gave it to me. Ugh! – so far Alexis had not lost a single contest to avoid the plod-work.

She rang off, after reminding me to look out my passport and cheerily wishing me success.

I tried to think of a weasel way to approach Kenelm Bates, but gave up after a minute's thought. There was

71

only one way to get through, and that was by pushing hard.

In the event there was no problem. Kenelm was obviously a professional, used to getting phone calls direct to his desk and keen not to drive anyone away.

"Kenelm Bates." What a smooth voice it was. You wouldn't call it fruity, although it leant towards that side in its intonation. This was a melodious voice, a voice that would go with singing in a choir and silly jokes and self-deprecation. It was a quintessentially English voice, parading education and a need to make other people laugh.

But I am giving my impressions of the interview that I quickly secured with him, not the sense of a single sound bite.

"I'm Mike Claver" I said in my phone approach. "I'm writing about Father Peter Mobile, the English leader of the *Pietas* movement. I wonder if you would give me an interview as part of my research, as I believe you may have known him and been on a mountain-walking holiday with him back in the nineteen seventies. Can you help me?"

"Mike Claver? - are you the journalist who writes those deflating articles in the broadsheets about the great and good?"

"I'll admit to that", I replied.

"I don't think you're going to get anything much from me" Kenelm said. "I just knew him as a teenager thirty years ago. I'll admit that there is something a little bit challenging about him, but I can't give you any great angle on him because I hardly know him."

"I'd find it useful, though, to get a handle on what happened in that Alpine tragedy. From what I've read in the press accounts back then, Peter Mobile came out of it with his reputation enhanced, if anything. An account by someone who was there would be a great help."

"Oh, OK" Kenelm easily agreed. After he had expressed surprise that I was already only a taxi ride from his offices, I went straight over to talk to him.

He had elegant offices, high in an old brick converted spice mill close to the river. There was a view out to the sea, just visible over a bank of distant trees. The walls of the wide wooden-floored rooms were covered with black and white pen drawings of old houses and workshops, each with a date and the neat italic signature *'Kenelm Bates'*. In the background there was a subtle and pleasing aroma of pepper and cinnamon and other spices.

Only Kenelm and a woman PA were in the office, but there was a sense of a good workload generated by another two desks obviously belonging to two separate employees.

I was ushered into a corner office to meet Kenelm Bates. He was in his mid-forties, with a gravitas aided by grey streaks in his hair. Natural grey, I would guess, because Kenelm was smartly dressed but

73

obviously not obsessed with his image. This was a cool guy. Did I mention the corduroy jacket?

He had a warm smile. We shook hands, coffee was organised, and he noticed my appreciation of the view.

"It is about the best you can get around here", he said. "When I got involved with developing this place, I put my marker on this superb corner straight away."

"You can only come down from a place like this" I warned him.

"Most people would be quite pleased to come up to it", he said. "How can I help you? I'm always intrigued when I hear the name of Peter Mobile."

"Yes, he is an interesting person. You knew that he leads the *Pietas* movement in England?"

"Those people! – yes, I did know and I wasn't too surprised. There was always this perfectionism about him, and I think *Pietas* is the absolute epitome of perfectionism."

"You used the word 'challenging' about him. Was he like that when you knew him in your teens?"

"Most definitely! Don't get the wrong idea about him, though. I'm deeply grateful to that man, and if he walked into the room or rang at my doorbell at home I'd welcome him in, not as an old friend, because I haven't talked to him for twenty-five years, but as someone who changed my life."

"How so?"

"Well you have to remember that we are Catholics. I myself still practise: it has always been a beacon for me. I'm a fairly, no, I'm an extremely liberal Catholic,

74

but I'm a Christian. I won't embarrass you with more, and I'd hate to have my views minced through your particular skill for exposing hypocrisy. But my point is that Peter was one of the people who helped me to sort out just what it was I could do in my life."

"Are you hinting at your vocation in life? – that's a rather Catholic term, isn't it?"

"You're right on the ball. He taught me that God was generous and had given me my life. I wanted to show my thanks for God's creation of me and that Christ had died for me. I wanted to give back everything I'd got."

"Did you want to become a priest?"

"You've got it. Yes, I thought I was going to be a priest. Peter encouraged me to give it a try, like the others who were on that mountain holiday, as it happened."

"Who were they?"

"I'll tell you if you can persuade me I should, but I haven't finished about Peter Mobile and my..." – he laughed in a mildly self-deprecating way – "vocation."

"Go on."

"I actually went off to a seminary when I was eighteen."

"That was three or four years after Peter Mobile left the parish?"

"Yes, but he was still relevant to the decision. I gave it everything."

"What? – the seminary?"

75

"The vocation. I spent my teenage years praying and Mass-going and opting out from ordinary life and it culminated with the seminary after I had done my A-levels, not particularly well, I might say."

"And?"

"I found out it wasn't for me after five hard years, and left and lived happily ever after. Slight exaggeration, but I did become very clear about what was worth doing in my life."

"And that was?"

Kenelm gave me a look which was part comic exasperation, part resignation. He opened his hands.

"This."

"I see. Spending five years finding out what you didn't want to do was useful for enjoying life thereafter?" I wanted it to sound silly, and it did.

"Yes, it was, and I owed it to Peter Mobile. I was such an idealist, such a would-be saviour of the world. There are a lot of people like that, and if they go to the limit of their powers they become class-one religious bigots, like those people in *Pietas*, and the suicide bombers and all the fanatics in the world."

"But you say it took exposure to that sort of vocation to cure you of all that. It sounds a strange argument."

"It is, it is, it is. But I have to say thanks to Peter Mobile for the cure, however painful. There was only one way I was going to learn my limitations, and that was what happened. I went mental in that seminary. I had a breakdown."

"I'm interested in whether you caught this disease from Peter Mobile, bigotry or religiousness or whatever, before you were cured of it so painfully afterwards."

"I don't think so. Maybe he helped, though. He was a truly kind, very matey sort of priest when he ran the Scouts, was it Senior Scouts or Venture Scouts? – actually they weren't so formal or organised as that, but it was more like that than anything else. It wasn't just kindness – he was on our wavelength. He was a muscular man, not much taller than us teenagers, and he had an infectious smile and jauntiness which made us all feel so cheerful and important, too. We were going to change and improve the world."

"Touchy feely?"

"Mm – I'd have to say yes. He liked wrestling with us – sounds dodgy from this standpoint, but it wasn't, you know."

"Are you happy to talk about the Alpine tragedy now?" I asked. "I'd like to reassure you that I feel I know what you are talking about. My former wife was a member of *Pietas*, and I can see why you might fear it. I certainly did, for exactly that rigidity of mind you are talking about. What I am always trying to do is to loosen the bad side of the psychological grip of religion. Look – I'm investigating the events of that walk in the Alps precisely because Peter Mobile may have skeletons in his cupboard, and they are worth exhuming even now."

Kenelm looked thoughtful. "It's not that I'm against what you are trying to do. It's not that it offends my sense of fairness to old Pete, and my respect for him. I just don't think there is any thing there to exhume, as you so nicely put it."

"Tell me who was there on that expedition", I asked. "You have already told me a lot that is useful in my picture of Peter Mobile. He still has enormous charm, but you make him sound a little more democratic than he appears to be today."

"We were all middle class kids" Kenelm said, "But mainly lower middle class."

"Who was on that trip?" I asked for the third time. Not that I didn't know, but I wanted the names from him.

"There was Anthony Mulherin, he was the posh one among us. He didn't go to our school, but was at a Catholic boarding school run by an order, a public school." He gave the name.

"What was he like?"

"We were all nice kids, and he was no different. Peter didn't proselytise, but you won't be surprised to hear that Anthony Mulherin became a monk or whatever they call it straight from school. We all felt we were all picked out for lives of holiness. Well, at least Anthony and I did."

"And was there anyone else?"

"I'm sure you know there was. Tom Benson. The boy who died."

"What was he like?"

"He was a wonderful person. Tom's death was a real tragedy. He was really gifted, and as good-hearted as you would ever hope to be. I don't think he wanted to be a priest, but I do think that Peter Mobile may have thought he could be. Tom was also liberated in a way that no one else was, including Peter Mobile."

"How so?"

"He came from a family of – wait for this – artists and naturists. You couldn't invent it, could you?"

"Nothing surprises me. But was that so unusual?"

"Of course it was. But there you see the social skills of Peter Mobile and his wide tolerance too. He was good friends of the Bensons, just as he was of the Mulherin family. Not to exclude yours truly."

"Did Tom Benson's naturism or whatever you call it affect his daily life, or the way you regarded him, or his attitudes?"

"Yes, there's something that happened that is an instance of that. Don't worry, we'll come to it. But an important thing about Tom was that he took stunning photographs of naturist subjects. At the invitation of the naturists, I might add."

"I find it hard to get my mind around this" I told Kenelm. "The way I think of naturism in the nineteen seventies is of a small remnant of old clubs founded in the twenties, with falling numbers and a tatty image except for – I suppose that's it – a magazine or two with beautiful pictures scoured avidly by horny teenagers."

"Well, I can't deny that, but the Bensons were committed and believed that where no sin was seen there was no sin. So did we all. And Tom was a brilliant photographer. They went abroad too, you know, naturism is much kinder to your bits in southern France."

"He was also an adolescent wasn't he? – it sounds strange to me. Does anything remain of his output?" I asked.

"There's one which is quite popular, while still relatively obscure, I must say, speaking as an amateur craftsman myself, called 'The Arrows of Innocence'. You may know it." I nodded. "But there were many others, landscapes and people and a whole variety of subjects. I wanted to have a show of them at his funeral, but no one would hear of it."

"Do any photos remain of that walking trip?" I asked.

"Not in the public arena, but if there did I can see what a paper like *Sunday Seven* could make of them."

"Nudes?" I asked. "Including Peter Mobile?"

"Yes, Tom took one, but it was completely innocent. It was the night before the accident. We were in a refuge not far above Chamonix, and allocated a family room. It was a big place – have you ever stayed in a mountain refuge?"

"No, actually, but I have a picture in my mind of a sort of youth hostel, but with everyone in giant beds

80

holding a dozen at a time. Each person in their sleeping bags of course."

"This one had some family accommodation as well. There were four of us in six bunk beds, and we were getting into our pyjamas after supper, when Tom suggested 'Let's have a naturist study of the Pilgrims'. Even then Peter Mobile called us all pilgrims – it was an idea we all loved, and a great excuse for walking holidays."

"What did Peter Mobile say?"

"Something on the lines of 'The human body is beautiful, and God has shared all of it in Christ.' And Tom set up a delay on the camera and took the photo. It was like a moment of dedication. Peter's words were solemn, so I don't think we had smiling expressions in that photo."

"You don't know?" I asked Kenelm. "Have you never seen this picture?"

"Let me tell you about what happened on the next day", he said. He was dodging the question.

7

"Next morning was so strange", Kenelm continued. "I'd slept very well indeed, we all did, usually, but it seemed to me that the others hadn't. Tom was red-eyed and stroppy, and something must have happened between him and Peter Mobile, because he was really so savagely angry. I didn't know what it was about, but I've had my suspicions since."

"You think that Peter Mobile made a pass at him, to put it crudely? Or worse?"

"I've always avoided guessing about this. I've found it hard to even suspect anything wrong, because I don't think Peter would ever do it, but obviously something upset Tom. I'm very confused about Peter Mobile. I know I told you that there was absolutely nothing dodgy about the trip, but maybe that wasn't right. There was something astray. It could have been that Peter's behaviour was misconstrued."

"Was that the cause of the accident?"

"Not directly, but then, it must have been, if utter fatigue and tantrums cause accidents. It seems ridiculous, but you have to remember we were all teenagers then. Now I've had my own teenagers I've had experience of screaming fits and abuse and storming out of the house in rage and all those crazy things they do, about nothing!"

"You're saying that it could have been something less serious than sexual assault or grooming?"

"Yes, I am. I'd have thought that being together in a small room with four bunk beds would make bed-hopping unlikely. Anyhow, *I* heard nothing."

"Did Anthony Mulherin?"

"I don't know, you'd better ask him."

"Well, what happened?"

"I woke up to Tom shouting that he wasn't going to stay with us any more. He wanted to go home, right now. He was effing and blinding, and really angry, but he wasn't saying why. He just kept shoving his stuff into his rucksack. He walked out with it, and Peter Mobile started dressing quickly to follow him."

"What did Peter say to Tom?"

"Peter kept on saying things like 'Wait! Have breakfast and we'll talk about it.'"

"Did he?"

"No! Tom was off, almost running. Peter said 'Come on lads, let's get after him.' Anthony and I pulled on our trousers and things and followed after the two of them."

"It must have been an awful shock to your system, waking up to mayhem like that."

"It was. I remember being breathless, not usual for me on those mountain walks. I was frightened, very frightened, I realise that now, but I couldn't name it at the time."

"I thought that you were going to tell me about an accident that happened long ago that was just something sad but unlucky. You're making it sound like a murder mystery", I said.

83

"No, there was no murder, it was unlucky, but I admit there was a bit of a mystery there."

"Go on."

"Tom raced off, went out of view towards a steep slope, and stumbled there, and rolled down and down, and – that was it! We could see him caught between two rocks below us. Peter went straight after him, straight down it was almost a precipice, and must have slipped and slid sixty yards down to Tom, and then he picked him up, put him over his shoulders, and started back again."

"He must have been very strong."

"He was, but I think it was pure adrenalin. This is where he became sensible though – he put Tom down and shouted to us to get the refuge people out to help with some ropes."

"So he was quite sensible then."

"Yes, and brave too, you could say. But it was no use. Tom was already dead with a broken neck."

"How sad!"

"It was awful. That was the end of that holiday, I can tell you. And though my admiration of Peter Mobile didn't change, there was always an element of faith in my relationship with him after that."

"Faith? It sounds like you are having to make an effort to trust him."

"Same thing, in the sense that I was aware of having to *try* to continue to trust him."

84

"So that is what happened, Kenelm. Thank you."

"I must emphasise that I don't know everything that happened. I think Anthony may know more. He cut himself off completely from Peter Mobile after Tom's death – that was the end of a good friendship."

"Did he do that on the day of Tom's death?"

"Yes, I think he did."

"Didn't he confide in you at all?"

"Not a bit! We are *English* lads, Mike. We aren't going to gossip our way into calumny or detraction."

"If I recall the terms", I said, "calumny is spreading dirty lies about someone which destroy their reputation. What is detraction?"

"It is just the same in terms of destroying someone's reputation, only what you say happens to be true."

"Of course, of course, the very fuel of gutter journalism" I said.

"Well, what I am saying is that even if Anthony knows that Peter did something wrong, he's not likely to tell anyone else. Particularly if the person involved in the wrong was a priest. Has Anthony gone on to become a monk? It wouldn't surprise me. So he's going to keep schtum, whatever happened."

"He is a priest now. But you can't discourage me, Kenelm, from following this up", I said. "I'll contact him."

I sensed that this meeting had almost come to an end in terms of information. "I've learnt a great deal today, and I'm grateful for all you have told me. I will get in touch with Anthony because I think there is

85

something here that is important in Peter Mobile's life."

"I don't want to be quoted."

"It's not an issue, Kenelm. I'll probably come back to you anyway. When you're researching anything, never mind something as delicate as this, you always have to go back to your sources."

I started to arrange myself to go from my seat in front of his polished desk beside the bright vista of wide blue sky. I knew that the question of the photograph of the naked young men could not be resolved then without prompting distrust. But I was curious to know why Kenelm had been so cooperative after showing that he could easily have managed a polite brush-off.

"I must go now, Kenelm, but before I leave I would like to know why have you been so frank with me? Given what you said about detraction? You'll know that any whiff of this story, innocent as it may be, will ruin Peter Mobile's reputation, even his life. Why have you taken this risk?"

"Maybe it's just that I would like to get this out of my system, confess it if you like."

"Have you never told your wife about this?"

"Not really, no."

"Didn't they ask questions about what happened at the inquest?"

"No, it may sound silly, but no one seemed to ask why Tom was running off in the wrong direction. Even back in Chamonix."

86

"Thanks Kenelm. I promise I will be in touch."

A few moments later I was back in the street, awaiting the taxi. On the way out Kenelm had shown me photographs of his children, and pointed out that his second son was now exactly the same age as he had been on the fateful walk in the Alps in 1979. Just fourteen years of age.

"I like to think that I am sensitive to the problems of adolescence because of my experience", Kenelm said.

I said a final goodbye. There was the chance of something else there, I thought: I would get back to Kenelm Bates.

The pub behind Waterloo was at about sixty decibels, I guessed. The writing gang were in the front, pushed up against the bar, impeding new customers trying to buy an honest pint of ale.

Bill was at the bar, the tallest and the kingpin among all my peers – no one begrudged him his success.

The ring of drinkers opened warmly as they exclaimed 'Long time no see' in a clichéd epitome of welcome.

"Hey Mike! Welcome back!"

Maybe my sulky period was over, I thought, even if the anger was still there. I talked to Clive, who was doing some telly work, and Ben, who was a sub-editor at one of the broadsheets, and even Steven (hey, even

Steven, who writes this stuff?) who had gone into TV documentaries.

We spent our time catching up on old friends who were not there, and comparing strategies to make a million. We wallowed in old-fashioned green, the envious rather than the environmental, as we brought ourselves up to date on share options and the success of less literary colleagues who had gone into public relations or TV programme creation – and at least had started their pensions.

Most of us had met in student journalism. There was an anti-public school bias among us, a disdain for the air-heads who had been our colleagues on the money-losing undergraduate magazines. Strong envy too, because they had found it so easy to get into the media through their family and school connections.

Well, we had forged our connections too. There was a buzz, the pleasing sound of people who trusted, liked and understood each other. No one quizzed me about the last eighteen months, because they knew all about it at second hand from Bill, but the pals said they were sorry about it, directly or indirectly, and I felt grateful.

Suddenly it was 7.30 and most of them had gone. Bill wanted to talk to me, and I told him about Kenelm's disclosures.

"That photo would sew it all up."

"The new one, Bill? – the three naked teenagers with the naked priest, eh? – 'The Pilgrims'."

"Yes, yes. You've got to get a copy. Get after the parents of the boy who died."

"Could I suggest that Alexis would do that better than I would? She's not done a stroke of work so far – though she did find Kenelm Bates in sixty seconds on the Internet, but I don't count that."

"You're right, she will do better with the family. But Alexis is a bright girl, you know. She knows more about this story than she's letting on."

"Well that must mean the Questor's office" I hazarded. "She didn't work there did she?"

"No, but I'm sure she has a connection. Anyway, she's a great lady and I hope the two of you get on well enough to make the Roman visit pleasant as well as getting the paydirt."

I considered Bill in the role of Cupid, but I didn't have enough bottle to tease him about it. But my curiosity about Alexis was strong, and I started to ply him with questions. Essentially I wanted to be reassured that she wasn't easy, someone wheeled out to amuse a friend.

Bill played the game for a little, and seemed to stand back a bit as he looked at me in a bemused way.

"Alexis is a good old convent girl" he said. "Isn't that enough?"

I nodded. I didn't know whether I wanted her to be a wild ex-convent girl or a demure and genial young Catholic. I knew she was exceptionally intelligent and highly critical of *Pietas*. One thing I was absolutely clear about was that I wanted to get to know her better, and now I had my chance. Our Roman visit would start within thirty six hours.

Next morning, I called the *Pietas* offices and tried to talk to Peter Mobile. He was at a meeting, so I plied the charm as hard as I could to get his PA on my side. I was following up on a meeting that was shortened, I said, but Peter Mobile had suggested that we might still talk later on.

"What's it about?" she asked.

"Could you tell him it is more personal than the last meeting? I hope he will understand."

"I'll call you back", she promised.

Alexis and I met at Heathrow at the check-in on the following day. She was in jeans and a blue-striped matelot top, and had a tiny bag for hand luggage.

I said hello warily, but I couldn't resist asking if Audrey Hepburn hadn't worn the same outfit in *Roman Holiday*.

"You know, you're absolutely right. What about the hair style?"

"The Princess cut her hair short, if I remember rightly. So you've had a *Roman Holiday* hairdo, Alexis?"

"I wish you were a young Gregory Peck", Alexis said.

"Ah, but you are a young Audrey, are you not? It does feel like a bit of a holiday to me."

"You won't need that sweater, I can tell you", Alexis said. "I travel to Italy quite a lot and by April there's only one thing you need – summer clothes."

After an hour of shuffling forward we at last reached the bar beyond Security, and sat down to compose ourselves with alcohol.

"How did you get on with Tom Benson's parents?" I asked Alexis.

"Well I didn't get the picture you want, but it was a very thorough and sad meeting."

"Opening up an old wound?"

"Exactly. His mother doesn't have any grudge against Peter Mobile, and never suggested for a second that there was anything but an accident back there. But there was a terrible sense of a wonderful life wasted."

She sipped her brandy.

"Did you see any more pictures?"

"Oh yes. The whole family is gifted, and the parents were obviously something in the arts world – but a little bit out of their time, I'd say. There were photos of the five of them, a lot of nudity, and some fantastic sculptures by old man Benson. He died last year, by the way."

"Have I ever seen any of his work?"

"Maybe. There used to be a sort of abstract figure he did on the South Bank near where the GLC was in the far past, but it's gone now."

"What about Tom Benson?"

"Our teenager was just as gifted as your Kenelm claims he was. Well, I think I can say that, Mike, but

91

let's say for sure that Tom had a terrific output. Fantastic for a boy of fourteen."

"Lots of nude studies? Odd for a little boy?"

"Rubbish. I looked at the whole portfolio and the nudes were a tiny part of that. Reportage more than studies. It just happened that one outstanding picture was the Arrows of Innocence, and that was Tom, as just another boy in the colony, photographing his peers for a naturist magazine."

"The other?"

"Quite comic, actually, a sort of Mamma picture, lots of big-breasted ladies behind a self-service table with all sorts of food, smiling at the photographer who is where the first client would be with his tray. So good! That one was in colour, with lots of round yellow melons. I asked Lala if Tom took lots of photos and had a huge pile of throw-outs, hoping to search among them. She said no, the rest had been thrown away."

"The rest?"

"Pictures of children playing games, nothing much without people in them. Good, no, *excellent* compositions, lots of black and white contrast, that sort of thing."

"Any sense that Tom was religious or gay? No equivalence meant – I'm just fishing for differences."

"No, just a much-loved son, doted on by his brothers and sister and his Dad, too. Such an awful, sad loss of life. If I ever thought it was someone's fault, like Peter Mobile's, I'd never forgive him."

Outside the airport it was raining and a gusty cold wind continued to blow. We set off for our gate, a little dampened by the thought of what was paying for our break.

My phone rang. It was Peter Mobile. I mouthed his name to Alexis, who listened attentively to my end of the conversation.

"Hello. I hear you still want to interview me" Peter said.

"Yes, I do" I replied. "But I've thought about it a lot. You know, Peter, that I find the position of *Pietas* a lot more attractive than I gave you cause to think when I saw you last Friday. I don't know what got into me this morning."

Peter said. "You know how Sarah Louise came to see me when she sensed your marriage was on the rocks. I am only sorry that my help didn't achieve anything. That time we wrestled, I know that I may have surprised you by what I did, but I can explain it. So we both have a reason to speak to each other without Alexis being there."

"Thank you, Peter" I replied. "I wasn't completely at odds with Sarah Louise about *Pietas*, you know. In fact, just before we called it a day I was proposing to come and see you again. But events worked out differently."

"I understand", Peter said. "I can't tell you anything about what Sarah Louise told me of course. But I understand you rightly, don't I? You want to see me about a personal matter, not because you're writing about *Pietas*?"

"It's a bit of both, if you can put up with such a wide brief. What has happened is that I was brought up against my unresolved anger about Sarah Louise when we met, and I want to get beyond it. I didn't want to behave like that, it just suddenly erupted. I want to talk to you about it."

"And your article on *Pietas*? What about your deadline? Still pressed?"

"Yes, so true! Meeting, soonest. Could we make it?" (I looked at Alexis for a suggestion, and she mouthed 'Monday') "... next Monday?"

"Eight o'clock on Monday evening. I'll give you an hour."

"Thank you Monsignor. Goodbye."

"Goodbye and God bless you."

I put the mobile back into my pocket.

"Maybe we'll have it wrapped up by then" I said to Alexis. "He doesn't seem to have smelt a rat."

"Don't be too sure. But we won't let it spoil the moment, will we?"

"What? He's the guy who is financing the whole thing, don't think anything else."

But Alexis was incorrigible, genuinely cheerful beyond the brandy she had drunk.

"Look", she said, giving me a dizzying smile, "we can get upgraded to first class if we play it right. Try to look like a member of the press, will you? Yes, get out a notebook or something. Let's pretend to be fiancées – look, I've borrowed my mum's engagement ring." She took a striking piece of jewellery from her pocket and slipped it onto her finger. Then she started to make self-conscious attention-drawing stabs in the air with it.

"Oh dear" I scolded her. This sort of behaviour made me wince, but so did my patronising words to her. What can you do with a bottle of bubbly like Alexis?

"This is a silly game, Alexis. I thought you were supposed to be intelligent?"

"Enough to know that you aren't going to buy me any champagne, even on expenses, are you?"

I gave her what I thought must be a shy self-deprecating smile, but which possibly came over as a silly smirk.

Not long afterwards in the plane, embarrassed but flattered by the stories that Alexis had told to get us to the First Class cabin, I became more negative in mood.

It was hard to stay in my reverie, but I tried. I had always promised Sarah Louise that we would go to Rome together. Why had we split apart, why had she gone for advice to *Pietas* instead of going for counselling, why was she so frigid despite all her deepest convictions, why had she gone off to work in Canada? How could I be to blame for all of this? But maybe I was. No, I certainly was. Bigotry? I was as guilty as Sarah Louise. There was a shadow over Rome, a sourness, an irony which would blight any feeling of pleasure and discovery

Alexis was naturally unaware of my feelings, but I guessed she wouldn't have much time for retro-agonising.

"Just look more loving, will you" said Alexis. Seeing the air steward looking our way, we kissed.

Alex was dazzlingly beautiful, even in sunglasses.

"You can take off your sunnies now" I said.

"Well, may Audrey be with me still!" She kissed them and put them away in her bag.

"You know, we will have to visit the *Mouth of Truth* and do a primitive lie-test. It's part of the *Roman Holiday* experience." That was my suggestion.

"We have to go dancing as well" Alexis replied.

It was a silly game, but we were enjoying it a lot.

"I'll ring my cousin as soon as we land" Alexis said.

Cousin? Did we need to meet her cousin? What was she hatching up now?

8

I got out my reading and tried to concentrate on other people's views of *Pietas*. Unlike *Opus Dei*, there wasn't a lot written about it. After fifteen minutes of reading and marking up quotes, I decided it might be time to quiz Alexis about her flirtation with *'the Noble Way'*, as *Pietas* was often called by its members. She didn't tell me the whole truth just then, but only when we were very much closer. I didn't realise how soon that was to be.

"I'm just reading an article here that claims *Pietas* taps into a chronic need for approval in timid individuals who want to avoid self-assertion. Does that chime with you?"

"It could be right – I'm such a shrinking violet, aren't I? But the movement isn't much into self-effacement. They want you to go out there and – "

"– do it for Jesus?"

"Yeah, yeah but that is too evangelical, they wouldn't talk like that. More God than Jesus. I really think *Pietas* can fit into any religious belief. Any creed where you are concerned about your own soul, or purging your guilt, or getting happiness or perfection or whatever superlative life-changing thing you want. For you. It's about self-obsession, but to be fair it tries to incorporate love for others into your self-perfection."

"Wow, what an analysis, if I could understand it. Well, what got *you* there? You sound like a first class cynic, just as bad as me."

"It's hard to say."

"Come on Alexis! You promised to spill the beans and this is the best chance yet."

"I didn't have a crisis or anything like that" she said. Something made me suspicious of that denial. She went on.

"I was on my conversion course – legal conversion course, not religious."

"You mean you're a lawyer?"

"Yes, I'm sorry, but that is why I'm teamed up with you. I'm not a journalist, I'm from the legal department. Bill thought we could get away with it, you know. I'm sorry Mike."

She turned her brown eyes towards me and looked sincere. I was in such a state about her that she could have been guilty of almost any deception and I would have forgiven her. Well. Almost any. I wouldn't have forgiven Alexis if she had said she was actually a man.

"Anything else to confess?" I asked her.

"Yes, there is. Anthony Mulherin is my uncle."

"You mean you knew all along that he is the whistle-blower?"

"I'm afraid so. He sent me the email and the picture, because he wants to spill the beans. But in such a way that it doesn't get back to him, Mike."

98

"Oh you bastards! You and Bill and the whole fucking bunch of readers of *Sunday Seven*." I can't do justice to how I felt at that moment. "You've stitched me into this thing with a pack of fucking lies! What a bunch of liars and cheats you work for, Alexis! What a stupid stunt! We needn't have gone through this entire charade if you had told me the truth at the start."

Alexis took hold of my arm, next to hers on the airplane seat. I was prickly and pushed her away.

"Mike, you weren't supposed to know. It's me at fault – I've just blown the gaff because…"

She was fishing for excuses or – could it be? – struggling to get an honest but painful answer out to me?

"It's just that I think…"

I admit that I wanted her to say that she was feeling some of the same things I felt for her.

I waited an age, and she said "You're absolutely special". She touched my hand.

I shook my head. I was angry, but also alive with joy, lost in a sensation that hit me in heart, in sex and in breathing. The skin of my cheeks felt hot. It didn't make any sense to me. I was furious, and then stopped in anger in milliseconds. How did she and I do that? I was amazed at the shock of joy that seemed to run up my arm as I touched and clasped her hand. This woman had suddenly dealt me something like a death-blow in its devastating effect.

99

We were silent for a while and then I said "As you were saying – you came across *Pietas* at your conversion course. What had you read before?"

"English at Kings College, London."

"Did you live at home while you were studying?"

"Yes, I'm a home girl. I've never lived on my own."

"And I thought you were a modern girl."

"I am, I am. Anyway, while studying to become a lawyer in Guildford, I met Elaine, who is still a staunch member of *Pietas*. She knew I was a Catholic, and when we were discussing the ethics of representing people you know are guilty, she said that I ought to have a good look at what *Pietas* had to say on the issue. So I read one of their pamphlets, I mean 'Studies', and went along to enquire about joining them. Mind you, it didn't happen really seriously until after I had left my first Chambers."

"So what did you like about them?"

"Well, I was used to moral certainty, that was what being a Roman Catholic was about. You have to realise, we are brought up to want to do the very best we can with our lives. Lying, like I've just done with you, and you have done with me…"

"I've never lied to you. And I never will."

"No, I mean when the two of us claimed to be engaged. What was I saying?"

"How honest you little Catholics want to be. I don't think that Catholics have a monopoly on that."

"You're right, you're right! But the thing about *Pietas* is that it is not nuanced in its approach."

"That's a new one to me. Nuanced?"

"Not nuanced. Let's go back to representing someone as a lawyer when you are quite clear that they have committed the crime of which they are accused. Most Catholic lawyers can cope with that. A member of *Pietas* won't do it. They take the toughest line."

"Look, Alexis, the way I see it is that *Pietas* could be attractive to someone caught in some tricky moral situation. Are you telling that you weren't trying to come to grips with a moral crisis in your life?"

"I can't see what you are driving at."

"Well, suppose you had discovered you were gay, or suppose that you had been tempted towards a married man? Could happen – though I hope it didn't."

"Why?"

"You know why."

"There was something like that. Well done, inquisitor."

She was quiet.

"Go on", I urged her. "I'm not making judgements."

We sat in silence for a while. The first class section of the plane was quiet with the rustle of plastic and the steward seemed to refill our glasses with something like deference. We didn't deserve it, but it was such fun!

I broke the silence between us. "We haven't cracked it yet. You were drawn towards these straight-talking, straight-living saints but you have since set off on a career of cheerful deception. I understand the attraction, I even feel it myself, but why flip over to this current cynical way of behaving?"

"You've got it wrong" Alexis said, curling her long lower lip in an irresistible moue. No need for botox there. "All this deception has been in pursuit of the truth about what happened with Tom Benson all those years ago, and why Uncle Anthony needs to reveal it."

I couldn't restrain myself from pointing out that claiming to be engaged didn't serve any purpose but getting free champagne, by tapping our glasses.

"Don't be so smug", Alexis said, turning her head towards the window, where the Alps were doing spectacular things some miles away to the east.

"And you denied there was a crisis a moment ago when you joined *Pietas*, and now you have just admitted there was one. Who's smug, Alexis? Who's a liar? What else did you get up to?"

"Well, let me follow up on that 'Do it for Jesus' idea. You won't be aware, maybe, unless Sarah Louise taught you, about clappy-happy worship and that sort of enthusiasm which the evangelicals have. *Pietas* is completely against that sort of thing. It hates it! No, it has solemn Mass, in Latin if possible, restraint and dignity and rubrics and so on."

"I'm with them there" I said. She gave me a funny look.

"What's that about?" I asked.

"You know, it's strange Mike, but I feel as if I am talking about myself as a completely other person."

102

"Why is that?"

"It's you. You don't believe in God, do you? You look at believers as if we are completely alien. I'm finding myself asking myself why I behave like this, and do I really believe what I claim to believe."

"That's a glance full of a hell of a lot of meaning, Alex. I'm going to take it as a compliment. So why the funny look at that point?"

"Well, I discovered feminism after I had joined *Pietas,* and I was thinking 'He'll think I'm dotty'. But it wasn't through reading a book, but actually at a prayer meeting. Not a *Pietas* meeting, of course."

"We're not really compatible, are we?" I said. "I can't imagine going to a prayer meeting. Ever."

"Well that's silly – what do you think of that *Rifugio* meeting? We said prayers."

"Dignified, dignified. But I'm guessing that the feminist prayer meeting was wild, the sisters dancing with bare feet and unbuttoned sleeves!"

"Oh shut up Mike. There was an element of improvisation, I have to say it, there was a sense of belonging to a sisterhood with a different way of relating to each other than just kneeling in a pew. That's how it started with me. But you know, I was getting something from them, that sense of being equal to men and deserving to be paid the same, a sort of mix of the respect I wanted as a person, and justice too."

"So you started to bridle against the *Noble Way*, eh?"

"Yes I did! The point is that *Pietas* members believe that women have a place which is subservient. They don't say that, but they do. They are completely patriarchal."

"That chimes with what I know about Islam and Judaism and almost all of the Roman Church too."

"Yes. There, that's it. Patriarchy reminds me of patristics, you know, studies of the fathers of the Church. One of the friends I made was Lucy Peer, who was into that, and particularly Saint Augustine. She had a field day teaching me where the ideas of inferiority of women come from, and the crazy picture Augustine had of sex. Anyway, I believe women are equal to men – in our language, equal in Christ. *No more slave or free, male or female, all one in Christ* – something like that. It's prophetic, it's something we work towards, it's justice and mutual respect, it's a great goal!"

"Alex", I said, "I can see that something turns you on. But why do you feel this need to get the knife into *Pietas*?"

"It's because they represent dumb deadly refusal to live and look at joy in life. They are against liberation. What is the biggest change to the way that we are freed from fear? – all of us, not just women? – it's contraception, and *Pietas* refuses to accept it, because the old Vatican bachelor-in-chief has pronounced against it."

Alexis' face was flushed, she spoke with passion. All grist for an article, even if I couldn't fully plug into the way she felt about this issue.

I went into the attack.

"Surely the Catholic Church cannot just be about sex and guilt and stopping abortion can it? I can't imagine trying to make converts on that platform."

"No no no!" Alexis replied. "It was the work that *Pietas* was allegedly doing for homeless people that turned me on. You know it goes with immigration, too – you'll find our bishops actually want an amnesty for lots of incoming people without papers who we are really exploiting in Britain. I wanted to help with some of that, now I'm a lawyer."

"Doing pro bono work for the homeless?"

"Yes, that's it. When we visited the *Pietas* school, you saw the way that the streams of children were separated in their classes – almost no ethnic minority children in one class, lots in the other. They deny that they operate any discrimination, but you can see it. It is the same with their work for the homeless. It's for everyone who is homeless, but is it? What they want me to do as lawyer is show that someone has no right to be here, so that we don't need to help them. I'm serious. The greatest moral grandstanding, but when you get down to hard cases there is no compassion, no need for compassion towards the undeserving. It's fundamentally unchristian, but they can't see it."

"I should have been taking notes. Enough already! What are we going to do in Rome?"

"I've got it all worked out, don't you worry", Alexis said, tapping my hand. "But let me tell you about another trait of hypocrisy in the organisation – relationships with other religions."

"Think instead of drinking a cappuccino in a café on the street."

"All right, all right. What do *you* want to do in Rome?"

"It's a bit overlaid with what Sarah Louise and I wanted to do there. We always wanted to visit Rome. It was so special for her, but I don't really know why. Maybe you would know what she would have wanted me to see. For me, it's just a distant memory of *Roman Holiday.* You do a wonderful Audrey Hepburn."

Alex said nothing, but squeezed my hand and we found we were kissing. I got up to walk in the aisle, and stood, waiting for the toilet to be free, looking out towards the distant Alps. There was a radiance about everything, and I felt a happiness which was quite without anxiety at that moment. I was smiling with pleasure as I looked at the children, particularly, but everyone seemed to be part of my dream of goodwill. The Arrows of Innocence were stretched in my vision, and the target was the love of this extraordinary young woman who had so suddenly come into my life.

106

If the mystery of the whistle-blower was connected with sex, it seemed that everything else I had learnt so far about the Roman Catholics was to do with obedience, purity, power and fear of independence of mind. There was a puzzle too about my own attitude to Alexis. Though I felt an enormous sexual attraction towards her, I refused even to hope for her love that night. Good convent girls don't do sex the first time they went out with a new boyfriend, did they? If she did, then maybe we didn't belong together in the way that I was already hoping we did. Unless this was a true coup de foudre – love at first sight?

I should have been in turmoil about these great questions, but I was not. I was up on the moon.

What was clear was that I had given up on all control of this project, except for getting the facts assembled. Alex assured me as we took our small baggage through the arrival hall at the airport that I was going to be interviewing Anthony on my own.

"He says he'd be too embarrassed with his niece there", she said.

"What's he like?" I asked.

"Oh he's lovely! I'm not one for priest worship, though my mum brought me up that way. But he's just so cuddly and warm and funny and very cool with it too. You know how old bachelors wear corduroy because they don't have wives to stop them? Uncle Anthony is like that at home. Outside, he's a model from a fashion magazine. In private, all baggy pullovers."

"He sounds like a woman's dream", I suggested. "Unthreatening, smart and utterly charming."

"Well, don't expect too much. He is my uncle after all. He's not gay, but he is celibate, you know."

"Any weaknesses?"

"It's no secret – he likes his food and drink. And he has had a problem with drink over the past year or two. But under control. He will find you a good restaurant tomorrow."

"Well, how does a priest live a life of luxury? – I'm guessing you are hinting at that."

"It's complicated", Alexis said. "You'll have to wait until we've got our taxi." We spent the next five minutes pushing through outside arrivals, and then Alexis resumed when we were in the queue outside.

"Anthony is a former member of a religious order", she explained.

"An ex-monk?"

"Ish. So he had taken a vow of poverty for life together with a vow of obedience, and he ended that."

"Why?" I asked.

"So simple! Grandfather died and left him a whole packet of wealth. Anthony decided that the money was better in his pocket than in the Order's. He got a chance to spread it around his sisters too."

"He must have been very popular back at the monastery."

"You bet! Anyway, he applied to become a secular priest, and was offered this job as secretary to the

108

Vatican Questor in England. He is the right person for the job too. Knows everybody in Rome, where he taught at one of the universities – the Lateran? – I don't know – for quite a while. Maybe he's a little stand-offish with some of the English bishops, but he is a cultural snob, you know."

"Ha, I guessed that. *Pre-eminent Victorians*."

"So he'll get on with you."

"You don't have a high opinion of me, do you?"

"You are lovely", Alex said and touched my cheek. "And you don't know how lucky you are."

We climbed into a taxi, and she gave an address to the driver in Italian.

"We're going to one of the oldest parts of Rome, and staying with my cousin and her husband. If he's around."

"Wow!"

It was a warm afternoon, and I took off my sweater and put it in my bag. Alexis remained small, excited and radiant: could it really be me having this effect on her?

"So tell me some more about your family" I asked.

"Well, there's only me and my mother at home. My father died when I was two years old, otherwise I'm sure we would have been a big family. But my cousins made up for it – there are sixteen, from two different Mulherin aunts, and almost all of them live in North London."

"All good Catholics, huh?"

"I wish you wouldn't keep going on about Catholics."

"We wouldn't have met except for that."

"All right, it's research, isn't it?" Alexis said. "Actually, describing them as good Catholics is way off. They almost all stopped practising in their teens, with plenty of fighting about it from their parents. The older cousins fought the battle with their parents, the younger ones copied their siblings because the aunts had given up fighting to make them go to church. Now four out of the sixteen go to Mass, and it's no secret why – they want their children to be eligible for Catholic schools."

"Oh dear. You don't sound bothered, Alex."

"No, I am really. The Church has let them down. They have been driven to where they are by the stupidity of the boxed-in Vatican bachelors and their jobsworth stooges." Alexis turned to look at me over her sunglasses. "I'm tired of this, Mike," she continued after a pause, "I don't want to rant like this. But look – we're here! Now no more 'research' tonight, please. We're just going to have some fun."

The taxi fought its way down a narrow street in an older part of Rome, near to the Piazza Navona. Restaurant tables stretched out on the right side of the street, faced by five-storey anonymous stone buildings with huge shutters, and no pavement anywhere. We got out of the cab by one of the tall wide double doors of one of these terraced mansions, decorated with brass plaques for businesses on the first and second floor, and then above them with names of residents printed in white or black on simple plastic plaques in contrasting colours. I spotted *Rowbottom* as a likely destination, and we climbed up towards the top of the staircase where Alexis rang the doorbell of one of two apartments set at right angles to each other.

Taller than her cousin and red-haired, Bernadette seemed to greet Alexis by using her small baby as an extra pair of lips. They danced together outside the door, hugging and hallooing with pleasure at being together. I felt myself a visiting academic, suddenly pushed outside the ring of intimacy, but my euphoria refused to evaporate. To be inside the magic circle of such simple love – I smiled to myself as I was introduced to Bernadette.

She handed me a key. Her face said "Who's this awkward guy?" and her tone was businesslike, as if this was the end of the meeting: "You're staying next door in the Professor's flat, Mike. The other key is for the main door downstairs, which is normally locked after it gets dark."

Mother and baby turned away into the flat. Alexis was obviously expected to join them at once.

"May I have a look at Mike's place?" she asked.

"Of course."

"Actually it's not such a boring business trip as I had expected, Bernie, and I hope Mike and I can go out and … and…" Her voice trailed off.

Bernadette looked amazed. "What, Alexis, not you...clubbing?"

"Father, may I go dancing?" Alexis said in an Irish accent.

Bernadette did a good version of a cool appraising look.

"To my knowledge this gal has never danced a step in her life" she said, turning into her apartment.

"I'll leave the door open" she said.

Alex and I went into the Professor's apartment.

9

The door of the Professor's flat opened directly into a large bedroom, dominated by a double bed. There was a desk with a PC and a chair, walls lined with bookcases, and nothing much else. There was a small bathroom, and light came from down the well of a spiral staircase. It smelled of books and wood, with savours of Roman pastries coming in through the single shuttered window.

The brilliance of daylight up the stairs was inviting. We were children exploring a holiday home.

"Oh, there's going to be a vista" Alexis called out.

The steps came up into a kitchen. All the walls were windows above the tops of the kitchen units and on one side we looked across the roofs of Rome towards the cupola of Saint Peter's. Its round hillock was not large at this distance, more like the top of a mound than a cupola, but it stood apart, undemonstrative but unmistakable. All around the roofs made an urban desert terrain.

"Oh it's fantastic" said Alexis. We stood with our arms around each other looking at each separate view. "I must thank Bernie for this."

"What about thanking the Professore?" came a booming voice from the stairs.

It was the Professor himself.

"I hope a good feminist like you is going to visit St Paul's Inside the Walls on Sunday" he said to Alexis, whom he knew from previous visits. "I shall be away, but it's where you pilgrims belong."

Bernie came up too.

"John is the Warden at the Episcopalian Church as well as being our kind neighbour", she explained.

I thanked him for his hospitality. "I'm pleased to do it for a fellow Brit", he said. "As you probably gather, I'm Welsh. My Professorship is with an American university here, though I studied in Oxford."

"You are a dear international saint" said Bernie. "And not light on self-promotion."

"Do use the roof for breakfast if you can work it", he advised. "It's the one time of the year when the temperature is right."

He left us. Bernie explained that John was famous for defending the rights of gay people to the Italian media.

"He is one of those people who change your attitudes" she said. "There is nothing in him except kindness and honesty."

We went down to Bernie's flat and watched the baby have her bath.

Alexis tried to persuade Bernie to come out to dinner with us. I had bought some champagne, and we drank it in Bernie and her husband's narrow living room: an instinct told me not to ask about her husband, Geoff.

114

"I'm just too tired", she said. "But you two enjoy yourselves, and I know just the place to go. Are you willing to take a bus?"

We were: it seemed to offer more fun than a taxi. Everything was new to me, and Alexis standing in a bus seemed to trail an invisible team of cameramen, lights and even paparazzi. Among the travellers there seemed to be a brief general moment of silent amazement at her beauty.

We found our dance in a marquee in a park not far from the suburban bus terminal. We bought tickets for food, drink and dancing. There were drums, a squeezebox and a saxophone.

I was enchanted by the spring evening, the pasta, the simple warmth of humanity, the music and the joy of dancing. There were couples in their sixties, fifties, forties and thirties with children and teenagers, but the twenties were just represented by Mike and Alexis. I felt a desire to belong to a world like this where children were taken to the dance and their shiny faces beamed with pleasure.

Once again we were the target of sly curiosity: presumed to be young lovers with what I hoped was a prescient, perfect perception of a reality as tenuous and real as mist over the park.

The accordionist did know the Lambeth Walk and everyone either picked it up quickly or was just pretending it was an English novelty so far undiscovered. With an 'Oi!' we floated back to the open side of the tent and looked out at the lights of Rome over the park.

I told Alexis that I loved her. I had never been so precipitate in behaviour in my life. My heart was full of dreams of love and argument, travel and children, but for the moment I had little to say about that. We started talking about her life and mine and swapping stories about the covert recordings and videos which supported her and my past investigations. Not even the dancing gave us a break in discussion.

Later we got a taxi back to our base and Alexis came into my flat.

I was afraid of a replay of the Sarah Louise scenario: and I was right to be. Our arms were wrapped around each other and there was nowhere to go except on that giant bed.

"We don't have to make love, Mike" Alex said. "We do have the rest of our life."

We went on kissing as we laid together and she licked my tongue and lips with her own.

Alex leaned back on the pillow and laughed, loosening her bra under the stripy sweater. "You're so silly" she said, and first I put my hands on her nipples and then went exploring to where she was warm and open.

But then the Sarah Louise moment.

"My mother wouldn't do it until she married" she announced. "I think so, anyway. But 21st century convent school girls won't do it without a

116

contraceptive. Even with someone they hope to marry. Have you got a condom?"

"No."

"Well you'd better get one", she said.

"That's a funny way to propose" I said, but I felt angry frustration.

"You hope. That's a statement of principle."

She moved to the door. It was only a step into her cousin's flat. She gave me a mocking grin, turned and pulled down her jeans to moon at me rudely but comprehensively for a fraction of a second.

She laughed and shut the door, then opened it again and looked at me – no doubt I looked miserable.

"I've always wanted to do that" she said, standing in the doorway and laughing so much that her shoulders and breasts shook with wobbly engulfing hysteria.

"You're silly, you're silly" she said again, and then "Tomorrow, tomorrow, tomorrow!" and was gone.

"Tomorrow, tomorrow, tomorrow" was what Sarah Louise said, day after day until I knew there was no tomorrow that I wanted to come.

"These bloody Catholics" I thought.

But it was different, of course, in laughter and fooling and the closeness to being together. But then it had been rapture when Sarah Louise and I had first met and her first caresses seemed to be the pledge of a future sexual love. Then it had all changed and my unconsummated ardour was just a pushing and pushing and struggle within the white sheets of the bridal bed.

117

I felt afraid of fooling myself that this was going to be any different. In the quiet of that Roman night I wallowed in the misery of the same damp depressing prison I had shared with Sarah Louise. She had married me in name, and we shared one home and one bed for a few crazy hope-filled weeks, waking each day to the possibility of real love, but shadowed by the growing knowledge of Sarah Louise's fear, confusion, sorrow and guilt. What was there but my anger, my sense of betrayal, her stubbornness and refusal to look for help except from her bloody *Pietas* and its novenas and prayers?

How strange a day it had been. I had lost all fear in speaking of a love barely beginning. What a lack of caution, yet what a relief it was to trust this teasing aggressive woman. Now I guessed so much more about her, and I was sure that she was no cinch for playing at romance.

I found it difficult to sleep. We were dancing, we were solving the problems of women in the world, we were making wedding vows. But I was sure of one thing – this lady was not just a feminist or a lawyer or a Roman or even a romantic – this was someone who might yet decide to share her life with me. If her religion permitted it.

These bloody left-footers!

We had only had one row, in the pub, so far. I hoped we would have many more.

118

I joined Alexis, Bernie, and baby Jennifer for breakfast next morning. It was Friday, and I had to prepare myself to meet Father Anthony Mulherin for dinner.

"Where's your camera?" Bernie asked me. "You've got this wonderful Audrey Hepburnish lady and no camera. What a waste!"

I hadn't taken a photograph of anything since Sarah Louise left me. But Alexis had come prepared.

Bernie pushed us out to do tourism. Alexis took me to the Coliseum and on towards the basilica of San Clemente. "You get more for your money here" she said. The church was dark but beautiful, with lights turned on and off to display the decorated dark ceilings. But it went on, downward, to where there was a fourth century church on which the newer medieval church was built, which we had just admired. Here it was more severe, but the faces of saints again shone out at us.

"More!" Alexis said, taking my arm and leading me down to a second century Mithraic temple below.

It was people who mattered to these Christians, I thought, and they were all holy people, saints. God's role was there in pictures of Jesus Christ, but the rest of humanity (excluding women except for Mary) was all over the place. There was a sort of stasis about these people shown in the mosaics and frescos, with

119

their honest eyes, blessing hands and stiff bodies, which I didn't really like. Was that the way they were regarded, as inert idols, or was it the result of the limitations of art?

On the way to lunch I took a picture of Alexis at the Bocca della Verita, the Mouth of Truth, in Santa Maria in Cosmedin. We were copying many other tourists, recalling the scene from *Roman Holiday* where Gregory Peck pretends that his hand has been bitten off because he has told a lie. In the photo Alexis looked cocky and cheerful next to the round and alien slab of stone, reputedly an old manhole cover.

"I've got to have some photos for my mother", she said.

"Why haven't we heard from her?" I asked.

"I haven't told her about you yet, darling" she said. "But I dare say that Bernie has."

"What is she like, your mum?"

"You'll find out."

"She must be marvellous to have you" I ventured.

"Put your hand in the Bocca della Verita when you say that, please."

After lunch on the Corso and a visit to the Trevi (more photos), we did our personal shopping in a pharmacy. We went back quietly to the flat to brief each other confidentially about the evening's dinner with Anthony.

The briefing was a comprehensive success.

120

I was on my own in interviewing Alexis' uncle. We met in a restaurant close to the Vatican with an opulent reception and bar. I was worried for a moment that the place would impede frank talk about abuse from the Catholic priest, but I didn't need to be. The atmosphere was heavy with curtains, and the tables were set well apart.

I didn't plan to tell Anthony that his exact words were going to be preserved for later quotation, but the first thing he said to me after we had introduced ourselves was "Turn off your recorder, Mike." I did so.

Anthony was in his mid-forties, and quite chubby around the waist, but with a younger looking face than his years might suggest. He was wearing a sotana, a black garment without any fancy piping, but undoubtedly tailored. He was slightly taller than average and broadly built, and looked more English than Irish to my untrained eye. He was born to parents who were both born in England, as I later learnt, whatever their Irish name. He had heavily rimmed spectacles that seemed standard at first viewing, but on further acquaintance proved to be designer glasses. I could see he had real style, but there was also a sense of a rather bigger-than-life sort of person, constrained in these clerical clothes, who was at heart a scruffy schoolboy.

It was our first meeting, of course, and these were first impressions. He had an eager face, despite all the clerical edge to his demeanour, a freshness that could not be confined. Even in the midst of the terrible disclosures of that evening he was able to laugh at himself and speak with delight about his niece.

He was in charge at once. "Your paper will be paying for this meal, Mike, I trust?"

"Why of course" I replied. Anthony occasionally put on a business-like way of holding himself, and my first impression was that I was meeting a priest-businessman. Like most first impressions, it contained a lot of truth about how he wanted his external character to be seen. But I was soon to find that *business* was just a tiny part of the man. He was a scholar, too, capable in winkling out the meaning in what he researched even when his naïveté seemed to mean that he couldn't possibly know what he was talking about. What I am trying to convey is his boyish lack of worldly wisdom, except for subtle wines and malt whiskies and power-plays hidden in the words of papal pronouncements.

As we got started on a delicate seafood antipasto, Anthony led the questioning.

"So what have you seen to set off this investigation?"

"It was a piece of a letter or email, Anthony. About two clerics. I surmised it must have come out of your office, and Alexis has confirmed that."

Anthony looked grave. "I can't confirm anything about that. I don't want to be identified as the whistle-blower, if anything can be done to shop these two, one for abuse and the other for concealing it."

"You'll forgive me, Anthony, but I'm not a Catholic and I'm a bit puzzled by this whole situation. Why don't you go to the authorities and say 'I've got something to tell you about these priests?' Why this devious way of making allegations which, forgive me for saying it, could be a whole pack of lies? Why this approach, especially when you remember all the claims that the Pope wants Bishops to go straight to the police when they have grave allegations of abuse?"

"Mike, you will have to play it my way or not at all. Look, I'm in a position of trust, and it could be that I've done some of those devious things you suggested. In fact, I *have* done them. But my allegations against these guys don't count – that's my problem."

"Well, I'm sorry, I just can't believe that."

"I don't underrate my power as a secretary to a Vatican official. But I'm not able to pursue this – believe me, this is a desperate measure. Shall we go on to my reasons for all this?"

But I still wanted to resolve my puzzle about the process of naming an alleged abuser: could it really be as difficult for a priest as Anthony Mulherin was suggesting?

"Anthony, look, one thing. Everyone has a voice. Even if a child feels no one will listen about bullying, they can still speak up, can't they? Or do they keep quiet to avoid more bullying? Not that I'm suggesting you are behaving like a child."

"Oh yes you are. Maybe I lack the proper courage."

"You better give me the background."

"Look, I don't want you thinking that I'm a devious plotter, Mike, with a knife out against old enemies. Before I give you the background, let me reassure you that the whole approach to *Sunday Seven* is the result of my having supper with young Alexis ten days ago. She brought up the question of Bishop Marcus Andrews herself."

"You mean she's driving this?"

"Not entirely. No, she told me, in complete confidence, which applies to you as well, about a dismissal case she was handling where a woman had been pushed out of her job in Marcus's diocese because she was too thorough in looking for evidence about abuse cases involving priests. It was a job the lady had been taken on to do. There was a locked filing cabinet to which she was denied the key."

"I thought Alex worked for *Sunday Seven*?"

"No, that newspaper happens to be a client of her Chambers. And the woman in the dismissal case happens to be someone I helped with a study of St Augustine's attitude to sexuality and women. Something that changed my own perceptions, as it happened."

I had no time to register my irritation at these further deceptions by Bill and Alexis.

"Right", I said, "she tells you about this incident. Forgive my cynicism, but it must be something that has happened in many dioceses all over the world. Hush up the dirt. And you would know more about that than I would."

"No comment."

"Well, Anthony, what drove you to this furtive manoeuvre? Was it Alex? You must have known something more, surely, to get you going?"

"You know, I have never told anybody yet what I am going to tell you. Parts of it, yes. But not all of it. I knew Marcus Andrews a long time ago when he was the secretary to the then Bishop in the same diocese he leads now."

"And you weren't impressed? What could he do to hurt you?"

"I feel it has damaged my whole life. What he did was witness my reporting two cases of abuse by priests and my being told that I was a liar and there was nothing to be done about it."

"That sounds far too extreme. We'll need dates and people, of course, but how can you have a case against a man who was there to assist the Bishop, not make decisions for him? He was just a witness of your complaint, no more, wasn't he?"

Anthony admitted Marcus' role was marginal. "Maybe I haven't got a case in the sense of an actual crime" he said. "I'll admit that the report about Lucy Peer's case for constructive dismissal is what has tipped me into this whistle-blowing effort. She was taken on to dig out the truth about abuse! That was in Marcus Andrews' diocese, I told you that, didn't I? It just pushed me over the edge."

Anthony urged me to savour the *Ribolla Gialla*, apparently a favourite with the restaurateur who came from Northern Italy. I was getting the impression that Anthony was an old client here. No matter – the paper would pick up the tab. But was I in danger of losing my story? Anthony had precious little by way of revelations so far.

"It must be hard for you, Anthony", I said, "but you'll have to bite the bullet about just what exactly happened. I thought that you were pointing the finger at Peter Mobile, but you haven't even mentioned him yet. I've got to hear what is alleged – and don't forget, it is a question of allegation. Using the gutter press to pillory someone for sexual abuse or a cover-up is pretty drastic stuff, Anthony. You must have something very *important* to justify it. People need to be able to speak for themselves when accusations are bandied about, and they won't get a chance, you know."

"But that's it, that's it" Anthony said with as much animation as he could muster. His voice did not rise, but his mouth seemed to have a greater firmness about it as he enunciated those words. "I spoke for myself, and I was not heard."

"What happened and when?"

Anthony wiped the corner of his mouth with his table napkin.

126

"It was when I was seventeen. It happened at school."

"You were a boarder at an RC school run by a religious order, as I recall."

"Precisely. I had decided by then to become a priest in the Order, and I was really in a battle with my father about this decision. He gave me so much grief, from my first memories of him, I was never good enough for my dad. He was a great businessman, you know, absolutely successful in his own area, and I was supposed to have that same sort of quickness that he had. But I didn't, I was a washout as a footballer or anything else. I was too slow learning my multiplication tables, for crying out loud! Not to mention my general shyness, made to perform in public before the most extrovert man I've ever known. I don't want to go on about it, but it explains that I was always in conflict with my father about what he wanted me to be."

"I understand perfectly, Anthony," I reassured him, "I know about it from personal experience."

He went on, registering that I was on side.

"Anyway, my mother was supportive about my vocation to the priesthood. So maybe you can understand that as I struggled with adolescence, you know what I mean, I leant a lot on the advice of my spiritual director at school, Father David. I fell under his spell, in fact. I didn't know the term for it, but he spent a lot of time grooming me."

"So was there abuse?"

"I thought so. It wasn't like the first time – "

"The first time?"

"Yes, it was less, less – "

"What?"

"Less genital, in fact not at all genital."

"Well what did Father David do?"

"He kissed me. I was shocked, and then angry, and I went to the Chaplain and told him. Mind you, when I say I went to the Chaplain, it involved breaking the door open to get out of Father David's room, crashing it and splintering it, and it was no secret that something had happened. I rushed straight to Father George's cell."

"They weren't all pederasts then?"

"That's a stupid statement, isn't it? God knows there is a problem about these priests but it isn't an epidemic."

I apologised at once. "Just take it that old prejudices are always just below the surface with me. I'm not priest-friendly, you know."

"Well, I wasn't either just then, I can tell you. But the School Chaplain, Father George, was absolutely straight and insisted on the whole truth. That was why I went with him to the Bishop to complain."

"What did the Headmaster think of that?"

"You know, it takes one solid good person to beat all the people who won't face up to the truth. Father George was that person. But when I think of it, really,

128

he didn't beat the system. He made them look shabby and I think they knew it, but he didn't beat the system. He didn't just have to deal with the Headmaster, you know, he had to deal with the person in charge of the religious community there as well. They hated all of this. And I hated being called a liar, because Father David said I had made it up."

"It sounds awful, but before you go on to what happened, can you explain what it was that let you get so close to this homosexual guy that he thought it was OK to kiss you?"

"Oh dear, oh dear. Why did I open this can of worms?"

"Listen, Anthony, if you were in a court they would be much more aggressive with their questions. If this Father David was taken to court, I mean, and had a defence counsel."

"Fair enough. My parents were happy together, I always fudge it, sorry, they were very happy actually with my sisters, but they always fought about me. I think my father despised me in some way, so I was miserable at home. I loved them dearly, but there was a great tension about living at home, and I was always glad to get back to school after desperately dismal holidays. I was scarily vulnerable and naïve - I can see that now. I was puzzled about what I wanted to do with my life, but one thing was clear to me – I had to have a life without the disdain I got from my father at home."

"Yet you knew that when you made a complaint against this priest, you would stir up all sorts of anger against you and a challenge to your truthfulness. Didn't you?"

"I said I was naive, Mike. I was always expecting affection and goodness, everywhere. I was a confused teenager, you must know that. But there was a grain of anger in me, even in that peace-loving frame of mine, which saw me through. It was when I considered what the two priests involved in the abuse had both said to me – both of them said exactly the same thing."

"So that first priest was the other name on the list? – Peter Mobile?"

"Yes."

"And what did he say that was the same?"

"Ha!" Anthony sighed. We both looked at the pasta put in front of us, and paused for a moment. The waiter removed our first wine glasses.

"I'm sorry about this", Anthony said. "I hadn't realised how much these old events still hurt me. Oh God!" He was swallowing, holding back tears. We sat still for a moment and Anthony raised a new glass, this time of a superior red wine from another corner of Italy. He gave me a professional cheery smile. But his tone was sombre despite this, like a man admitting to having lost a fortune or getting caught out in a fraud or some other disgrace which showed him to be a fool and even a scoundrel.

"Look, I'll tell you what they both said, I'll tell you, but don't expect it to mean as much to you as it does to me."

"I'm on tenterhooks."

"Wait. It is a phrase without any sex in it at all. Now Peter Mobile was full of sex, though he would deny it I'm sure, and used to talk about Christ's penis. Don't wince. Jesus Christ Our Lord was a man, and he had a penis."

"Save me from this!"

"Mike, he had a point, and it is just embarrassing that he *would* be the person to make that point, wouldn't he? Circumcision, naked baptism, buck naked on the cross – Peter was insisting that all of our bodies were holy, and Christ showed that."

"It's embarrassing stuff."

"He would stand up for it even today. That sounds silly doesn't it? Sorry."

"There's not much humour in all this, Anthony. But you say that it was not this that hurt you so much, but something both priests said to you. What was it?"

"They both said. They both said." He tried again. "They both said 'God loves you even more than you love yourself'."

"And that still hurts you" I said. "Why? Because they were both the biggest fucking hypocrites you would ever meet?"

"No. It was *'God loves me.'* It was that message coming from someone who really knew that it was

131

true. It was something I wanted to believe, and I was being told it by a liar."

10

There was nothing much I could say as I watched this middle-aged cleric struggling with recollections of the two abusers.

After a moment he went on. "It was betrayal, that was it. I could never listen to that phrase again, I could never use it. For a while I couldn't believe it, in fact now I think about it, I don't believe it. How could those miserable charlatans have ever known that God loved them more than they loved themselves? I grew to hate that – that mawkish religious ... I want to use the S word, Mike. Utter shit. You see, I'm disgusted and ashamed."

"So what happened at this meeting? Just what did you accuse them of doing?"

"It was more about Peter Mobile than about Father David. Father George, the chaplain, insisted that I explain that it was this recent experience 'with a priest at school' – I wasn't to give his name – that had got me there. He made it clear that he, Father George, had dragged me kicking and screaming to make this protest. Old George had got it right. Peter Mobile had instructed me that I must never tell what had happened under pain of mortal sin, to avoid scandal."

"How did that happen?"

"Mike, it's so awful what I went through. The indignity, the humiliation. I've not told you what happened, but I will, and at the end I went to confession to that bastard..."

133

He was almost crying now.

"You don't need to tell me everything you know, I'm just trying to get a hand on the story, Anthony. The allegations, you know? Can you talk about it dispassionately at all?"

"Yes, well, back to what Father George said. He insisted that there was no question about mortal sin, he didn't see it that way at all, and he was made of the right stuff, like I said, absolutely intolerant of lies and evil. But it didn't make any difference. The old Bishop there refused to believe me. And George and I had to go back for a second visit where we didn't even see the Bishop, just his then Secretary, Father Marcus Andrews."

"Whatever happened, you seem to be very agitated, Anthony, about not being believed. They would believe you now, wouldn't they? A past professor of the University here, are you not? A distinguished cleric? Surely you could walk into the Pope and tell him the truth personally, couldn't you?"

"You could be right. I'm just getting my courage up to do something. You don't know how damaged you are when you are abused and not believed, I don't think you can guess Mike. I have never felt the least bit sure about being someone who is pure. Do you know what that means?"

"Well, I wasn't brought up a Catholic, but I like the idea of purity, and, if you don't mind, I would say you are someone who embodies it."

134

Anthony's eyes opened wide, and he laughed in a quite cheerful way. "How on earth can you say that?"

"Well, it's Alexis of course. She regards you as the best of bachelor uncles, kindly and absolutely clean, 'pure' if you like, though I doubt she would ever use that word."

"Well, I can't hide the fact that I am delighted to hear that. But I feel soiled, I feel violated, I feel that I am dirty in the deepest way, and that there is no digging out of that filth. It's as if I need absolution, even though I know I don't, it's a feeling, Mike, of shabbiness and guilt."

"I don't have to understand all this, Anthony, but I do need to know some more about what you alleged about Peter Mobile and what happened."

"It gets worse – I haven't said it yet, Mike, but Peter Mobile was at the second meeting."

"So there was you and the school chaplain, Father Peter Mobile, the Bishop and his secretary, Marcus Andrews?"

"Not all of them – like I said, the Bishop didn't have the good grace to turn up. Just those two – Marcus Andrews, present as the Bishop's secretary, and Peter Mobile, present as an aggrieved party. I was pilloried by those two, I still feel the shame of having to say what Mobile had done, right in front of him and the others, still strongly unsure that it was right to make any complaint at all. Mobile had said it was mortally sinful to do so, you know."

"You said that already. Means? – just what?"

"Means I would burn in hell if I said anything about it."

"Well, presumably after all these years it is possible to say just what Peter Mobile did, isn't it Anthony? At least to me, an adult who doesn't believe what you believe about what Alexis tells me is detraction."

Anthony was looking more relaxed after the strain of talking about the interviews with the clerics. He twitched his nose and dabbled at his lips with the table napkin again, sighing as another empty plate was taken away.

"The meat is always good here", he said. He went on, in a narrative way with less obvious emotion.

"We have to go back to the refuge beyond Chamonix in 1979. There were three of us, three lads all from Peter Mobile's parish, where he was a curate, and Peter himself. It happened at night in absolute pitch darkness. It was me and Tom Benson and Kenelm Bates, as well as Peter Mobile, of course. I was fifteen and the other two were just a bit younger."

"Wait a minute, are you sure about the pitch blackness?"

"You're on the ball, aren't you?" Anthony said. "I've thought a lot about it – maybe there was a little light from the emergency exit sign. I know I want to think it was pitch black, so I don't feel so guilty about what happened."

136

"Are all Catholics like this? Do you have to analyse your motives in such detail?"

"We're not all crackpots, just me, I hope. We are trained to look hard at what we want to do and winkle out secret selfish motivations. Let me get on with it."

But it took him a moment or two to continue. He went on quite swiftly, then, as if he had rehearsed it.

"I was in one of the floor bunks, and Tom was in another. Kenelm and Peter Mobile were in the top two bunks. There were two other bunks with no one in them. It was quiet, I was getting ready for sleep when Peter Mobile came and touched me on the shoulder. He said 'Are you awake?' I said 'Yes'. He said 'Why don't you come over to the spare bottom bunk – I'd like to talk to you.'"

'I didn't say 'Why?' or anything like that, because I couldn't do that – I had too much respect for him. We sat on the edge of the bunk and I felt scared at once, because he put his arm around me. Then he started on the grooming. Talk of the sacred holiness of the penis, it makes me sick, how Christ was involved in all of this ghastly stuff. All the time he was whispering in my ear. I was terrified. My heart seemed to be beating so hard that you could hear it, and I remember that especially because of what he said after he had told me to lie down and followed after me. He was naked. He whispered 'I can tell the talk of these things makes you excited, your heart is beating like a hammer!' I said 'I'm very scared, Father'.

137

"There was no sense of pleasure then?"

"That's a real problem, Mike, for my conscience. Maybe that is why I always feel do guilty. At the start I felt a sort of prickling of curiosity and excitement, but it passed. I'll spare you the details, but he wanted to bugger me, and when I wouldn't let him he wanted me to handle his holy sacred organ for him. I was supposed to be learning about sex, he said. He refused to realise I was terribly terribly scared. Did you read about that awful American case, where Father Murphy said something like 'You know that God wants me to teach you these things?' It was that sort of patter, the bastard. I guess that his logic was that he wasn't masturbating, either, if he could get me to do it. But I wouldn't do it – thank God. I wasn't even tempted to touch his sacred organ.. It wasn't a short business either – the whole thing must have gone on for more than an hour, I would guess. Maybe less, but it was exhausting. Telling me all about the mechanics of sex, as if he was instructing me. This muscular man pushing at me, stroking my arms and legs, trying to persuade me that I needed to know and love and understand his – God! – his bloody penis. I was tired to start off with, but this was impossible.'

'He gave up. I went back to my bed and fell asleep quite quickly. But I was anxious and frightened, and the sound of whispers woke me up. It was Peter Mobile and Tom Benson. I tried to persuade myself that I was dreaming. I didn't dare to speak, so I pretended it was a dream."

He went on. "It was awful, Mike, and it has haunted me ever since."

"It sounds as if you were at the suffering end, why do you blame yourself?" I said.

Anthony looked sad as he quietly said "I didn't speak out. Maybe if I had, Tom would be still alive today."

"You're speaking out now."

"Mike, Mike, I was a coward. All I needed to do was say something right then and turn on the light, maybe wake up Kenelm, and there would have been three against one. But instead I lay there, stupid, pretending and pretending that I couldn't hear, pretending I was dreaming it. An absolute funk, disgusting, and I had no moral courage, I thought, because I had committed a mortal sin."

"For heaven's sake, Anthony, you didn't choose to be on the receiving end of that monster's seduction. And you weren't seduced, were you?"

"I feel as if I was seduced, and I know it's silly, but I can't ever get rid of my obsession with it. I'm compromised with myself before God, my voice is unheard because I have been seduced. It doesn't make sense, but that is how I feel. I'm a nobody, I am unable to be heard speaking the truth because I am a sinner, someone who took some pleasure in old Mobile's gropings and suggestions."

"Listen Anthony, in the end your conscience has brought you to the point that you are willing to speak the truth again. Because I take it that you told the

Bishop this before, when you were seventeen and the events were much closer to your memory."

"Yes, that's right. This would be a second telling. But they won't believe me, will they?"

"I think that you might have problems with your Church people, but other people will be ready to listen to you, and believe you too. For the record, I believe you. Because of the detail. Because of your obvious suffering, Anthony. I just wish we had some more evidence."

"Can you see now why I got so close to Father David, the teacher who kissed me? I hated my father, I can say it because I've told you so much, and I was betrayed by Peter Mobile. I was always looking for another father figure, and after my seeing through Peter Mobile, Father David was just that. You wonder why I am so fond of my family, my nieces and sister and sisters-in-law and all the family. It's because I know I can't trust anybody male, especially in the priesthood. I'm scared of being betrayed again, Mike, that's why I went for this pathetic approach to the newspaper."

"You're in a bad way" I said. "The way you talk, I get the sense that you feel that whistle-blowing about Peter Mobile will damage you in the Church. But I can't see that. From what Alexis says, you've got a private income, so why would loss of office be a problem? Do you have ambitions to be a bishop, or something? Forgive me, I don't know how the system works, except that it's, well, medieval."

140

"Look, if I make these accusations it will be me who is treated like a pederast, not those two. The fact of all the frenzy at the moment about clerical abuse will make them even more angry with me. I love Rome and the Church and I know everybody of any importance around the English-speaking hierarchy worldwide. It's a life I love. It uses my skills. It keeps me from becoming an old alcoholic recluse – I could be that so easily. Or stuck in some godforsaken parish visiting the old."

He laughed, a self-deprecating laugh as he urged me to drink up. "Hey, I'm not supposed to think or say things like that. But talking to you has made it easier."

"So what do we do now?" I asked. "You feel you owe it to Tom Benson to see that justice is done, don't you?"

"To him and to me, and if they won't be fair to me, then I can do it for him."

"What I can't get over is how Peter Mobile is seen as such a saint despite all this history" I said.

"That's because you haven't understood the Christian belief in penitence and the grace of God" Anthony replied. "Not that anyone knows about his – sin, shall I say?"

I thought about the problem of evidence. "I think we have got to get a copy of the picture Tom took on the night before he died", I said. "You haven't mentioned it, but I have talked to Kenelm Bates about what

141

happened in the refuge, and he says that Tom took a picture of the four of you naked. Do you recall that?"

"Yes I do, and I feel so ashamed about it."

"Why, did it give you a thrill?"

"You know Mike, for a non-Catholic you have a good grasp of the Catholic mind. It could be that – it's one of the reasons I never feel pure. I distrust anything I feel that is remotely connected with sex. But no, that isn't the main thing. I'm ashamed because it was all part of Peter Mobile's silly grooming, can't you see? But we didn't see."

"Tell me about your next morning."

"It was a nightmare. I was so tired and I felt rough and as if I had enjoyed being sinful – yes, it was my perception that in some way I was guilty of enjoying those gropings, even though I didn't."

"Yes, but what about Tom? Did he say anything? Did you compare notes? – sorry, that came out wrong, but you know what I mean."

"We didn't have a chance to do that, because Tom was already dressed and pushing at the door to go. Peter Mobile seemed to wake up about then and he asked Tom what he was doing. Tom said he was going back to Chamonix, and returning home. He shot off. Peter said 'Let's go get him' or something like that – I know I felt that I had to get up too. No, I recall, Peter shouting 'Let's talk about it!' and 'Wait!', but the next thing I remember is pounding along on the path, with Peter Mobile ahead of me. You know what happened, don't you?"

142

"Yes, I'm up to date on Kenelm's account, but what about you? What happened?"

"Peter Mobile wasn't quick enough to reach Tom, and he fell. Maybe he fell because he was trying to avoid Peter's hand. I don't know. He fell. Down the mountain. Peter went down after him, it was precipitous, picked him up, but didn't get far. Then it was me running back to the refuge, with Kenelm ahead of me, and the ropes and the warden and his chaps, and poor dead Tom pulled up ahead of Peter Mobile."

"So the only other witness to what Peter Mobile had done that night was dead."

"Yes. It was always going to be my word against his. Kenelm was spared all of it by being asleep."

I interrupted the flow here because I wanted to give Anthony my view of Peter Mobile.

"I've met Peter Mobile, of course, and I wonder if this man you detest has in fact changed in any way. I mean repented, become something of a saint, Anthony. It sounds daft, doesn't it, but I was really impressed by him. He seemed to have a sincerity and a devotion to the very best – I shouldn't be saying this, but do you agree that maybe he has changed?"

"Maybe, anything is possible."

"Mind you, I can't be so sure about that. I'm one of the people who has wrestled with Peter Mobile, and he ended the session by peering down my pants at you know what."

143

"And you give him the benefit of the doubt! You were indulging him, you realise that?"

"There's an aura of holiness about him, for heaven's sake! I detest and distrust him now, but I'm trying to be open to the other possibility."

"Listen" Anthony said, "the man always was a stunner. Absolutely clear eyes, straight back, a wonderful sincerity which meant – what? Piety without any connection with ordinary feelings, sentimentality. Cruelty, even. I think he identifies God and himself, and there's not much difference between the two."

Another plate came. Anthony asked after Alexis and warned me to take great care of her. He approved of our visit to San Clemente and advised a visit to Saint Peter's.

"If you can see just what you are taking on when you oppose the Church it will prevent you being triumphal" he said ruefully. "I do want to stop these people, but I don't know if I've got the courage to do it."

"That's where that photo of the four of you naked would be so helpful", I said. "It's enough to establish that things were dodgy."

"If I had ever had a copy I would have destroyed it in my quest to avoid detraction", Anthony said. "You know what I mean – scandal."

"What I don't understand is how, after all this experience of bad behaviour you went on to become a priest" I told him. "Didn't you want out of the system?"

144

"No, it's only now that I wish I had taken another turning. The pinnacle of imitating Christ is becoming a priest, and I never wavered in that. There was a search for security too, away from the wild sexual feelings that I suffered, not all the time, but I felt they were evil and would take me over. Being a priest meant that I opted out of all that, and I had a refuge from guilt. I had been warned in the confessional that if I spoke about anything that had happened I would burn forever in hell. I could give up everything to God as a priest so he wouldn't hold me guilty of anything. Yes, I had to put up with those two priests who were dodgy, but they didn't destroy the goal I was trying to reach. And did reach. I never dreamed of blowing the whistle until now, you know. It's just that I've thought a lot about all those children molested by priests, not only in Ireland but the huge numbers in the USA. After all, I'm someone who has suffered this, and I know that it is difficult to be believed. I know it's bigger than anything we know about so far, and it has gone on for my lifetime and beyond. With everyone's connivance, but mainly the clergy."

He looked thoughtful.

"Mike, I don't know if I can do it. But if I can, maybe other priests will come out of the woodwork too. We're all afraid of being taken for abusers, you know? Or regarded as damaged goods, whereas we were perfectly crystal pure before."

"Listen, you've made your cry for help, we'll find a way", I said, inwardly uneasy at the thought of what the uproar was going to cost him. "I've got two more questions for you. First, have you ever come across any other instances of child abuse in schools and parishes over your career?"

"Not at first hand. But there have been so many stories. It's not just children, it's not just boys, you know. Curates who arrive from some other diocese, even some other country, and within six months they've gone again, leaving some people very troubled. Young and older women, children of both sexes. Uncontrolled, hushed up. That was why Alexis' appeal for my help meant so much to me. The business of abuse isn't over yet. The bishops need squeezing for the truth."

"I'm sorry I can't be as definite as you would like" he went on. "But that's it, secrecy, concealment, protection of the holy hypocrites who are ordained like I am."

"How many clerics out there are abusers, do you think? As a percentage of the total?"

"It's not a question I can answer easily, Mike. Five in a thousand maybe? No, it must be five in ten thousand. I can't tell you, but I think it is not that many, really. But even one is too much."

"Well, there are four hundred thousand priests worldwide my research tells me. I think even one in ten thousand adds up to a lot of abuse. Second question" I continued. "You know we have a copy of

146

a missive to someone in the Vatican giving the two names of the priests you are accusing. Can you admit that you sent it out actually as a Vatican Questor's official document? Or at least got it ready to send out, but sent it to us instead? Why didn't you discuss it with the person I know to be your boss?"

Anthony answered "Maybe I can answer that obliquely. You are here to interview the Papal Questor for England, aren't you? I have an idea. Come over with Alexis to the Palazzo tomorrow, and I'll give you a rare glimpse of a part of Rome few people ever see. You can pop in to my office and then I'll introduce you to my boss, and you'll *find out* why I can't discuss it with him: I judge."

"That would be wonderful, as well as useful, I suppose. So that's it, Anthony, is it? I know why you want to shop these people, and it is entirely personal and based on their behaviour a long time ago. If you believe in repentance, then they should be left alone, shouldn't they?"

"What about belief in righting the wrong? What about stunting my life as I struggled to have a sense of my own worth, which I could only achieve by being some kind of dumb suffering saint? What about that, Mike? What about stopping it happening again? – not through those people but through the system?"

"All right, all right. I don't know where we will go with this, but I've been brought in to investigate. Should I go and see Bishop Marcus Andrews?"

"And confront him? Yes, please do. I'd like to do it myself, and maybe I will. Don't expect it to be very fruitful, though."

"Well, Anthony, thanks for choosing a wonderful restaurant. You know I'm not completely ignorant of the Catholic Church in England. I married a *Pietas* member, but it didn't work out."

"I'm sorry to hear that. But come on! – you're the man who wrote about Cardinal Manning in *Pre-eminent Victorians*! It's some time since I read it, but it was such a witty send-up of Lytton Strachey. Didn't you do research about the left-footers when you wrote that? The English RCs?"

"I did, I did. But it was an undergraduate spoof, in fact, and if you go back to it you'll find it was pretty sketchy. Mind you, nothing seems to have changed with the RC Church in England since the Victorian era as far as their bishops are concerned. Poorly educated Vatican-loyal bigots."

"You are so bigoted yourself, Mike, how can you talk like that? I admit they don't have the Oxbridge education of the Anglican bishops, but by the standards of the universal church they are pretty liberal and even radical and generally honest and – I'll admit to being an Oxford intellectual snob, but despite that – damn good company."

It was a slightly sour note on which to end the meal, but I was used to a sense of unease in myself after wooing subjects for information which was going to hurt them.

I could not see what was going to happen next. I felt for Anthony, who had drawn the short straw in life but had still preserved integrity and even a cheerful radiance about the future. Could I avoid an awful mistake?

As we left and shook hands, promising to meet at 10.30 next morning, I asked "How do we play this with Alexis? You didn't want her to come, did you?"

"Tell her whatever she should know, Mike. It's just that I couldn't tell her directly about this myself. That's why you're involved. I'm glad - I trust you."

As I walked back to the Professor's flat through the balmy night streets I wondered if I was worthy of his trust.

11

The Professor's little flat seemed more like an extended space around a bed than ever, as I prepared for sleep.

It was too late to knock on Bernie's door. I was saddened by what Anthony had suffered, but I had no idea how Alex would react to what I had learnt. She had to be told everything. Not that *she* had told me the truth.

Here I was, suddenly plunged into difficult moral territory while falling so deeply in love. I put down the burdens for the night and soon dropped into deep sleep.

I awoke abruptly. It was still dark. I was just capable of making out Alexis' features as she sat on the edge of the bed bending her head towards me.

"How was it?" she asked.

I puffed a little, waking in sharp shots of adrenaline as if I had just fallen asleep and was reawakening with that awful fear of dropping off a precipice.

Alexis grasped my arm reassuringly.

"It's only me" she said.

"Only you! 'Only you can make the darkness bright'!" I sang. All the adrenaline had moved instantly away from the part of me that was concerned with Anthony and his allegations to another part which warmed to the joy of her presence.

"Wait" she said softly, and I said "It can wait."

150

It was barely starting to get light when both of us woke up to the peace of a summer's day when we wanted to be nowhere else in the world but that high stuffy flat, quiet in each other's arms.

There was scarcely a sound from the street far below. "Let's get up" Alex said, "I've got some coffee and rolls so hard you can bang in nails with them. Let's do what the Prof suggested and go up on the roof for breakfast."

I followed her up the spiral staircase to the half-glass cube of the kitchen. We didn't turn the light on. There was a glow all around the horizon, and we stood looking at the panorama of rooftops as the coffee machine started to warm up.

"I want to ask you something very special", I said. "Can we turn away from that little lump over there?" I pointed towards the tip of St Peter's which was just proud of the skyline.

"Sideways to the sun?" Alexis replied. We looked towards each other. "Alexis, will you marry me?"

"I will", she answered. We swirled about the small roof, laughing, whooping, kissing, whirling and overjoyed.

I put on my best serious face. It wasn't hard for me to go into nagging mode.

"Alexis, now we are going to get married I want to ask you why did you bloody lie about this business of your uncle? You knew that it was him from the start, didn't you? I expect that he told you about Kenelm

151

Bates as well, so your pretence about looking him up was ridiculous."

"Have some coffee darling, and you can tell me about Uncle Anthony."

I told her the whole sorry story, and while she seemed to consider it from a legal angle she was obviously moved by pity and then by anger.

"We'll nail these bastards" she said. "We've got to find that other picture."

"But there isn't a legal case against anyone, is there?" I asked. "Not unless Anthony starts the ball rolling by making official allegations to the police. From what I saw, he's really afraid of doing that."

We munched the hard rolls, now dipping them into the coffee, now spreading on some Nutella we had found in the tiny fridge.

"What's the time?" Alex asked, as the hot sun was suddenly above the horizon.

"Why?"

"Because we've got to talk to my mum and go to Mass in St Peter's."

"I don't know which one strikes more fear in me" I said, getting a funny look in return.

"They are no threat to the good" she said.

"We're not married yet, you know" I replied. "Don't forget that I've had a trial marriage before."

Alex decided it was too early to call her mother, so we got showered and dressed in our separate 'official' dwellings, kissed baby Jennifer bye-bye and set off to the giant cathedral of the apostle saint. An early bus

152

took us quite close, and we walked across the big piazza.

We went inside St Peter's and found Mass at a chapel where the language was English. I was fairly familiar with the Mass due to my time with Sarah Louise, and I liked its quiet predictability and lack of tambourine-whacking evangelism. But there was something puzzling here, namely Alexis' keenness to receive Holy Communion (I knew it was always 'Holy' for the Roman Catholics). In my pre-marital instruction with Sarah Louise at *Pietas,* the need to avoid sex before marriage was stressed again and again. Catholics, guilt, sex was it? – yes it was, yes it was, sex, sin under pain of eternal damnation. I remembered an old Graham Greene novel, *The Heart of the Matter,* where one of the ways an adulterous husband tries to keep the secret of his infidelity from his wife is by his receiving communion. Scobie was not a born Catholic, but he sweats on the belief that he will burn in hell because of this, because to receive the Lord's body unworthily – not in a state of grace – is to ensure eternal torment. *Pietas* certainly subscribes to that scenario, but Alexis seemed to have another set of beliefs.

What a relief. Could it be that there were other Catholics like her?

Still, I didn't know if she was making a point about her beliefs about sexual sin by receiving communion, and there was no more to it than that. Alexis was obviously supremely happy. She was deeply in prayer that I knew must include me.

It was simple. I felt that urge to be good, no, be supremely holy and happy and secure that everything I did was right and good and even blessed by God. I could see that being a Catholic was a way of living your life. But being a member of *Pietas*? – never. I would have to explain my feelings to Alexis.

I did some of that as we walked towards the seminary where Anthony was going to introduce us to his boss, the Vatican Questor. Calling Alexis' mother was postponed until after the meeting.

We walked up to the old seminary side by side as I told her about Sarah Louise and our marriage. It was too hard for me to speak these words directly facing Alexis, but at times I turned to her or felt a reassuring squeeze of my fingers.

I told her how we had never lived together until our marriage. As best I could I talked of our problems – I didn't want to put Alexis off me. I reminded her that she had known Sarah Louise.

"Yes I did, but it was two years ago when we first met" Alexis said. "She seemed a bit of a waif, Mike, she was unhappy. I thought that was why she was exploring *Pietas*. But she is a born Roman Catholic, isn't she?"

"Yes, that was the root of the trouble, I think. She was seriously afraid of sex, Alex. I think we should have lived together and waited to get married, instead of what happened. It was a lightning romance…"

154

"There's a pattern here, I detect, look out."

" – and a terrible anti-climax."

"Come on, Mike! You can't put all the blame on a Catholic upbringing can you? Is that what you are saying? Warning! – Catholic teaching can cause you to be prudish, priggish and frigid? Millions of RC girls can prove you wrong!"

"I don't know. We got close to being lovers at the start, but she was really afraid of letting go. She stopped loving me, but said she didn't, she refused me, it was a nightmare. I tried to get her love back, but it was as if she were mentally ill, that's the only way I can describe it."

Alex grasped my hand extra strongly and said "Did you have any reason to reproach yourself Mike?"

"Some times I was harsh, I was sarcastic, I sneered, I hurt her. I didn't woo her, I expected her to be ready to make love, and I couldn't bear her refusals. A thousand reproaches now, but not then. I didn't know how self-obsessed I was, I had no idea. I was working flat out and being very successful. We weren't together enough. I know how these things go wrong, Alex, maybe that will help *us*."

"So what happened?"

"I tried to persuade her to get counselling, that meant both of us of course. She wouldn't. So we went back to *Pietas* and tried to get help there. That was when I was really desperate, that was when I wrestled with Peter Mobile. The *Pietas* people were all useless,

155

while they seemed to be full of consideration, they were full of duty and absolutely devoid of love. Sarah Louise moved out and we went through the annulment process. But the way I saw it and still see it is that it was all caused by *Pietas*. She had been flirting with them, you know what I mean, for a long time before she left me."

"Why flirting?"

I found it difficult to justify the word, which I could only do by using it to describe my paranoiac suspicion of any interest in *Pietas*.

We walked on in silence, climbing the road beside a long tall brick wall that was at the side of the huge gardens of the seminary we were to visit. The gardens were invisible to us over the wall except for occasional poplars and the tops of roses and other climbing plants reaching out into our narrow lane. How could Rome hold all of this beauty, so close to the centre of the city?

"Did she want you to join *Pietas*, Mike?"

"Of course she did, Alex. I wrestled with Peter Mobile…"

"*Flirted* with him."

"Oh shut up Alex. I wrestled with him precisely because I was wondering if going over to *Pietas* would put things right. But I couldn't sacrifice my principles and agree to join it just for her sake. It would have cheered her up. I can fool myself, you know. I could have done it. But when I thought about it, I knew it

156

couldn't be – not that and a happy marriage. Someone peering down my trousers didn't exactly help, either."

More silence, more squeezing of my hand. Then we were there, at the great door of the seminary, set in a brick tower just back from where the lane took a right-angled turn. I rang the bell and the large pink-faced figure of Father Anthony soon appeared, coming down a corridor with windows looking out on the classical garden of the seminary. As he came towards us, smiling to see his beloved niece, I studied the IN – OUT display showing who was to be found in the building. There was space for ninety people, I surmised, but only eight names were shown as occupants. There were a lot of empty rooms in this palazzo.

"You'll have to wait in the annex around the corner I'm afraid, Alex" he apologised to his niece. "Women aren't allowed here. But I'll try to get His Excellency to come down and meet you."

"Thank you, Uncle" Alexis said with simulated hurt. "You should have warned me."

"It just shows how out of touch we are with the female sex" Anthony said. "Even the aristocrat mothers of priests aren't allowed in here, I should have told you about this, Alex." Anthony didn't seem that bothered, though, as he turned to me and boomed "Come and see the Questor!"

He led me along the corridor and finally knocked at a door reached through a spartanly furnished suite of huge rooms used by the priest students for reading, TV and table-tennis.

Anthony instructed me "Call him 'Your Excellency'".

We entered an office which had the same lack of furniture as the other rooms we had seen, but with filing cabinets, a PC and a fax and one large antique desk and a throne-like chair in which sat the Vatican Questor.

He was a small self-assured Spaniard with glasses that made him look like a torturer from a World War II movie. Looking again, I saw a Spanish diplomat and cleric who wore glasses, about sixty years old.

I recalled my original approach for this interview. It was the wind-up in which I claimed that the Roman Church had no more authority than the Anglican Church because Catholic MPs couldn't be relied on to toe the Vatican line. The Prelate indicated that Anthony and I were to sit on the sofa. A man in a white overall came in with some coffee almost as soon as we entered.

Anthony introduced us. "Thank you for seeing Mike Claver. Mike is a journalist with an interest in the Catholic Church in England. I first heard of him over five years ago when he wrote a book which included an account of Cardinal Manning's place in the English Church in Victorian times. He has questions for you."

His Excellency Xavier de Raton said nothing, but stared at us solemnly.

158

I pitched in. "I am interested in the authority of the Roman Catholic hierarchy in England" I said. "I put it to you that membership of the Church by people in politics and senior positions in the Civil Service means nothing in the 21st century. The Bishops or the Pope can make proclamations, but no one will obey them except a few members of ultra-faithful groups like *Pietas* and *Opus Dei.* Your Church is on the level of the Anglican Church today. "

The Spaniard looked towards me with a stance as rigid as if he were posing for a photograph. He said nothing.

My training was to sit quiet and wait for some reply to my opening onslaughts, so I sipped my coffee and waited. Anthony seemed to back this approach, saying nothing and not budging an inch. The Spaniard stared at me without a movement of his face.

Outside there was the sound for a brief moment of someone kicking a ball. Then it was quiet again.

What seemed like two minutes passed. I wondered about the Questor. Did he suffer from Parkinson's disease or what? Why wouldn't he say something?

I waited, casting a glance towards Anthony from time to time. He was a ruddy colour suggesting some concealed tension, but his outward posture was unflustered. Finally the prelate spoke.

"His Holiness has made it clear that the Anglican Church does not possess the plenitude of ecclesiasticism" he said, with an accent that was Spanish. His English was odd and sometimes

159

incorrect, but his gist was quite clear. "The infallible nature of the teaching of the Roman Catholic Church on matters of faith and morals is guaranteed by the continuity of our orders of priesthood from the time of Christ."

"I am aware of your argument" I replied. "I'm saying that in practical terms many parts of your teaching are ignored by law makers and administrators who are nominally Roman Catholics. Not to mention almost everyone who is married."

"Not every Catholic is a good Catholic", he replied. "But most of our truths are practised, the loving concern for each other that is the mark of the Christian."

"No doubt" I answered. "I think you can't claim to have a monopoly of goodness, can you? But what about issues to do with abortion or medical uses of foetuses or the care of orphans by homosexual couples? Do all your Catholic MPs come out to back the Vatican line?"

"Anathema. They are to be anathematised if they do not" the Questor said, not raising his voice, but with a quiet satisfaction.

"I don't understand you. Do you mean excommunicated? I haven't noticed any of that. So I put it to you that the Roman Catholic Church has no power because it is so lacking in authority."

"We do not lack authority. We are the repository of the teaching of Christ" he riposted. I persevered.

160

"You believe that, and you do have power, I agree, if others share that belief. But I'm saying to you that they don't share all the beliefs that have the Roman Catholic brand name on them."

We drank more coffee and paused for a moment. I was falling into a mistake that I associated with the first months after Sarah Louise and I parted, namely a wild aggression that was destroying the sort of charm I needed to coax incriminating remarks from my interviewees. I nearly wrote 'victims' then, and that was my problem: I did want to find and nail an opponent, and this cleric was the best hate figure I had met so far.

But Anthony had arranged the meeting to show me why a direct approach to this prelate would be a waste of time. I needed to keep things going.

I changed my tack. "I mentioned *Pietas*, as a group within the Church with great orthodoxy and obedience. Do you regard them as model Catholics?"

"It's a strange question Mr Claver. Obedience and orthodoxy – it goes without saying that they are good Catholics."

"Well, I was thinking about the way that unthinking obedience to an unchanging agenda is associated with fascism in the British public mind", I said. "Fascism is indeed anathematised in the Church, isn't it?"

"Of course it is."

"But was it always like that? I'm thinking of Mussolini and Franco." I hadn't meant to be so aggressive, but it slipped out. I would have to give up investigative journalism, I feared, if I went on like this. But the Questor was not put off.

"Shall we adhere to the Roman Catholics in England and your hypothesis?" he said with a steely smile. "The Church is not a secular power in the current age. It is not united to secular powers anywhere in the world. It has moral power, and it preaches to a world that is sometimes deaf and sometimes contrarian. You are saying that the Roman Church is not as powerful as the Anglican Church or no more so. Maybe. It does not matter. That is it."

"But Your Excellency, can't you see? A moral power is only as strong as its advocates. Your voice is diminishing because your moral coherence has gone. And the scandals of clerical abuse and cover-up have diminished it even further."

"What about the Church's opposing the Iraq war or its opposition to nuclear weapons?"

"What about it? Has it made any difference to anyone anywhere in the world?"

The Questor was not discomforted. He glanced at Father Anthony and said "You were right to get Mr Claver to talk with me. He needs instruction." Then he turned back to me.

"It is dry, these abstractions, is it not, are they not? Let us consider someone who is to become a saint quite soon – Franz Jägerstätter. He was beheaded in 1943 by the German army for refusing to fight in a war that he considered unjust. He exemplifies the moral authority of the Church."

I bit my tongue. I knew that the man in question had made his refusal to fight against the best advice of most of the churchmen in Austria. What had obedience meant there? This Austrian farmer had been disobedient to the main body of the Austrian Church's direction.

But I had to be diplomatic. I could see what Anthony meant about his hopes of getting anywhere with this old Spaniard. I tried to reintroduce *Pietas.*

"Jägerstätter is a wonderful witness and I have read his biography, Your Excellence. Thank you for pointing it out to me. But I wonder if you could make any comment on *Pietas* and the future of the Church?"

"The group are not the Church, but they are a shining beacon within it. I can say with assurance that the Holy Father shares this perception. It leads the way in its commitment to the practice of Christian, yes Catholic values in the world today."

Anthony coughed and came into the conversation. "Actually there are two Members of Parliament in *Pietas*" he said. "One in Scotland and one in England. So they are a small but important presence. They are represented in the Civil Service too, and in leading companies. They have visibility Mr Claver, and some authority."

Anthony then turned from looking directly at me to take in both of us. Very slowly, sitting quite straight and looking at both of us, Anthony spoke strongly, as someone not to be silenced.

"Your Excellency, this morning I told you about my experience of abuse at the hands of the current Ordinary of *Pietas* in England. I have spoken about it to Mr Claver here. I would like to discuss with you, in the presence of Mr Claver, what should be done about this matter, Monsignor Mobile's abuse of a child, myself."

The Questor's eyes stared at us through his rimless glasses and he made some barely audible whimpering noises as he shook his head from side to side. We watched as he opened and closed his mouth again and again. I was surprised too, but Anthony turned to me and touched my arm as if to say 'I owe the courage to do this to you.'

There was a knock on the door, and it opened to the bright sound of Alexis' greeting.

"Hello! I've just walked round your wonderful gardens. Can I join you?"

The Questor stood and walked past her in silence, shaking with anger.

"You should never have come in here!" he shouted. "It is forbidden to your sex! Even the mothers have never entered the seminary at the ordination of their sons! Get out of here at once!"

We stood silent and watched him rush down the corridor, driven from his own office by a need to escape from facing the issue Anthony had raised.

"Where's he going?" Alexis asked Anthony.

"He needs to get word up to his superior in the Vatican", Anthony replied. He gave us a wan smile. "That's what authority means, you know. He's not worried about me, he's worried about himself. He's terrified of doing the wrong thing. I should never have told him, you see? That's what he thinks. Life is difficult for him now. He could have just ignored what I told him, but now I've involved you, Mike, way hey!"

He smiled in self-deprecation and said, turning to her, "Alex, I'm sorry, but you'll have to go. Coming in here is even worse than pederasty in that old fruit's mind."

"What's happened, besides my one-woman rape of a Roman seminary?" Alex asked.

"Anthony has just told the Questor that he is going to denounce Peter Mobile for you-know-what, Alex" I explained. "What about that?"

"I'm so pleased for you Anthony" Alex said. "I knew you would get your courage up. It is the right thing to do, never doubt that."

"Should we both go now?" I asked Anthony.

"Just wait a bit will you, Mike? I know I'm going to need your help."

12

We accompanied Alex back out of the office through the elegant salon with its tatty furniture back into the long tall corridor and walked to the outside door. There was no sign of the Questor or anyone else at that moment.

"What exactly happened?" Alexis asked.

"I got my courage up to raise the issue with His Excellency", Anthony said.

I chipped in. "That was a brilliant idea to tell His Nibs that I was just as much in the know as he was. He has got to do something now."

Alex said "Actually I've just wreaked havoc with the priestly nudists in the garden too." She laughed. "I almost thought that His Eminence..."

"...Excellency..."

"...had seen the chaos and someone had run in naked to report on me. Isn't he hateful? Or is it just that he's a misogynist?"

"Both" I said.

Anthony asked me if I'd like some coffee, and turned towards the distant kitchen. As he set off he said "Don't let this spoil your fun, Alexis. Give your Mum my love when you give her the news about Mike. But don't tell her anything about this yet, will you?"

Alex stood holding the side of the huge door to the seminary and showed me a serious face.

"Mum will have to wait. I need to let Bill know the latest events. This is going so much faster than we ever

166

expected. It must be you, Mike. You've made Anthony feel he can speak up for the first time."

"I feel so sorry for him" I said. "But that lunatic Mobile deserves everything he gets because of this. Anthony has no idea what he has lost because of Peter Mobile's abuse."

"You don't think he went for the priesthood *because* of the abuse, do you?" Alexis asked.

"You know, I wouldn't be surprised. I think an experience like that – with two clerics, one after the other, even *because* of the years between – must have left him feeling that sex is a uniquely damaging and dangerous thing. That he himself could run off the rails so easily. So maybe he should be a priest and avoid it altogether. Maybe that's why your Church is so odd about sex, you know? It has seen so many supposedly holy guys turn into sex freaks. It only needs one in a thousand and the message gets around."

Alexis looked as if she wanted to be somewhere else, no doubt phoning Bill about events to date. Her boss-lady persona, God bless it, was taking over again. Not that it was ever successfully concealed from my eyes.

"I'm pretty sure things have to move back to the UK now" she said. "I'm going back to Bernie's and I'll phone Bill on the way. I'm sorry."

"Why are you sorry? It was always a business visit, and we've done the business just fine so far, Alex."

She moved up to me and I put my arms around her. There were no clerics around to be shocked at our affection.

167

"Mike, we can go on in London! I haven't even talked to my Mum yet! She's going to be so surprised!"

"Alex, Alex, I need some more Roman background. Let's at least stay until Sunday night, tomorrow. Please. Things can still happen here you know."

"I want that too. But I can't promise. When you've finished here, get Anthony to come back to Bernie's. We've got to plan the next steps."

At that point Anthony reappeared, followed by a white-coated man with a coffee-pot. We went back to the office where I sat on one of the uncomfortable chairs.

"She's a remarkable woman" I said.

"Yes she is" Anthony agreed. "She asked me for *my* help and now *her* help has completely changed my life. For the better. Thank God I've faced up to it."

"Anthony, remember you asked me to turn off my digital recorder when we met?"

"Yes. You did, didn't you?"

"Of course I did. But I've got it here with me. If the Questor is going to take some time, maybe we could start to prepare your statement about the incident?"

"It has to be done. Not a press release Mike, please, not yet."

"No no, I mean the statement you'll need when you talk to the police."

"Do I have to do that?"

168

"Anthony, even if you were never going to do it because of what the Church decides to do about these allegations, you would still need to convince your superiors with the facts. And if what you have hinted is true, then only the threat of it all coming out in court is going to make them take you seriously anyway."

Anthony nodded. "Let's get going" he said. We started to record an account of the events in 1979. It kept us busy for the next three quarters of an hour.

"Where's His Excellency?" I asked. "Will he reappear at all? After all, it is Saturday."

"I'll go and talk to the staff. They'll know where he is. There's a phone up in his bedroom and he'll be using that. He'll be in real trouble, you know, without his secretary. Ha! Serve him right!"

When Anthony returned with yet more coffee he told me that the Questor was still holed up in his cell upstairs. We talked a little about Anthony's beliefs.

"No, I was never likely to have been attracted by *Pietas* once I had passed through university. My Order had a connection with Oxford and I read theology there. You learn to go beyond the formulae of different statements of what people believe, do quite a lot of study of the scriptures, and you get the whole system into a sensible focus."

"So you become a sort of liberal agnostic, Anthony?"

"No no no. You – I mean I – believe in God revealing himself in Christ. But I don't necessarily feel I have to talk about it in some special way – Jesus would be born from sexual intercourse just like

169

everyone else, and the idea for example of his virgin birth would just arise because people of the period had funny hang-ups about sex. And still do."

"So you can't say that sort of thing to the ordinary Catholic, huh?" I asked.

"That's right."

"Well if you have to live in a strange world where what you really believe can't be said, isn't it all hypocrisy?"

"Maybe, Mike, but there's this too. We love Christ because he was so in the face of hypocrisy and self-justification, so keen on us being non-judgemental, and so good! All the miracles. Do I believe in them? Yes, I do. They are quite full of personal details and lots of joy and an anti 'You're sick because you sin' ethos. So I love him and the Church he created and I just wish it was as intelligent as its scholars and some of its theologians."

We talked more as the clock ticked on. This was turning into a tough day. Outside the sun shone and Alexis might be sitting at a café table with Bernie and the babe, but I was here, waiting on the whim and fear of an old Spanish cleric.

Anthony had three inspirations. "I'll use the kitchen staff to take a message up to the Questor that we are still here. I'll ask them to wheel in some sandwiches. And I'll start to type this stuff up as a proper statement."

The inspirations lightened this sad Saturday for a while. I felt grim because the evil of Peter Mobile was

170

manifesting itself here in the funk of the cleric at facing a sudden and nasty truth. For I never doubted for a second that Anthony had told the truth. Why had the Questor not just discussed it with us like normal human beings? If he had thrown a wobbly, shouted his disbelief, even hit Anthony in his anger, I could have accepted it as part of the process of swallowing such a destructive fact. But nothing but funk, fear, furtive scurrying to the wainscot where the other cockroaches lived.

"Who will he talk to?" I asked Anthony.

He remained the eternal English gentleman, ready to entertain with surprising facts about the Roman church.

"*There's* a question. You see, all priests are assigned a diocese, and as I'm in a diplomatic job, I am working for the diocese of Rome. The Bishop of Rome is…?"

"Not the Pope, is it?"

"Precisely! Because we are diplomats. In practice there's a Vatican official I report to, and I don't expect much enlightenment from him."

"Now look, I'm no worshipper of the clergy, so I share that perception. But Anthony, you don't seem to have a high view of these Vatican folk. Really, you're letting the side down aren't you?"

"Don't be a hypocrite, Mike. We're in a place beyond diplomatic words just now. I am probably already dismissed."

171

"That can't be! Shoot the messenger? Look, if you are to be interviewed by any of these people, you should take someone along to support you."

"Mike, will you come with me?"

"Of course. But you will need a lawyer when you get to the UK. I don't know where you will have to go to report the incident, but I expect it will be back where you all lived in 1979."

"Can't Alexis be my lawyer?" Anthony asked.

"No, I don't think so. There's the other case and there might be a clash of representation. Too complicated."

At that point the door opened quietly and the Questor slimed in.

"For today you are relieved of your duties as secretary" he announced to Anthony. "You will have an interview with the Cardinal Sidesman at noon tomorrow, in his office in the Vatican."

"Thank you, Your Excellency. I want to be accompanied by Mike Claver at the meeting. Could I let the Cardinal know about this requirement?"

"He is away at the sea today. I doubt if he will permit it."

"I plan to go to the police in England as soon as possible and depose the facts with them. I have them written here, and I advise you to read them."

The Questor took the copy that Anthony had printed out only minutes before, casting a practised eye over the document. Whereas he had looked fearful before, now he was matter of fact and deadpan once again. I

172

sensed that he already felt that everything was less of a threat because the whole matter could be condensed into four typed pages.

"Thank you" he said. "Please get in touch with me about tomorrow's meeting. You can stay here during your time in Rome. For the rest, I advise you not to return to our office in London. You know why this issue is so sensitive."

"You know it might make more sense to cancel tomorrow's meeting" Anthony said. "I can't see what purpose it will serve. I've made up my mind."

"In decorous and meek obedience to your Bishop, who is His Holiness the Pope, you must have this meeting. You are under obedience to so do." The Questor sounded prim, but his face suggested that he was relishing the power of righteousness. He had obviously retaken possession of his office, so we shambled out into the corridor and faced each other.

"Hey, let's go have a drink" I suggested.

"Never so welcome!" said Anthony. "Have you seen the gardens? Would you like to?"

"Come on Anthony, we need those bevs" I said.

"Just take a look Mike, two minutes, I promise. If you left Rome without seeing this, I'd never forgive myself."

We walked out over a small lawn of surprising greenness to a wide brick arch beyond which were the long formal gardens so tantalisingly hidden from the street by the seminary's tall walls. Espalier apples and damsons lined the narrower paths and tall poplars

173

teased the eye with the promise of never-ending gardens beyond interior walls. Fountains, arbours, even a statue at a corner all made this place an outpost of Eden. In the distance there was a swimming pool, and we spied a naked sun-worshipping student reading a prayer-book Anthony told me was called a breviary..

"It's amazing" I admitted, "and thank you for showing it. It raises so many questions in my mind, Anthony, I can't avoid it." He knew that I was looking at the Church in Rome and finding it wanting.

Anthony at last decided to take off his sotana and put on some leisure clothes. After he had changed we left the seminary and started to walk back towards Alex. She told us by phone to take our time as she was doing some shopping with Bernie and baby Jennifer.

"Let me show you a little church on the way", Anthony said. "There's a nice little bar just beyond it. Work up a thirst, you know? Am I giving a bad impression?"

"You sound real to me, not like that boss of yours" I said. "What shocked me is that huge building with so few people using it. It should be open as a park, at least. And those priests are living the life of Riley."

"No vocations, that's why it is so empty. Don't worry, it will be sold off in the end. That's what the Catholic Church is about now, selling off old assets to prop up its dwindling cash flow."

"And support its lifestyle?"

174

"To be fair, those young guys will never have it so good again in all their lives. And they do have a lonely life you know."

"They chose it, I thought, out of a desire to be priests?"

Anthony shrugged. "I can't argue with you."

In the shoe-searing heat we hot-toed away from a wider avenue into the narrow shade of a side street. Along its busy frontage Anthony opened an unexpected tall gate that went into a courtyard beside a small church. It was a narrow tree-lined garden, contained within the tall side walls of the large houses on both sides next to the church. By a lion-head fountain, trickling welcome water from its brass mouth, there was a bench. I sat down.

"My feet need a rest" I said. Anthony ploughed on into the church.

There was no sound except the soft splashing of the water in the fountain. I looked around me. The leaves of a fig tree next to me filled my nose with a sweet breath, and a pigeon was cooing below the eaves of the church with the quietness of waves lapping at low tide. On the brass lion's cheeks there were droplets of moisture, and on the architrave of the fountain an ant was moving towards a tiny hole in the mortar between the big stones of the wall. Peace.

Anthony returned from the church.

"Thank you for that" I said to him. "You missed the best" he replied, "The church is fantastic."

"Well the churchyard is wonderful, and Rome is incredible, and Alex is better than both of them."

"And the wrong-doings of the Church got you here. Well, here is something else which is hidden and nothing but good. Let's go have a drink."

Anthony drank the first beer rather too fast: he was grabbing at a way to escape from his dilemma.

"I need another – sorry, I'll go ahead of you here in the booze, you don't think I drink too much do you?"

As he took a gulp of the second glass of the cool drink Anthony let me in on the reasons that had precipitated his action in contacting *Sunday Seven* and his niece about the abuse in his own life.

"It was this" he said, tapping the side of his glass. "It's a miserable tale, but just before I left the Order that I used to belong to I was asked to go to a Retreat Centre, so-called, to help by giving a talk and a day of being available for priests on retreat. I thought! It was this spooky place near Stroud, which looked a bit like an enclosed order, you know, all high walls. A prison, I mean. Who should I see there but his nibs, Peter Mobile. He pretended not to know me, and I was enraged. I said 'Chamonix, remember? Or at a certain Bishop's office?' "

"He ignored that. 'What are you here for?' he asked me, 'internet porn, full sex or the bottle?'

" 'I'm giving a talk' I said, ' and I don't need to ask what *you* are here for.'

176

" 'You fell for that, did you?' he sneered at me. 'You're in denial about your alcoholism, aren't you, and they got you here by that trick.'

" 'You bastard!' I said, 'You can talk about denial!' '

" 'Oh yes? You're thinking how pleasant it would be to have a good tot of vodka just now, aren't you?' '

" 'Peter, I didn't expect this' I said. 'I'll admit it would be nice to get up to the Amberley Arms for a meal, and I'll do that if I want to.'

"He asked me if they had taken away my stocks, meaning my bottles.'

" 'What are you on about?' I said, 'I don't carry drink around with me, at least, not yet.' It wasn't true, though.

"Why am I telling you this, Mike?" Anthony said to me, his face now quite ruby with the beer he had consumed. "You have to know what an insect that man is. He said 'Hand over your hip flask' and held out his hand out for it.'

"I told him it was nothing to do with him, and reminded him I was there to give a talk on the relevance of the Trinity in St Augustine's theology. He was absolutely scathing. 'You're here for alcohol abuse, Anthony' – that was good for someone who had pretended he didn't know my name – 'haven't you realised?'

" 'Well, we both know what you're here for, don't wc?' I said.'

"But he acted as if he didn't know what I was talking about. He was right, too, I mean about the drink. I was there as a warning about my drinking, I realised that as he said it. I was in denial, you know. But what made me seethe was that he was there to teach the way of holy restraint. As the English Ordinary of *Pietas*, no less."

Anthony went on. "It was an awful moment, it was like suddenly being stabbed, by this disgusting pretty-boy hypocrite, the hound of humility. I hate him, I know I shouldn't, but I do."

"So what did you do?" I asked Anthony.

"I did have my hip-flask in my pocket, and I took it out and poured it over his head. And I left. When my Superior asked me about the Retreat he knew I had stormed out. I could tell he had heard about the hip-flask incident, but still he was sort of respectful. He knew I was looking at leaving the Order, of course, so he stood back a bit. They didn't want to lose me. Or my inheritance. Between you and me, that weekend did a lot to stop me drinking for quite a long time. But it fired up my resolution to shop that awful bastard on his bloody moral high horse!"

"So that's when you decided to get after him?" I asked.

"Yes, and there were things about him being promoted to the Archbishopric that came through the office, and when as it happened the name of Bishop Marcus Andrews came up as well, I wanted to go after them. It has taken a hell of a lot of prayer and anger to do it though."

178

We encouraged each other and talked about tomorrow's meeting, and left the café rather later than planned, with renewed resolution to nail the offenders down.

Alex was sitting at an outside table at the café just near Bernie's and our apartments. She beamed at me, waving her mobile phone.

"I've just called Mum and she's on the line here Mike, so say hello."

I took the mobile and told Alexis' mother that her daughter was going to marry me.

13

I heard "Michael, Mike, how wonderful!" from the mobile, in a voice which was rich and like Anthony's in its intonation and pronunciation. "Congratulations!" it went on. "No surprise that I've never heard of you with a daughter like Alexis! You're very lucky, young man, you will have so much to live up to, and you are very unlucky young man, so much to live up to, I did say both, but I am so happy for you, Mike, eh? And when did you meet?"

"I know I'm lucky, yes this *is* Mike, we met – oh dear, it was last – golly, I feel as if we've known each other all our lives, last *Monday* was it?"

"You have known her so little time, Mike! My daughter is a very successful young woman, and she has never even been out with a man before, so you be careful, she must have chosen a great one, you know what am I saying? But you know what I mean, Mike, we both know about her wonderful gifts?"

Alexis grabbed the phone and said rather sternly "We'll have known each other for two weeks next Tuesday. I heard what you said. You know damn well that I have been out with men before."

I took the mobile again and my future mother-in-law said "When you come and see me I'll give you the strengths and weaknesses of your fiancée. I am glad to say she is always aggressive and stubborn."

"I know it already, what do I call you, prospective mother-in-law?"

"Letizia. She tells me you are good-looking, dark and wear glasses."

"Yes, that's right. I imagine Letizia that you are petite and as beautiful as your daughter? She looks just like Audrey Hepburn here, you know, a little more feminine in her hips but even more beautiful."

"Yes, yes yes, you should be careful with your flattery, but are you a lawyer too?"

"No, I'm a writer."

I held the mobile away from my ear as Letizia made a slightly gasping sound which was quite audible to Anthony, Alex and Bernie, who all laughed aloud.

Alexis grabbed the phone from me and shouted "Mike's in the media! He's a freelance journalist and non-fiction writer. His articles are in the papers you never read, the heavies. He's an intellectual. And to answer the next question, he's not a Catholic."

She turned to look towards me, giggling and shaking a little with excitement while she told her mother "Mike will bring some of his articles in the original papers in which they appeared when we get back to England." I nodded. "He says of course he will. So see you soon Mum, possibly Monday, maybe tomorrow, but very late. I'll call again. Your daughter is going to be a married woman, don't doubt it!"

I thought I heard an exclamation from the mobile, but I couldn't be sure. Alexis ended the call with kissing sounds.

"Has your Mum got a problem about writers?" I asked her.

"Not at all, not at all! Not as such. She has exactly the same problem about window-cleaners and jockeys and schoolteachers. It's just that unless you happen to be a lawyer or a doctor or a wealthy, let me stress a *wealthy* aristocrat her daughter will be marrying below herself. That's the way she thinks."

"Was your father a lawyer?"

"He was a dentist. A Catholic dentist, of course, pulling out Catholic teeth. Why hide it? But don't forget, I'm the only person Letizia has got."

"Except for her brother Anthony and her two sisters and the twelve nephews and nieces" Bernie chimed in.

"Look, I'm completely out of this" Anthony said. He had been gurning his pleasure at our news about being engaged so far, without actually opening his mouth, but now he was able to express his pleasure that the two of us were going to marry.

"When did this happen?" he asked. "I thought you hardly knew each other. I can't say how pleased I am that you are going to marry, though."

Hugs, handshakes, promises to drink to it later on, and then Alex wanted to go straight back to business.

But Anthony had sensed the elephant in the room.

"Look, I know nothing about you Mike, and I hope to learn more later on. But I had a sense that you were involved with someone in *Pietas*, isn't that right? Did you mention it, Alex?"

Alex frowned. "I may have done. Can we get on with the business?"

"Sorry, I'm a clod I know. But you've got to tell me – you're all looking at each other there, I may be self-obsessed, but there's something I need to know."

"It can wait" Alex insisted.

"I've got to spill the beans" I said, addressing Alexis in particular. "Your uncle needs to trust people, first and foremost. You and I and Bernadette and Letizia and your family are the only people he feels he can trust. We've got to tell the story."

I told Anthony about Sarah Louise and the annulment. Bernadette listened avidly too.

"Well where is this lady now?" Anthony asked. "Sarah Louise?"

I had three alert and interested listeners.

"She's in Canada now, working for a branch of a right-wing clerical sect: the European ones may even include Holocaust deniers. Somewhere right of Pope Benedict, I'm afraid."

"It strikes me you were well rid of her" said Anthony. "I'm sorry, I'm such a clod, I didn't mean to say that Mike."

"Anthony, Sarah Louise is a woman of great intelligence and power, struggling with something that probably goes back to her mad mother. And I happened to love her. Can we move on, now? Have you talked to Bill?" I asked Alexis.

She shook her head slightly to signal that discussion in front of Anthony was not a good idea, I think, rather than that she had not talked to him. It was Saturday: Bill would be busy putting tomorrow's *Sunday Seven* to bed.

"What's happened since I left you?" Alexis asked.

"I'm suspended" Anthony explained. "But I can use the seminary as a bolthole. I'm not allowed to travel to England. But the big news is an interview with the Cardinal Sidesman tomorrow at twelve o'clock."

"I've offered to accompany Anthony for the interview" I told Alex. "And maybe he'll need a lawyer for the English police, Alex. I explained that you would be unlikely to be able to help."

"Look, this is private stuff, isn't it" Bernie asked. "Shouldn't I butt out?"

"We can talk about it after you've been to the Rifugio" Alexis said. She turned to me. "You know, the crypt of the Episcopal church where the Professore is a Warden? Bernie always helps the asylum-seekers on Saturday afternoons. I'm going to do the baby minding for her. It's just a couple of hours isn't it, Alexis?"

"Yes, but you men ought to come and see it. You promised the Prof to go to morning service there tomorrow, but if you have an interview at noon you can't do it. So you've *got* to come *now*. Yes, even you Uncle Anthony. You can cope with slumming it in the crypt of the Episcopalian Church, I'm sure."

184

"Is that all right, Alexis?" I asked her, wondering if I was already married to her in spirit. Well I was, I thought, and it made me happy and a little nervous.

We set off, leaving Alexis in charge of baby Jennifer, and caught a bus towards the railway station. Bernie explained that the Centro per Rifugiati had been started by a Ugandan Episcopalian priest called Joel Nafuma, who had been a refugee himself. The Episcopalians were an American branch of the Anglican Communion, whom most people had heard of in connection with their liberal attitude to gays. They were under attack from conservatives and the African Anglican Bishops, in particular, who were anything but liberal in attitude.

"This is the church where the Prof is a Warden", Bernie explained again as we travelled towards Stazione Termini. "It's the first church in Rome to have ordained a woman priest, but I bet it won't be the last. Uncle Anthony you are out of the ark" she exclaimed as the bus lurched towards the side of the road. He was making little moues of amused disdain at the idea of women priests.

The Chiesa di San Paolo entro le Mura was more like a neo-gothic brick church in Birmingham than anything Roman. It had mosaics created by Edward Burne-Jones. It was impressive in a Victorian Church of England sort of way, and mainly patronised by Americans and other English speakers.

But Bernie was full of the day-centre she wanted us to visit, down the steps and in the crypt of the church.

"This is the best place that asylum-seekers can go to in Rome" she said proudly.

There was a noise of human chatter as we went through the wide doors at the foot of the steps into the crypt. The background colour was that of sand, the predominant tint of the Muslim asylum-seekers' clothes. Against that amber the Africans stood out for their black skin and bright clothes. I looked around for women's' faces, and found them in a corner of the large central area, with two dozen children. I tried counting the numbers present, a standard drill for all journalistic reporting, and reached one hundred and ten. Almost eighty of them were men, probably all under thirty years of age. Take away the helpers, difficult to distinguish from the helped, as they were also wearing tracksuit pants and T-shirts, and the remaining number were young women.

Bernie introduced us to the Manager, a middle-aged Iranian who had lived in Rome since before the refuge started. Bernie went off to help with crayons and drawing books for the children while Yousef explained what the refuge did. There were three case-workers helping with paperwork for applications for visas, and another two interpreters who helped out as the need arose. "Many people here are in a line waiting for this help" the Manager explained. "While they wait, they talk and drink coffee and get told how difficult it is to become an Italian citizen."

Anthony was intrigued. "I never imagined this was going on", he said. "How many people come every day? How many do you feed?"

"One hundred and fifty come in. They wait outside for us to open. We think that at least another thirty new asylum-seekers arrive in Italy every day, and many come here on their way to other places."

Anthony asked if there was anything he could do, and was sent off to help Bernie and the children. I told Yousef that I was a journalist, and asked permission to question his helpers.

They were a mixed bunch, with one thing in common – they all wanted to help. "Why do I help? Would you let your children sleep in the street if you could find them a bed?" So one Italian lady volunteered, confusing me because I had thought the refuge was closed at night. "It's a way of speaking", she explained, as the Rifugio was indeed only open during daylight hours.

Another was an American post-graduate student who spoke Arabic. "I felt I need to help. These people don't want to be here you know, for the most part. They have been driven here by the Iraq situation, or they have been victimised in Afghanistan or pushed out of the Congo."

I asked him if he was an Episcopalian, which he was, and then if the other helpers were from the church community too

"No, I'm a rarity", he said, "there's all sorts of believers here and those who believe in nothing. Look at Mohamed Adam over there – he is a Muslim, but he helps out here every day of the week."

I sat down for a moment and looked around me. There were faces showing signs of suffering in the way that the eyes searched the floor. For many their body-language of stiffness and humped shoulders, mouths set in a downward curve and tightly held hands all spoke silently of desperation and fear. The faces of the helpers were outward-looking, calm, not quite cheerful, and undemonstrative.

When we left, I asked Bernie how she could do this work when it achieved so little for the people there.

"I don't know", she said, "but the world would be a sadder place if someone didn't help. You can't tick boxes here. There is no reward, but I feel it's something I can do."

"What do *you* make of it?" I asked Anthony.

"I'll need to think about it. It's completely outside of my daily experience. But I am impressed."

Back at Bernie's again, Alexis announced that we needed a planning session. I was sure she had been on the phone to Bill. Forbidden to drink anything alcoholic until the discussion was over, we settled under the awning of the café-restaurant in the narrow street below Bernie's and the Professor's apartments.

188

"We need to sort you out Anthony", she said, dropping the Uncle once again to indicate that this was business. "Why do you want to talk to this Cardinal Sidesman person if you have made up your mind to shop Peter Mobile to the English police?"

"Good question. I want to acquaint him with the facts and let a process of justice according to Canon Law start against Peter Mobile."

"Sensible. With the statement you have completed with Mike's help it shouldn't take him long to decide you have a case, should it?"

"I don't know. There could be plenty of delay as the case is considered for acceptance by the Canon lawyers. I don't really expect a decision to investigate and have a hearing until after – I'm guessing, but I shouldn't be far out – maybe eighteen months. But they will only go on to reporting things to the police at that time."

Alexis seemed satisfied with these replies. "I get the picture. You can't afford to wait on the Church's justice system."

"No" Anthony replied.

"Why bother with the Vatican people at all then?" I asked.

"Because I am a priest and that is the right way to go about it. From a practical point of view I have to be whiter than white if I am to remain a priest, too."

Alexis looked grave.

"Have you thought of the chance that the British police might decide not to proceed on your evidence, Anthony?"

"What?" I asked. "A distinguished cleric? Why would they doubt him? When they consider for the first time the possible contributory factors to poor Tom's death?"

Alexis turned to me.

"It may surprise you, but the police can play exactly the same card as the Church to refuse an investigation. That the benefits of refusing to prosecute or even investigate will outweigh the social consequences of letting it all alone. Especially after over thirty years."

"But what if the Vatican puts me in purdah?" Anthony asked. "If I'm forbidden to do anything with the civil authorities until the Church investigation is over?"

"You tell us" Alex suggested.

"We're getting back to my fears of my own wimpishness again. I intend to say 'Sorry, but I'm going to make my complaint right now'."

I said "Anthony, don't say 'I intend to'. Say 'I will'."

He smiled and said "I will, I will. *I am going to the police in England now.*"

Alex said "That means from a practical point of view we ought to leave Rome tomorrow afternoon and get out to the police headquarters on Monday morning. OK?" I guessed she was thinking of the need for speed

190

for the *Sunday Seven* story. But Anthony seemed to have the same sense of urgency, fortunately.

"What about Kenelm Bates?" I asked. "Shouldn't Anthony see him first and bring him along to the police station?"

"It could be just as sensible for the police to approach him separately, so it doesn't sound like a stitch-up between the two."

"Well, I still want to talk to him, but maybe about something more general as background to my research" I said. "And ask about 'The Pilgrims' picture. You know, the four young men unclothed."

"You can do it. But the key interview still remains – Bishop Marcus Andrews. You want to get to him, don't you Anthony?"

"Oh yes I do."

"We'd better be clear why you want to talk to him."

"I want to tell him that his decision to disbelieve my evidence has left me embittered for years, and that I decided that my conscience won't let me go on without justice."

Alexis asked in a mock-male voice "But why have you come here to tell me this? This has nothing to do with me!"

Anthony replied. "You will be approached by the Vatican for your corroboration of my account, as well as by the police. I just wanted to make sure you hadn't forgotten about it." Anthony looked enquiringly at Alexis for approval.

191

"You know", she said "we will all look silly if he suddenly says 'I have a very slender recollection of all this. I don't know, from my experience of the diocesan archives, that the files even exist any more."

"Ah!" Anthony exclaimed, looking moderately triumphant, "but here is where I play the insider ticket. Your behaviour isn't at issue, M'Lord. This sort of information however could be crucially relevant to the future of Monsignor Mobile as an alleged abuser." Anthony looked like a parody of conspirator, pink-faced as ever and slightly uncomfortable with the role of a serpent in the school play.

"It sounds too wicked to come from you, Anthony" I said. "Do you seriously think that sort of argument would work? That he will be malicious against Peter Mobile?"

"I do", he said, "but I don't have the weasel skills to put it over. Anthony Mulherin, the tempter from hell!"

"You are being naive, Anthony" I chipped in. "He won't want any part of this. Allegations of cover-up? – not me, guv."

"This dialogue has helped me to see things better", Alexis told us. "If we could crash in on him without any warning as to the topic we might get further in our goal, which is to have a written account of what happened back at your interview with the then Bishop's Secretary, Peter Mobile and Father George back in 1982."

"How would I play that?" Anthony asked.

192

"Well, you might not necessarily let your superiors and the Cardinal chap know that you are off to England, so there's a chance they wouldn't tip Marcus Andrews off about it. But you would need to be much more tentative in your meeting with him. Nothing urgent, that you had just been thinking about it and so on."

"It doesn't sound like a recipe for getting much documentary help, does it?" I asked.

"But suppose Anthony could suggest with a nod and a wink that he was investigating on behalf of the Vatican Questor, in connection with certain new appointments in the Church?" Alexis' brown eyes scanned ours fearlessly.

"Oh fine!" said Anthony with disgust. "We've covered variants of that. It just happens to be a pack of lies, that's all."

"Not entirely" she said.

"Oh shut up Alex" said Anthony, closing that approach down.

"Is it likely, Anthony" I asked him, "that Marcus Andrews might refuse to support the truth about your meeting with him? By the way, I'm assuming that we can't get hold of Father George, can we?" Anthony shook his head: he made a sign that meant Father George was dead. Anthony went on "You know I do fear that he won't tell the truth, crazy as that might sound. My experience of being disbelieved has left its mark here forever."

Alexis asked us for our choice of alcoholic drink, indicating the business was over for the moment. She addressed Anthony in family style.

"Now Uncle Anthony, one last thing. If you are asked to swear, take a solemn oath that you will not give details of your complaint to anyone else except an authorised superior in the Church, what will you do?"

"I will say that I cannot do that."

Alexis looked grave. "That is good, honest and liberating. But it warns those concerned that everyone needs to be tipped off because a maverick is in the system."

"What do you want me to do? Swear an oath and then go back on it straight away?"

"Wait. Can your superiors really ask for your silence to be bound by oaths like this? Surely in natural justice they can not?"

Anthony stroked his cheek and his chin. "No" he whispered to himself. "They can't."

"Think about it" Alexis suggested.

The drinks arrived and toasts were drunk to the fiancés and future success.

"And now" I declared, "I'm going to ring up my family to give them the good news. I'm going to talk to my one and only parent – my dad!"

I got him and it was an immediate anti-climax. He was as hopeless on the phone as he was everywhere else except the bar of the Marlborough Arms. I was

194

doing all the talking for the two of us, over-enthusing about Rome and how much he would adore my future wife. I felt embarrassed, so I kept the call as short as I could while it still sounded jubilant: at least at the Roman end.

Alexis said a few words to him, listening to a brief message from him about something and then passed the phone back to me. Had he dented her joy by some nasty remark? – I almost didn't dare to ask.

"What did he say?" I asked her, but she waved away the query, "Another time, another time."

It was to be our last night together in Rome. Alexis said she had a lot of organising to do in connection with early flights and changed arrangements, so she would be out of commission for two hours. We decided that I would walk Anthony back to his seminary, and he would point me on the route to where Alexis and I could continue our dancing of the night before.

As we walked up to Anthony's seminary palace, I quizzed him some more about the celibate life.

"Is it as lonely as we imagine it, Anthony?" I asked him.

"I don't know" he replied. "I've never known any thing else."

"Well, do you have old friends you meet, do you ever go out to dinner with them, you know what I mean?"

195

"There's just my family, really. Fellow academics when I was here. We were never allowed to have *particular friendships*, you know."

"What, for fear of homosexuality or what? I take it that *particular friends* means close friends?"

Anthony shrugged. "That's right. Because of fear of homosexuality, why not admit it it? And fear of sexual liaisons with women, much more to the point with me. But the main thing is to steer this lonely path through life, not attached to where you live or your companions or anything except the vocation. It's easier, in a way, if you don't really trust anybody anyway."

"Devoted to your vocation?" I queried. "Or do you mean devoted to your work?"

"Yes, both, but especially to be Christ to everyone around you. I know I'm talking to a sceptic, but maybe you can get a glimmer of that sense of – unreachable holiness? And why I might have longed for it?"

"You know, Anthony, I've been surprised at what I have learnt over these few days. For someone with a real grievance about the way he was abused and disbelieved, you seem remarkably well-balanced as a person. How so?"

"I have my sisters and their children. Nothing ever stopped me from seeing them, and they claim to have dented some of my pompousness, you know?"

"But you have an attitude to women which strikes me as utterly strange, Anthony. You obviously

196

worship them in principle, but you seem to think they are inferior in some way."

"Does it show?" he asked. "Does my fondness for the bottle show too? Speaking of which, why don't we stop here and have a beer, Mike?"

The café was a last outpost before the green residential area leading up to the seminary on the hill. Anthony quaffed the beer with some pleasure, accompanied by a small pasta. I had yet to eat.

"Let me tell you about my friends and women" Anthony said. "Our order runs a few parishes around England, and one of my pals was put there as a curate. He had never met women before in the course of training, I mean not as adult people who weren't relatives. He was just bowled over by one of them, and now they are married. She has nothing to recommend her as far as I can see, at all."

"What on earth can you mean?" I asked.

"No university degree, no enquiring mind, no intellect."

"Good God, Anthony, what an almighty snob you are! Are you saying that women are inferior intellectually? How can you say that, with your niece so obviously brighter than either of us will ever be?"

"Oh dear." Anthony shook his head. "Maybe it's just that particular woman, because I did meet Lucy, that friend of Alexis, as my pupil for her thesis about Augustine's attitude to women and sex. I was supposed to be teaching *her*, but *she* opened my eyes."

"You mean she woke up your sex instinct?" I said, nudging him to indicate I was teasing.

"You pick the vibes quickly, Mike, don't you?" Anthony said, laughing. "You know, when I think of her I have to say that is a woman I could marry."

"Joking or serious?"

"That's the problem. If I made my protest, went off and got married, it would blunt its strength completely. The mind of these old celibates is that if you marry, you're discredited. You were always a sex-obsessed sinner, so what you say is not worth listening to. Priests have to be absolved from their vows of celibacy you know."

"Anthony, I still think you have come out of all this a better person than I would have expected. Provided you are not an alcoholic, yes? I'm asking these questions because I want to understand what abuse has done to you as a person. But it seems to me that it wasn't the abuse but the way you were educated by the monks that has really damaged you."

"Oh God" Anthony said, "I can see myself wallowing in self-pity with a bottle of whisky as company." He pulled himself upright and laughed.

"Shall we get on?"

But we had another beer and talked some more.

"I want you to really take on board that you have suffered something dreadful, Anthony" I told him.

"I feel that" he replied. "But it was the way they wouldn't believe me that made me suffer the most.

And maybe I was less of a real person as a result of that."

"Anthony, tell me. Did you ever have doubts about being a monk and a priest?"

"Of course."

"Did you feel as if your experience of abuse and disbelief meant that your doubts didn't matter?"

We started to resume our walk in silence. Finally Anthony said "Yes. Yes, that is true. The first time I took charge of my life was when I told the Papal Questor what I was going to do about Peter Mobile. Yesterday."

The huge portals of the seminary were bright up at the end of the road where I said good night to Anthony. I walked on in part darkness towards my rendezvous with Alex.

The dancing was everything I had remembered and even more. We ate our supper, danced, and confided yet more of the histories of our lives to each other. I realised that our real struggles to tell each other what had happened in our lives was moving towards Alexis telling me about the crisis that had pushed her into *Pietas*. It was clearly hard for her to talk about it, but vital to us both. I found her sympathy was a solace as I told her more of the sad history of my split from Sarah Louise. Alex told me about Bernie's problems with her marriage, which sounded encouragingly temporary.

Today there was a jazz fiddler instead of the accordion player. As Alex danced it was as if Stéphane Grappelli's violin was the shape of her shoulders and slender back. Her feet moved sideways and forward and back in the bright animal world in which we were playing. Her face lit up, and she was laughing at me in sheer joy, looking into me with ridicule and love and meeting me in a place where I was especially silly and silly and laughing with silliness.

Around, back, parading, stopped, electric again in a moment, with fabrics of jeans and blue stripes and bright flowers seeming to stream from her glorious hips as if in a tail visible only to me, a long bridal tail of willow and twist and archness.

We came up close to each other and she whispered close to my ear, tickling it with her breath and tongue. She said "Mike has anyone ever told you? You dance as if you'd filled your pants."

14

It was Sunday morning. I left our bed and climbed the spiral stairs up to the apartment's galley kitchen, the bridge of a ship coasting above the ruffled sea of Rome's dark old roofs.

When I called Alexis up to join me for the breakfast I had prepared on the roof, she told me that she had not slept as well as I had. "We've got a tough day", she said. "I've booked three places for five thirty this afternoon, and we've got to get Anthony on that plane."

"OK" I agreed. "But how we pressure him onto the plane I don't quite know. I sense he is finding this whole business very tough. That's why I want to go with him for the interview with this Cardinal wallah."

Alexis complimented me on my coffee. "Bill and I have had second thoughts about that and about the visit by Anthony to Marcus Andrews."

"Why?"

"We need to do everything that gives us a chance to nail the abuser and the concealer of the abuse, and nothing that shows our hand. I'm afraid that we will set too many alarms going if we show our faces now. There's a chance of surprising them into the truth – that's what I believe."

"Alexis, I'm easy, if you think that Anthony will agree to your plan."

We agreed to try to steer him along our path.

"He doesn't know what will hit the Roman Church in England if this comes out, does he?" I asked. "I don't think you do really either. The sheer dirt, the sniggering nastiness of the *Sunday Seven* readers, the cynicism, the destruction of faith, the confusion of messages about gays and pederasty and – well, isn't that enough?"

"Fear for the institution, eh?" Alex sneered. "Spoken like an intellectual and moral superior. Males mustn't be pilloried for sexual violence ever, must they? The poor old reader of *Sunday Seven* is too dim to see the difference between a loving gay relationship and a rape of a child by a pederast, eh?"

"Alex, I'm sorry. We see it slightly differently. Either you are totally naive or I am completely into the male sex domination world."

"Look, there's no point in standing back and saying 'Oh dear, we can't punish this criminal because he belongs to a holy institution'. I've heard them argue that nailing a woman religious, a nun, for some evil deed wouldn't matter to the Church because nuns aren't priests, are they? Don't you worry about the effect on the Church of punishing its bad apples. You go for justice or you don't, Mike, do you hear me?"

I heard her.

Alex had forgotten nothing in her planning. After packing our bags we left them with Bernie and her husband Geoff, who had arrived back from a nasty assignment in Afghanistan the night before. That was their marital problem, nothing more. It was just like me to think that everything was much more serious than appeared, and everyone was concealing it. There was time to exchange our great information about our engagement, and then Alex and I set off to see the *Pietas* church and watch the 'pilgrims' at their prayer.

"It's just a quick visit", Alex explained, "so that you can talk about it with Peter Mobile when you see him tomorrow night. You won't get the subtleties of worship, but at least you can learn something about them. Then we're going on to Anthony's seminary for Mass with him – a sort of family affair. You will be marrying a Catholic, you know."

Didn't I know it! – even if she was a liberated Catholic woman, there was never any prospect of a registry office marriage with this young lady, and I never thought about it for a moment except to reject it. There would be a church wedding.

The *Pietas* church was medium-sized, baroque and over-endowed with bright painted ceilings showing scriptural scenes and earnest saints in billowing robes. There was a strong smell of incense. There were statues with votive candles burning beneath them at every pillar and niche. The chapel of Our Lady was especially striking, almost seeming ready to catch fire from the carbon trails from the paraffin of the long white tapers and their yellow flames

It was nine thirty, and the building was full. Alexis gave me a whispered running commentary on what was going on. No one gave us a glance.

They were a normal looking collection of Italian people to my eyes, but among them there did seem to be both women and men with a body stance that I took to be one of adoration – extreme reverence, self-consciously lowered eyes, an amazing shuffle in their movement forward to communion, a way of holding themselves that had been learnt but was also reinforced by a visible in-your-face belief.

I didn't like it, but that was not the point. Was this any different to the way that many human beings behaved in other churches or synagogues, temples or mosques?

The congregation moved forward to receive the hosts from a priest in a white surplice with an open pattern of lace like an extended see-through vest, running down from mid-chest to knees. He wore an obviously old-style outer vestment I learnt was called a chasuble, notable for the beauty of its fabric and its fiddle-back shape. The communicants opened their mouths and the host was placed on their tongues by the priest. After communion the priest seemed to take an enormously long time cleaning and drying the chalice. He held a silvery plate up to the light and brushed at it for a long time, as if looking for minute crumbs. Alexis pointed out a red lamp hanging in the sanctuary, and a high niche on the back wall where there was space for a special showing of the consecrated host in what I recalled as being a sort of baroque display unit made of gold.

Alexis made a deep bend of her right knee again as we tumbled into the aisle and out of the church.

"Wow! I'm glad to be out of that" Alexis said. "Stifling!"

She explained some of the features of *Pietas* worship to me. It seemed that they were very taken up with the idea of Christ's presence in the host and wine, and insisted on this absolute attitude of respect and worship to what they regarded as the divine presence of Christ, right there.

"Catholics all believe in that real presence" she said. "But you wouldn't think from the way the *Pietas* members behave that he was an actual human being who bled all over the place when he died, would you?"

"What was that about the sanctuary lamp?" I asked her. "And the priest facing away from the people? I've not seen that before."

"It's all connected. At the end of *Brideshead Revisited*, you know, the 'old English Catholic family' novel by Evelyn Waugh, he writes about that red lamp showing Christ's real presence and never deserting the believers. They just light the lamp when the Blessed Sacrament is there, virtually all the time, and keep it in the tabernacle at the back there. There's a lot of nostalgia for that strength of reverence for Christ being there in the bread in the tabernacle. In England some Roman Catholics were tortured and burnt because they believed Christ was there in the host and wine. Some

205

of the English *Pietas* people are social climbers, and they like to feel aristocratic and ultra-orthodox and all those stuffy things, and this is part of that nostalgia. They just love the courage of the recusant martyrs – at least the English ones do. *Pietas* loves Latin too. Not to mention the Pope. But we need to move on."

"Well, Alex, you sound completely free of them now. I'm surprised you still go to church."

"Tease! We'll see what Uncle Anthony can do for us."

She was referring to having Mass at the seminary, said by her uncle. It happened soon afterwards on that busy morning. All I can say about it was that it seemed mercifully short, Anthony was warm about the two of us in his snappy sermon, and it really did feel like a gathering of folk who cared for each other around a dinner table. I could understand what they felt, that Christ was there, but he was a Christ without that majesty that *Pietas* people seemed to worship. Anthony didn't seem to be so hung up on cleaning the sacred vessels, either.

Anthony smuggled out a small suitcase masquerading as a laptop holder. He had called a taxi and we went over close to Vatican City for coffee and a last briefing from Alex.

We got Anthony's report on the Vatican meeting late on that Sunday afternoon when he appeared at the last possible moment to board our plane at Da Vinci airport. Fortunately, the flight was delayed.

"They threw the book at me" he said. "Honestly, I was left feeling that *I* was the person who was guilty of abuse! It was terrible!"

"You, Uncle? You?"

"Yes dear, your Uncle Anthony. Aaargh! Just pour me that beer will you?"

"Don't prove them right, Anthony" Alexis said.

"Well they are right about my less than perfect character, you know. That's what I mean about the book they threw at me. They had in the head of the Order I so recently left, the old holy boy. They went over the whole saga of my inheritance and my leaving the Order to get the money. So I look like a right little money-grabber. Who could believe someone like me? Get the drift?"

Alexis was annoyed at them. "How palpably unfair!" (Yes, she really does talk like that, quite often.) "You know Mike, my granddad had Anthony over a barrel on this one. He always hated Anthony joining a religious order, so he decided to give all his money to Anthony and if Anthony turned it down it was all to go to a charity instead. Not a penny for the daughters, either. Of course if Anthony accepted it, the Order swallowed the money. So he left the Order, took the money and shared it with the sisters. Action of a mean man?"

Anthony laughed. "Action of a disobedient man, they thought. They were right, too. And my dad was pretty canny. It got me out of the Order all right."

"But what about the allegations you've made? Did they quiz you about them?"

"Oh yes, yes. We went over the whole thing again, aided by the magnificent document that you helped me to write, Mike. That was fantastic. No matter how they tried, they couldn't destroy the testimony."

He went on. "Then they made more attacks on my character. They dragged in someone from the Pontifical Institute to attack my orthodoxy, who waved around a paper I wrote when I was lecturing here. It was a little bit avant garde, maybe, and tucked away in what I thought was an obscure Dutch monthly. The previous Pope hated exploring new ideas even more than this one. But they didn't really follow that up very well, because they know it just isn't true. They tried a little blackmail too. They mentioned two old female pupils of mine, one of them a nun, and I can't think of any reason for doing that except to rattle me if there had ever been any hanky-panky. Desperate stuff on their part, and so shabby. Then they changed tactics. They started on the loyalty and scandal thing."

"Meaning?"

"Was it of benefit to make these criminal accusations so long after the events, and after the blameless and indeed holy life – yes, old Peter Mobile, the living saint! – of an exemplary priest? If indeed there were any truth in what I had alleged, and how could there be? – but if? If there were a smidgeon, my word, not theirs, they talked about a 'minisculum of verity' – I'm reinventing their pompous language – well shouldn't it be better to forgive, like the Lord, and 'Go, sin no more?' Ha!"

"How many of these guys were there?" I asked. "Because if there were a lot, it will be around the system by now, and there's no hope of creeping up on the Bishop or Peter Mobile and going 'Boo!'"

Anthony sipped his beer.

"Maybe it's a little near the cusp. There were four folk – the Questor, whom you've met, the Cardinal Sidesman, the head of the Order and the academic from the University. Not a huge number, but someone could be blabby there. Maybe one chance in four that someone will blab."

"So what happened next? You were there for hours."

"Well, they took me off for lunch and we had stiff conversation for an hour. Then the Pontifical Institute guy, who is American, did I mention that? – tried a charm offensive, just him and me in another office, all concerned about the anguish he knew I was suffering. He even talked about counselling – thirty years after the event! He tried to persuade me, I think that was his drift, that I was in need of psychiatric help, that I was mentally sick. Yes, I can see where that would have left me. They would have tried to persuade me that this was a delusion on my part. I feel hatred as I say that, because I know it would have destroyed me.'

"I didn't bite much, but tried to look grateful. Then came the good buddy stuff, where he told me that there would be an investigation to see if there was a case, and I was given the name of a Socius, a sort of legal representative I think. Then we went back to the Cardinal's intimidating office, with an enormously high ceiling so it seemed quite small but I swear you could have converted it into a squash court. The tactic seemed to be for them to shut up then, and wait on me to be penitent or something, maybe aggressive, I don't know, but I sensed the need to keep quiet. They might have noticed me looking at my watch, though."

"The silence stuff again" I laughed. "I thought it was just that he wasn't intelligent enough to formulate the words."

Anthony gave me a direct look. "Your problem is your arrogance about these clerics. Maybe you can't control your disdain Mike, but at least you could hide it. The tone of the meeting was calm and intelligent, no matter what you think. *I* can make allegations about them, not *you*. Understand?"

I was reproved. Anthony felt that I patronised him as well as all other priests.

"All right" I said. "High quality Tom and Jerry stuff. Next?"

"I was stuck. I wanted them to lay down some requirements to which I would agree. "

"I know what they wanted" Alexis volunteered. "If they could get you to formulate a plan then you would have ownership of it and be more likely to keep to it."

"I suppose so. After a lot of vacant chat, I asked if I could go. That enraged them, and they went around the whole thing again. They kept on asking if I was going to file a complaint. I said 'This meeting and the document you have are my complaint to you, the Church authority.'"

"So I really forced them to ask me about complaining to the police. Was I silly? I don't know, but I was getting to the end of my tether."

Alex asked "How did you answer?"

"I said that whether I complained or not depended on their response to me about these allegations. I thought that was a good let-out – they wouldn't realise that I regarded our meeting as their shabby answer to the allegations, anyway, and I felt absolutely in the clear to go to the police at once. I started to make movements to go. It was close to three o'clock by then."

"I could see them looking at each other" Anthony continued. "I just hoped they weren't going to play the solemn oath card, but I didn't say that, of course. I did say I was grateful for their kindness in hearing me so carefully, and I tried to get away with their trust in my good will. Not a chance!"

"Who was it?" Alexis asked. "The papal diplomat that I met? The Questor?"

"You are right, dear niece" said Anthony. "He reminded me that I was under contract to work for him,

211

and he required me to do my secretarial duties in Rome for the next four weeks. Now I knew that I had to appear to take that on, so I said that I understood exactly what was wanted. I thought that was enough, but no such luck once again."

"Why not just tell a lie and say yes?" I asked.

Alexis gave me another of her looks. "We're taught all our lives not to tell lies, Mike. Anthony would find it almost impossible to lie."

In a mock Thames-basin accent Anthony said "But after, I done a whole lot worse! The Cardinal Sidesman got a bible out of his desk and gave me a statement which he asked me to swear to."

"What did you do?" I asked.

"I refused. And then things suddenly took a surprising turn. They started to try to persuade me that the abuse I had suffered was just too trivial to make any fuss about."

We were not that surprised by Anthony's revelation. For a concealer, any argument would do.

"Yes, trivial!" Anthony went on. "Put against all the sufferings of all the children in Ireland, Australia, the deaf boys in the USA as well as hints of new cases in Belgium and old cases in Germany, what had a comfortably-placed well-adjusted old cleric like me have to complain about? Come on, Father Mulherin, don't be so petty!"

"But did they get you to swear an oath?"

"Yes, I swore it. I decided there was no point arguing about my alleged pettiness, or was it the trivial nature of the sin? – so I gave my solemn oath."

"I hope you've got a copy of the oath" Alexis said.

"Yes, I knew you'd be proud of me when I asked for it and got it. There it is. No sooner had I sworn it than I was out of the door. Looking completely subdued and cowed and obedient, I think."

Anthony beamed. He did not look like someone who felt guilty of a great sin in making a false oath.

We looked at what he had been asked to swear and sign.

"I actually typed this too", Anthony said. "Lucky I'm a secretary or there would have been someone else in on the secret."

> *'I solemnly undertake in the sight of God and the Holy Church to make no complaint to the civil authorities about alleged abuse in 1979 until an investigation by the Church authorities is concluded, and only if the investigation shows that such complaint is justified.'*

"No witnesses' signatures?" I asked.

"Not needed" Anthony explained. "To break this oath is to be guilty of a mortal sin. I'm a sinner now, in a big way."

"Or so they will think, Anthony" Alexis said. "But you know they can't stop you from following the path of justice even by oaths. The guidance from the English Bishops, which is being used as a model, is that criminal abuse has got to be reported to the civil authority, anyway. The police. This oath is ridiculous. But let me keep it for you, it's precious too! You'll be fighting these people later on, and they have given you a weapon. Put the place you signed on it and write down the names of the people who were there, won't you?"

The flight was being boarded now and we were set on the next step towards justice.

"Did you get any written agreement that they would look into your allegations?" I asked.

Anthony nodded his head. "I didn't, but I'm sure it will come. I was trying to appear to be someone who was biddable, you know."

I reassured him. "I don't think you could have got much more than you did, Anthony."

"It's not as if they would lock me up and arrest me, you know. Even if the Vatican *is* a separate state."

"No", said Alexis, "your job was to get out of Rome to report to the police – without them tipping off the two clerics today or tomorrow. You may have done it. Good old Uncle Anthony!"

The flight promised to be blessed by perfect evening weather, and I knew the Alps would give me a feeling of exaltation. I would be sitting beside a most forthright and beautiful woman with whom I had travelled into Rome some three days ago, and who now planned to marry me.

I had to prepare myself for my interviews on the next day.

So why did Alexis need my comforting arms earlier that afternoon, when we talked of her conversion to *Pietas*? I want to tell you some of it because Alex thinks that what provoked her move to *Pietas* helps to explain the power it can have in some people's lives.

She was determined to share the difficult secret, and we walked in the shade of the embracing colonnades around the piazza of St Peter's, speaking and listening. It was all to do with a married colleague in her Chambers (at that time, almost three years ago). Alex was deeply ashamed, but no matter how many times I said *'You don't need to tell me this'* she insisted on going on.

She had to explain why she had suddenly come to repent what had happened between her and this man. I had to know because I must understand what she had learnt and why repenting meant that her life was changed forever.

It was excruciating for both of us, but I needed to hear and understand her. There was and is a maverick streak in Alexis. She is a serial enthusiast, and that is her charm and her weakness. Certainly, as far as our future together is concerned, it is something I need to be aware of. But in the story of her affair with a married man and the way it worked out I know that whatever cause or person comes into her enthusiasm radar, her direct love for affection and respect between us is what drives her and keeps her who she is.

Alexis called herself a homebody, but it was her ambition to match the performance of her women peers that pushed her towards social climbing. She was a high flyer at her legal conversion course, and mixed with the children of the legal professional class for the first time. With her good looks and ability to think on her feet Alexis was popular and her academic success made for glory. I don't know about the boyfriends of those days, but there was nothing as serious as marriage.

The fourth Chambers she approached gave Alexis a pupillage. Still cautious in her romantic attachments, perhaps because of her deep links with her widowed mother, Alexis looked like being a perpetual spinster at one stage. But then something snapped, and the successful young barrister decided that the world of love affairs could be as open for her as for everyone else. Alexis began to be away from her mother at the weekend, staying with 'old friends'. Not so old, in fact.

The crucial event that changed Alexis' behaviour happened on a Friday afternoon before what was to be a weekend together with her married lover in the same Chambers. There was a rush on, and they did have a great deal of work to complete, it was true. But Jeremy was supposed to go with his wife and son out east of London to their cottage for the weekend. So

Jeremy's wife, Jenny, drove into London and actually had a place to park, briefly, as a visitor, close to their Chambers. He had got the only key to the cottage, so poor planning, or probably weak lying meant that she had to come in to London to collect it. Jenny had looked forward to the country weekend and wasn't going to miss it, even if it meant being on her own with their baby until Sunday afternoon.

"We were having a meeting with the client", Alexis explained to me, "so when Jenny turned up with the baby I was sent down to hand over the keys. I didn't mind, I thought, this was all right. Think of me as a woman who knew her attraction and was the complete master of her life."

"Mistress?"

"Mistress of her life, yes. Not *a* mistress. This was two people who enjoyed each other's company, that's what I wanted it to be."

"So what happened?"

"It stopped me in my tracks. Jenny was a person who was strong and well able to cope with her husband's wandering tendency, I'm sure. But it was Ben, their baby, who got to me. The little baby was sitting in his chair in the back of the car, fast asleep, and I thought about his vulnerability and I remembered losing my dad when I was so small, and I said nothing to Jenny, but I put the key in her hand and went straight back to the meeting with a feeling like a lead weight in my chest. I was accused by that child. Do you understand?"

"I need to understand. Was it just that there was a baby? What do you mean?"

"It was worse than I said. I wanted to say 'What a beautiful baby!' to her, and actually I always feel cheerful when I meet mothers with babies, maybe it's a female thing, but it's what life is about. But I said nothing."

"I see. All you wanted to do was say 'What a lovely baby'?"

"I just caught her eye, Jenny's, the wife – the wife we were deceiving. She wasn't gimlet eyed, you know that sort of look? She wasn't angry, she was something else. She was hurt, but putting on a good face, and I couldn't talk to her about her son because I would only hurt her more."

She stopped. There was more to say. I put my arms around her. She sobbed. "I kept thinking about my dad dying, I had a memory of being visited by one of my aunts with her baby, my cousin, and seeing him in the car just like this baby. I was crying for myself."

We were silent for a while. "And that got you into *Pietas*?" I asked.

"It made me repent. I had been someone who was cruel to another woman and her child, and I couldn't live with it. I couldn't be ordinary any more, someone who talks easily to mothers about their children, and I hated that. I hated being silenced by my own selfishness."

"Did you break off with Jeremy at once?"

"Soon. I wrestled with my conscience. Finally I told him it was all over. I told him what an unfeeling shit he was to send me down with the keys to his cottage to his wife, too. That had hurt me when I thought about it. Why was I so? – blind?"

Alexis was over the worst in this confession, and from here on I saw the cheeky lady who had mooned to her would-be-lover for fun.

"So tell me about what happened next."

"Don't get me wrong if I seem to be a little detached about it. I have to mock myself a little. My problem is I get very committed, you know."

I didn't doubt it.

Alexis told me how she had gone to confession to be forgiven by God, and what an enormous relief it was to have done it. "I felt new and pure and unthreatened by hell, and ready to do my best."

"You believe in that hell stuff?"

"I did, I did. But I was new and light-hearted, almost the same girl you see here today."

"Well, what happened?"

"I felt that I'd gone astray because I had forgotten about the teaching of the Church and I had been too lax. It was easy to go back to *Pietas*, which I'd started with when I was doing my training, remember? They were so local, and they stood for everything that was hardest and most unchanging in Catholic teaching. But for me it was a real religious conversion. I went in for things I had last tried as a schoolgirl, like fasting and wearing an itchy belt as a penance – I know, I was crazy. I couldn't sort out what was superstitious in the old stuff, so I said all sorts of prayers to reduce the suffering of people in purgatory, I went in for indulgences, don't let me bother you with them, but they were one of the grievances of Martin Luther. Only these weren't sold, to be fair."

Alexis knew I wasn't really keen to discuss all this. My knowledge of all this stuff was based on Sarah Louise and what I had researched for *Pre-eminent Victorians.* I pressed her to tell me about what drove her out of *Pietas*.

"So you were the most devout Christian in the world, and no doubt *Pietas* were keen to have you as a trophy barrister. How did you become disaffected?"

"I got so weary of the effort for perfection. I was praying incessantly to God in all the moments I wasn't working, and I got tired of the sound of my own voice. I was barking! I had to do everything to perfection, so it was almost sinful if I didn't sharpen a pencil perfectly. Makes for a good researcher in a legal practice, let me say. Have you ever reached the point with work where you're worn out, but you push yourself on to do more? I did that all the time, I said more and more prayers, but I needed something else, to talk to someone else with a brain, to be connected to ordinary life."

"Did you find a pal in all this?"

"It was a good woman friend, Lucy Peer, who you will meet."

"The lady in your constructive dismissal case?"

"The same. She's a tower!. She was in *Pietas*. Its whole purpose is being loyal and being seen to be loyal to Church teaching, but we both discovered the hierarchism…?"

I said "That's not worthy of you, Alexis, come on, what do you mean? I want you to say the word."

"Fascism in *Pietas*. But first we noticed the patriarchy in there, the lowly esteem for women. It never occurred to me before then that stopping Catholics even discussing the ordination of women as priests is about as fascist as you can get. Yes, the last Pope did that! I just took it for granted that the Pope was speaking up for revealed truth."

"How did you come to talk about all of this with Lucy?"

"Oh Lucy has a sense of humour, you see. And a sense of reality, not all that piety-speak stuff. Yeah, our dear Lord Jesus – forgive me Mike, it just slipped out – was fond of calling a spade a spade, and if he saw that the little old lady giving a quid to Oxfam was a much nicer person than the corporate representative donating ten thousand, he would say so. We were on that tack. We reckoned that if the first Christians were able to see they were equals, even as slaves or men and women, because of Christ, it should work for us in the Church. We should have women priests."

"The Anglicans have done it" I said.

221

"Yes." I noticed that it didn't seem to be a very enthusiastic yes. Alex went on "We couldn't help thinking, Lucy and I and so many other Catholic women, *'What if?'* What if women were priests? What if there was no real barrier to it except engrained patriarchy?"

"Hey, what if we get married?" I asked. " *'What if'* has got to be the first step towards joy for human beings, and if not that, for understanding."

"Yes" Alexis concurred. "You see, we can dream of such wonderful things, and then have them."

"Yes, but *what if* you don't like walking in the mountains?" I asked. Our conversation went off on a whole new tack. We both liked mountains, so that was all right. And we both loved children. Enough! Alexis went back to how she abandoned *Pietas*.

"All of the problem about women's status came clear to me more slowly than finding out what was wrong with what I was doing for *Pietas* for immigrants. I was supposed to give pro bono legal help to some asylum-seekers. I was really involved and it was clear as it could be, it was a really good thing to do! There's lots of *Pietas* lip-service to this sort of thing, but then I couldn't help noticing that the whole ethos of the organisation was anti-equality. Fascism was all over the organisation."

"You mean that what we suspected at the school is a policy? Keep non-European children in separate classes from the Brits and EU diplomats' children?"

"There's no policy statement, but – yes."

"So you stayed in *Pietas*, but started to be stroppy?"

"Critical. I was ready to argue against the unspoken consensus."

"And you couldn't get a hearing?"

"It's like talking to the brain-dead. The best will leave *Pietas* but we were all in a specially Catholic delusion. Can you guess?"

"Universal delusion. I know what you are going to say. Stay with the church or the party or the department or whatever because only the critics within will it ever bring about any change."

"Yes. Just that. And the next leader of the Labour Party, or the next Pope or whatever will be a great reformer and take everything back to its true roots. You wish."

Alexis hugged me. We had to find the bus to Da Vinci Airport.

"I knew you were the right one from the moment I saw you" she said.

"All we need to do is keep on agreeing with each other about what's to be done and we'll be together forever."

"Arguing about what's to be done, I think" she replied.

We were to put that to a severe test on the next day: the day of the three interviews.

223

We caught up with the news about the abuse scandal on the plane. The Irish Cardinal was still 'considering his position' about whether to resign because of the abuse there. Rowan Williams' comments on the loss of credibility by the Roman Catholic Church in Ireland were just part of the background of more news of scandals and reactions everywhere in the Christian world.

Anthony leaned towards me and said "Well, even if we don't rock the establishment with our revelations, I still think they have destroyed themselves. I can't see His Holiness getting a warm welcome in England in the autumn. I hope he doesn't."

Accepting a drink, he added "When I look at the suffering of these poor children at the hands of the priests, I do have to feel that what happened to me was peanuts in comparison. They'd got a point. Are we doing the right thing?"

"Look Anthony", Alexis said, "the fact that you happen to be a wealthy middle-class man doesn't change what you suffered in any way. You have all been abused, and it has hurt you and affected your life. Hold on to this – justice!"

We settled on our journey. I tried to plan my approach to Peter Mobile, in particular, by entering into the way he saw the world: if I could do that.

Don't get me wrong about my method, and please don't take me to be a complete cynic. I had always had my best results from my 'debunking' interviews by cosying up to the person interviewed and seeming to take on their every belief. Actually that requires more than acting skill: you need to know what the person facing you really believes. You even need to believe some of it yourself. At least for the duration of the interview.

One thing I had noticed across all these religious people: they had deep devotion to Jesus Christ. It kept coming out in things they said, but so too did their picture of Christ as a person. He was friendly, concerned with the outcasts, very human for Alexis. She was touched by an account of an appearance of Christ after the crucifixion by the grave where Mary Magdalen was looking for his body. She took him for a gardener in the story, and Christ made himself known by saying 'Mary'.

That was the sort of risen Christ she worshipped, indistinguishable from the lowly worker. Divine, of course, but you might not see that and he wouldn't care. Personal too. 'Mary' might almost be a line in a Mills and Boon novel. But the Jesus Christ of *Pietas* was someone else – all powerful, a judge, the creator of a Church with absolute authority in teaching what was right and wrong, and with this caste of priests continuing to ensure his presence in the world by their unique power to make him present in the host and wine of the sacrament.

I knew which Christ I preferred. I was on Alexis' side.

I decided that I would get up my courage and challenge Peter Mobile about the way he had peered at my genitals when we had wrestled. Then I would challenge him about what happened in the mountain refuge, using everything I knew from the press reports, Anthony, and Kenelm.

Tomorrow would be hard, with the Bishop to see, if he would see me, and Kenelm Bates, whom I counted on getting hold of even without an appointment. Then Peter Mobile in the evening.

Well, Bill had certainly given me enough work to do, and we had completed it so far at breakneck speed. I bet myself that despite all this, I wouldn't get much work from *Sunday Seven* beyond next Wednesday – and I was right.

15

Next day was Monday, and I woke in my own bed back at my flat – alone. Alexis wasn't given to discussing why she made her choices, and I was happy enough that she had chosen to marry me. But as we had travelled in from the airport on Sunday night she made it clear that Anthony was going to stay with her and her mother, and plans for our living together before we got married – 'moving in' – would have to wait. I am afraid that Alexis is someone who can change her mind, but I had not sensed in what way it was going to happen.

Monday's first two tasks were to see Bishop Marcus Andrews and Kenelm Bates.

Objective one: get Marcus Andrews to admit that he had seen Anthony and Peter Mobile and Father George from Anthony's school on Monday April 21 in 1982.

Objective two: get Kenelm Bates to agree to be a witness at any proceedings against Peter Mobile.

Objective three: to get Peter Mobile to admit to abuse of Anthony in the refuge on Friday 5 August 1979. Well, I could try.

Enough work, and far too speedy. Before going out to the provinces, I had to actually get the first two to agree to talk to me.

I did it. Bishop Marcus Andrews associated my name with prestigious daily papers and said yes, to my surprise. I wondered if there was a move among the English bishops towards disassociating themselves

227

with the Vatican's clumsiness in handling the clerical abuse scandals. After all, as yesterday's paper had reminded the public, the English RC hierarchy had been the first to take on reporting these cases to the police. Mind you, that wasn't until after 2000, a little bit too late for Anthony.

Kenelm would talk to me too. He wanted to learn more about my investigation into Peter Mobile.

While I was on the train to my destination, Alexis rang.

"Could you do a little investigation for me at the Episcopal Office please, Mike?" she asked. "I'm interested in the office layout. Ask to use the loo. Just make a note of where the PCs are, how many workers, where the filing cabinets are – you know the sort of thing an industrial spy would report on? It's for Lucy in my constructive dismissal case. You remember, she was supposed to help abuse victims but she couldn't have the key to the filing cabinet with the files in? She wants to photograph it, and will be coming down with me. She wants to go in, surprise them, take a snap and get out fast. Only she can do it, but you can look out for the cabinet which fortunately is distinctive. It has big red tapes running at the top of each drawer. Otherwise it's a standard grey three drawer filing cabinet."

"Alex, knowing you as I do, I'd say you were preparing a burglary."

She laughed. "Well, now you mention it, if you see any alarms make a note of where they are too."

"You can fish for it!" I said. "If you see Bill before I do, pass the message on to him too."

"Don't take it too seriously, Mike. If you can do it, do it."

"Listen, I'm just taking on board the fact that Lucy of the dismissal case is the same pal of yours who studied St Augustine's attitude to sex with Father Anthony Mulherin."

"Yes, I told you that, but what of it?"

"Nothing, nothing! I'm beginning to see that your role in all this is central, isn't it? No reproach.."

"Good luck with the clerics" Alexis said, ringing off.

The Episcopal Offices were not large, employing no more than seven people, I estimated. I explained to the receptionist about my appointment with the Bishop and she telephoned him to check where we would meet.

She replaced the phone. "He wants you to go to Bishop's House" she said. "It's five minutes walk from here or a minute in a taxi – not worth it."

"Well, I left the taxi outside actually, so I can go on. But could I use your loo first?" I asked.

"By all means."

I walked through the office slowly, memorising its shape and the layout of desks and cabinets. I spotted the one with the red tape. In the loo I made a sketch as an aide memoire, and returned to Reception.

229

When I got back a brown-overalled man with a two-wheeled trolley was deep in conversation with the receptionist. Apparently he was instructed to take one of the filing cabinets over to Bishop's House where I was going. I thought how ironic it would be if it were the one containing the information about Anthony's 1982 meeting with Marcus Andrews (then Father, now Bishop Andrews). He wasn't supposed to know that I was going to be asking him about the 1982 archives. I hoped he didn't.

Across at his home the Bishop greeted me at the door and took me into a large living room furnished with unfashionable old armchairs and sofas against dull walls. What struck me as the biggest giveaway of the lack of any feminine presence were the curtains, hung badly, apparently dirty even when pulled back as they were to show a large and well-treed garden.

Right down to the scuffed carpeting, this was not the mansion of an American Bishop, but more the creation of a committee of lower middle class English women and the wish of the priest incumbents to have no fuss.

We got on reasonably well. The Bishop had easy manners, taking me into his kitchen to make me a cup of instant coffee. He was taller and better looking than I had expected, yet another proof of my chronic anti-clericalism. This project was at least making me aware of my stereotyping habit.

"You're lucky to get me at such short notice" he said. His voice had some of the reassuring melody and authority of a Douglas Hurd, and more than a hint of a posh accent. "Today is my day off and I'm playing golf early this afternoon instead of my usual morning stint" he explained. "What can I do for you?"

We talked about my writing a profile of his career, as part of an article about the leadership of the English RC bishops in tackling the abuse crisis.

"I suppose there's no way of escaping from that?" he asked.

"Believe me" I replied with as much force as I could, "You're better off running with the press than hiding from them. The scope for misrepresentation is high, even for a cleric like you. What I'd like to do is just get some answers on stock questions, the issues that surround the Roman Catholics in England, and then make some notes about your career."

"Fine." We covered abortion, contraception, AIDs and the prohibition of condom usage, RC schools, and adoption of children by gay couples. That was what the media wanted in an article about the Roman Church, after all. Oh, abuse as well, but we would get to that. I was glad to have my digital recorder with me – he knew and permitted it – because I had no desire to pillory him with inaccurate replies. It was as if he had rehearsed the answers to these questions a hundred times, and knew he could weather the suspicion of the Vatican that he might be unorthodox while sounding at least aware of liberal disgust at doctrinaire rigidity.

"It is about law-making, not the compassion that Christians actually show" he said at one point, trying to shake off the 'sex-obsessed Church' label.

After spirited replies to questions on the dwindling number of priests and faithful in his diocese (he played the Polish immigrant card) we went on to his career. I asked him about his accent.

"You're one of a Wigan Catholic family with five children aren't you? How come you don't have a Lancashire accent? – in fact, no hint of it?" I got no answer except a shake of his head in disbelief and we went on to his early life, straight from school into a seminary. Except for a period at the English College in Rome, his experience had always been within the diocese of which he was now the Bishop. That allowed me to ask about his experience as Secretary to the former Bishop.

"Oh you have done your homework, haven't you?" he said. "I didn't actually go straight from Secretary to Bishop, you know – there were two Bishops in between. I was a parish priest."

"That reminds me of something that we left out of our general discussion", I said as if it were so easy to forget. "Have you ever had to deal with allegations of clerical abuse in your career as priest, parish priest, Secretary and Bishop?"

"When you mention all those jobs, well, sadly, I have dealt with some cases, yes. But since the Nolan Report you know we have a very robust structure to deal with these issues. Allegations are always reported to the public prosecutor. Every diocese has an assistant dedicated to resolving the issues around allegations of clerical abuse. We are creating a process to deal with abuse which is quicker, more transparent, and more sensitive to the victims. And to the falsely accused, may I say."

"I'm sure you are state-of-the-art in your bailiwick, Bishop" I volunteered. "but what about the cases back before Nolan? Some of these cases may come out of the cupboard this year you know."

He raised his eyebrows. "Really?"

I went on "There was a rule that you had to get your complaint about abuse into the police within a six year period, I think – but now an appeal to the Law Lords has been successful, you could well have cases going back to when you were the Bishop's Secretary here."

I realised I was coming on too fast here, showing my hand with a little too much accusation and not enough sympathy.

Bishop Marcus gave me an appraising glance and straightened his shoulders.

"Our job is to see that abuse doesn't happen in the future and that justice is done to those who were abusers in the past. We worry about the abused people too" he added, almost as an afterthought. "In my diocese we have someone whose special job is to look after those who have been abused. Nationally there is a body for the protection of children and vulnerable adults – I won't bother you with the name, which is going to change. You know, if you want to talk about this issue, you need to research it and come back to me. I can't claim I'd be overjoyed to talk about it, but if you think it merits it, I'll talk to you."

I wanted to say 'You're not about to tell me what the Roman Church in England has paid out to victims, are you?' I knew one of the published figures for the USA was almost $400 million, and that was a low one. I kept a rein on my tongue.

"I do understand", I said, "but I'm just warning you that American punitive damages for old cases may be about to arrive over here. Mind you, I'm presuming that anything that has come to the Bishop in the past by way of accusation will be in your files and available to the Public Prosecutor or a complainant."

"Oh yes", he said. "We have our own legal procedures in the Catholic Church which is called Canon Law. Documentation has to be kept. Sadly, we were not as alert to Canon Law in the seventies as we are today. That had implications for falsely accused priests, you know."

"Would someone making an accusation under British law be able to use those Canon Law documents?"

"You know, I can't answer those sorts of questions Mr Claver. I am not a Canon Lawyer. I don't think it is central to what is my vocation in life – which is looking after the spiritual welfare of everyone, be they Catholics or anything else, within my diocese."

Marcus Andrews was signalling that the meeting was over. As we made our way towards the door I said "I have a personal interest in an abuse case that goes back to the 1970s. You will recall Father, now Monsignor

Peter Mobile, who was a priest in this diocese when you were the Bishop's Secretary."

"I do, I do!" he replied. "As it happens, he gave a presentation on *Pietas* at a recent meeting of the Bishops."

"But you may also recall a young man called Anthony Mulherin, now Father Anthony Mulherin, who made a complaint against Peter Mobile in 1982 right here in this diocese, with you as a witness."

"I really can't reply to that" Marcus said. "I'm sorry, I can't recall it." The Douglas Hurd voice seemed to sing with intelligent regret.

I shook hands with him at the doorway and set off down the suburban street, nursing a fierce feeling of failure. Had I ever really imagined he would be willing to talk about this old case? What a stupid question I had asked, inviting him to shut up. Why hadn't I just asked him if he remembered Anthony Mulherin? He had squeezed out of any real interrogation due to my ineptness. Actually what I felt even more strongly was angry with Alexis, a seething wild rage that occupied me for most of the fifteen minutes it took me to reach Kenelm Bates' office, where my task promised to be so much simpler.

I checked my list of targets. One. *Andrews recalls Anthony's visit?* Complete failure.

Two. *Kenelm willing to be a witness?* We would see.

Kenelm was everything I had remembered, funny, frank, relaxed, amusing and the provider of a damn good cup of coffee.

"You look as if you need it" Kenelm remarked. "What's the agenda today? I can give you half an hour, maybe more if needed, but I don't think I have anything much to add to what you already know from me."

"Kenelm" I said, looking him straight in the eye, "I could ask for what I need from you in two minutes and be out of the door at once. I will be quick, but can you help me with some general questions first? There *is* an issue about abuse according to Anthony Mulherin, as you suspected, but I have questions about how priests could ever be abusers. I haven't really cracked understanding what Catholics and particularly the clergy believe about sex. I'm beginning to think that it is essential to understanding why abuse happens and why it is hidden. For one thing, how could fellow priests and people preparing to be clerics not know that there was someone who was likely to be an abuser living among them? Why didn't it show?"

Kenelm was dismissive of my question. "Come on Mike, how would anybody know about these things? These were people trained to be modest and not to be curious about colleagues' orientation, for heavens sakes. And never to talk about sexual things."

"I thought that everyone had to confess their sins? Wouldn't the priest be aware and put a stop to it?"

"Naive Mike, naive. They wouldn't confess it until they were caught out. Mind you, the confessional is important when they are fighting for being kept on as priests."

"How so?"

"I'll need to explain a bit. We believe that people are able to change with God's help – grace – and do so. So part of being caught out as an abuser would be to make a confession at that time. The problem has been that bishops have taken that repentance and purpose of amendment as something they had to accept – it was part of their faith in God, almost. Some of them have admitted they were too naïve in believing in instant change."

"It seems a strange way to look at things, Kenelm – that the sin of the priest is what really matters in these awful cases of abuse. I got that sense from you, am I right?"

"Oh yes, you are. It's the sinner's immortal soul that has to be saved, that's primary. The abused are innocent, so you don't need to be so worried about them. But listen, I think I'll have to tell you my experience as an adolescent and then a candidate to be a priest if you are ever going to understand this, Mike."

"Well, let's give it a try."

"Why not? I'm talking to you as someone who is a father here, and I want you to remember that the people who have educated our priests have never been fathers. I am a father of teenage sons."

"Why would that matter?"

"It matters because the clergy have a pre-adolescent and adolescent mindset about sex. In fact, in my view, bordering on infantilism. The unmarried Roman Catholic clergy, I mean. And they aren't able to see outside of it because they have no experience of proper adult sexuality."

"So? What does this explain?"

"It explains their obsession with sexual acts."

"Acts? Striptease?"

"No no no, Mike! Actions, if you like. The purpose of sexual activity is to produce children, right? So anything that doesn't fulfil that purpose has got to be wrong. Get me? There are lots of sexual acts that must be wrong. That's the way they see it."

"Yes, but I still don't follow why the obsession with sexual acts is tied in with being an adolescent."

"You've forgotten what being at that age involved, Mike. I have two sons in their teens now, so I am reminded that it's all novel and vivid and wildly pleasurable beyond all their dreams. And if they masturbate they feel ashamed, and it doesn't fit in with their view of themselves or their friendships with others."

"Yes, but they get older, it all comes into perspective doesn't it?"

"Not if you're a candidate to be a priest, it doesn't. It's a heroic struggle. Listen, we were told that if we wanked we would burn in hell forever."

"Wow! Imagine carrying the fear of that around with you! And you are saying that those sorts of attitudes are prevalent in the clergy of the Roman Catholic Church of today?"

"Absolutely. They are scared stiff of sex because all their experience is that it could be a disturber of their sense of purity and goodness. That comes from being stuck in adolescent mindsets."

"So feeling interested in sex and normally excited was regarded as sinful by you guys" I said. "Not at all a natural urge."

"Sort of, yes. The urge and interest was terrifically genital too. Small children don't have so strong an idea of the personality of others, especially of the opposite sex. They think about sex in exactly the way that pornography attracts men. Featuring models, pictures, not people."

"Kenelm, so if I understand you, the abusers were quite childish in their attitudes to sex, and maybe fell into abuse almost by accident."

"Yes, sort of. There was wickedness there, you know, but I'll grant you that it could have surprised them when they got started. My own transgression from celibate purity – as they would see it, and I did too – was a kiss in a sacristy with a beautiful young woman."

"Let's go on to whether I understand you rightly, though, Kenelm. Other priests are unlikely to be aware of the abuse, so that's one let out. And they share the same view of sex, anyway."

"Yes, the whole caste of priests is not savvy about their own sexuality. They hold off the temptations, finally see a fellow cleric fall into abuse but find it hard to believe it as ever happening. They are like little boys, Mike."

I said "I think I might have been the same if I hadn't been brought up with the chance to work with and have fun with the opposite sex. I haven't told you, by the way, that since we last met I have proposed marriage to the most beautiful lawyer in England? Ha ha ha!"

We talked about it and Kenelm got my address out of me and quizzed me about where we were going to live. We had more coffee, and then returned to our discussion.

"I'm trying to explain how the clergy look at women, how their pre-adolescent outlook makes them incapable of understanding tenderness or attraction or even sexual intercourse except as dodgy or evil. And they're outsiders in their peer groups when they are at school, too. They can't help feeling they are missing something, like I did, but they are comforted that what they are missing is actually wrong."

"I'm getting the picture, and now you explain it it's not so surprising, really" I replied. "But is there something I'm missing when I say that holiness seems a possible attraction to me? You know that each time I have met Peter Mobile he has given me a little taste of his message, and it was – it was good, it was attractive, 'strive for the best'. Not that I think he is very attractive as a personality, given what I know of him now."

Kenelm leaned forward to make a strong point. Creator of this wonderful picture-lined room with its warm timber floor and its vista of water and boats, Kenelm wanted to show how abuse didn't just spring from perverted human desires. He wanted to persuade me that the very shape of the institutions that formed all clerics permitted some to abuse others and led their colleagues to shelter them from justice.

Kenelm spoke emphatically. "The point about these holy folk is that they are utterly self-absorbed! Self-obsessed! Utterly lonely, distrustful of hugs and touching anyone, ambitious to be wise and respected, lonely, lost, absolutely lost. Sorry, it makes me so sorry for them. Full of the ultimate ambition – to be holy ones of God, to be saints. That's what is wrong with all this. And how do you motivate these young men to continue to struggle on for perfection? I'll tell you. You keep on bringing out the model of obedience to God the Father, namely Jesus Christ, and motivating them by telling them they are his representatives on earth and share his priesthood. Salvific! Terrific! Celibate!"

"Means?"

"What?" Kenelm asked.

"What is the consequence of thinking yourself so holy, when by your account they are all a bunch of eternal adolescents anyway, and well aware of it?"

"No problem to understand. They persuade other people to believe the same thing that they do. With that they get lots of respect and bolster their sense of their own self-worth, which is all to do with what they aspire to be. They get parents who are happy that their children are friends with 'Father'. Lots of respect in the past, before the scandals."

"Have I missed something here, Kenelm? You are telling me that these young men don't know about sexuality, and yet at the same time they are raving adolescents, and then some of them go out and abuse others? This is Rowan Williams sort of stuff. Too complicated for me."

"Drink up your coffee. Right, I'm just doing my best to explain. Don't forget that only a tiny number of these chaps are ever involved in abuse. There shouldn't be any of course, but it is not something universal, it is tiny. Now those abusers get to the people they abuse because everyone knows they can trust a priest. That goes for abused women as well as children of course. I hope that clarifies some of the puzzles. What you have to understand is that for these priests almost anything could turn them on and be sinful."

"So? How does that explain abuse?"

"It doesn't. But it is just to say that the abuser may start out innocently and find that he is subject to temptations of a simpler type than actual full-on abuse. As we look at it we identify it as 'grooming', but the priest abuser may not even realise what is going on. I'm not trying to excuse him, of course, because it is abuse directed at children."

"Correct me if I don't understand you, Kenelm, but you might mean that the cleric doesn't really mean much harm but suddenly he finds he is kissing a child, and he is quite surprised by this himself."

"I'd accept that as an example. So going back to the pilgrims when we were in the Alps with Peter Mobile, I would never have expected him to plan his hanky-panky, if he did do it, but it would spring upon him, in a sense."

"That's why we're talking, Kenelm. I think I've got hold of your argument, which is really one of a self-perfectionist ethos practiced by unmarried men in a strong clubby institution? I added the last bit – but is that fair? Oh, and they are quite ignorant of women too."

"Yeah, that's quite good. The Church doesn't have a way to fit sex into the lives of its priests. In practice, it rejects the fact that they have normal sexual instincts. As a result of its self-perpetuating way of looking at sex, it has only got a small place for sex in married people's lives too. Forbidding contraception or using condoms to avoid AIDs both go back to this puzzlement about the purpose of sexual acts. There has to be only one model which is good – full intercourse to create a baby. Not adolescents trying out their tackle. Not the young couple who want to save to buy a house before they have a baby, but still

243

want to make love. Or couples who want to get to know each other before marrying. Or want to educate a child rather than have another eight children."

"There are liberal Catholics aren't there? *You* don't pay attention to the teaching, obviously."

"Yes, but we would *all* be liberated if the message came out right. There is something sinister and silly about what is going on, and it is killing the Church."

"You still love it then?"

"I do, I do. We Catholics believe in a full-bodied person called Christ, and we really feel he is close to us, right there at Mass. He is easy to love, but we want him to go on being present at Mass, and that means we need ordained priests. They don't need to be unmarried."

"Well now, were you never ordained?" I asked. Kenelm ignored the question. "What about the ex-priests who got married?" I asked. "Couldn't they educate the celibate clergy about this?"

"If only. They are the fallen, the ones who have abandoned the search for sanctity on the high ground. No. They are failed priests. Our message is poisoned, to their ears." Maybe Kenelm was saying he had been ordained.

"But hold on" he continued. "I've told you more than you deserve, and you've told me nothing about progress on the Peter Mobile story. What is happening?"

"I can't tell you all the details, Kenelm. You should be approached by the police to get your version of what happened that night."

Kenelm quizzed me and I told him that Anthony alleged abuse against Peter Mobile on the night in question and was certainly going to report to the police about it during the day. "He may already be there" I said. "Would you be willing to be a witness?"

"Of course. But I didn't see anything, I slept very soundly. But as I explained, I had suspicions. Poor Anthony. But most of all, poor Tom."

"Suppose your suspicions are right, Kenelm. Would you see Peter Mobile as a serial abuser?"

"Of course not. I feel he is a good bloke, like I told you. But he does illustrate the whole thing about sex with the priests, doesn't he?" He turned away for a second and then said "I'm going to find that picture for you – the Pilgrims. I've hesitated because I think showing the picture of us four as young men in our birthday suits will give a completely wrong impression. The picture is not evidence of abuse. But I've just argued myself out of that by what I have told you, now I realise that. I've been in denial about all this, but you forced me by coming to think it all through. I didn't want to shop Peter Mobile. But you've heard my views. He belongs to all of that, and just happens to be gay on top of it. I know he is doing a great job for the Church, for good living, holiness, all that. But the system has to stop."

He gathered his breath and went on with vehemence. "Abusers run the Roman Catholic Church – that is the truth. The priests have made 'No Sex' the way to have power. The first power was power over themselves. If sexual urges can never be simply good for human beings to feel and explore, then it is easiest for those who must never lose power over themselves to have no sex at all."

I reminded him that Peter Mobile probably had transgressed that, but Kenelm said it didn't affect his argument.

He went on. "But suppose some priest goes into fornication, child abuse and adultery? All power would be lost with the loss of the holy caste's credibility. So they deny that it ever took place, or conceal it as much as they can, belittle its importance, downplay it, make it invisible."

Kenelm concluded. "That is why we need to speak out. Abusers and deniers of abuse are running the Church. And the root of the abuse is their fear of sex."

It was my chance to beg again for the photo of 'The Pilgrims.' "Thank you Kenelm. If you have that photo it would be a real plus."

We had more chatter as we slowly went back to the door of the offices. Kenelm was a practising Catholic, but he thought his children would not be. "It's too complicated for them", he explained. "We had hopes for spreading a message of joy after the Second Vatican Council, but the Church has gone backwards since then. If my boys learn that contraception is wrong in their RE lessons, and their parents say it isn't, what can you expect except indifference?"

"Did you find you had to change your attitude to life after leaving the seminary?" I asked Kenelm.

"Yes, of course. I started to enjoy life for the first time. I seem to have lost a big goal, to be holy, and have lots of little joys instead. It's about caring for people and doing what you love doing. Like all this", he said, indicating the building, the office, the pictures of his family and the view. "I'm proselytising for optimism."

He showed me down to the door. Where before we had admired the photos of his wife and family, this time he paused to make up and give me an envelope with some literature about his practice.

"What about the 'Pilgrims' picture?" I asked him again.

"You'll get it. Meanwhile, you've got to promise to give this to your fiancée at once" he cajoled me. "Men don't worry about structures – they just take them for granted. It takes a woman to make a home out of a house. Apply that to this abuse and sex issue if you will, Mike, the answer is the same. Look to the women for a solution!"

"I will. But what about the picture?"

"I'm almost 100 percent sure you should use it, but I'd like you to call me later to tell me exactly what you are planning. I'm dead serious, Mike. I'm into grudge against clerics, Anthony Mulherin obviously is too against Peter Mobile, and maybe you are in grudge as well. I think you should think more about what you're going to do with it from the point of view of a lawyer."

"I promise to do that with Alexis. Can I call you back tomorrow? The deadline, you know."

"Any time, I mean that, any time. We all need space for reflection, not knee-jerk reaction."

As I went away I remembered the time it had taken for the Vatican officials to even acknowledge some letters despatched to them about abuse. Months. No danger of a knee-jerk reaction there.

16

I went along the waterside to a hotel and ordered an Orangina, sitting outside at a table to quieten my adrenalin-taut nerves.

What a fiasco that first meeting had been, even if the second had been so promising. What sort of a dupe was I, to think I could ever get any useful admission of anything from the Bishop?

I called Alexis on my mobile.

"Did you get the picture from Kenelm?" she asked.

"He's looking for it", I said. "And he will give evidence that he was there if approached by the police. Where are you?"

"Never mind, I can't say, Mike, but how about the four of us having lunch together?"

"Sure, who's the fourth?"

"Lucy Peer, remember? She got the whole thing going when she came to me about being dismissed by Bishop Marcus Andrews."

"And she's here? You haven't told me half of this Alex, have you? Well, yes, come on over here by the quayside will you? It's just near Kenelm's office and it's very nice."

I had got my notes in order by the time Anthony, Lucy Peer and Alexis arrived an hour later. Anthony and I recognised the same hang-dog feeling in each other at once, but Alexis was bubbling with self-satisfaction and delighted that she had sprung Lucy on

Anthony and myself as the ultimate surprise in our investigation.

Lucy was in her early forties, dark, composed and decorous. She looked just like the ex-nun that she was, with a plus, that she was another no-nonsense girl like Alexis. We got on at once. What intrigued me was the chemistry between Lucy and Anthony, however.

I shook her hand. "What brings you here today?" I asked her. "This is where you worked for Bishop Andrews, isn't it? I think that you and Alexis have been up to something nefarious, haven't you?"

She smiled. "I've just pointed out some features of the office where I used to work" Lucy said. "It's quite painful for me, you know. Particularly when I think that I'm not likely to get anything like fairness out of this diocese."

Anthony chipped in on a breezy note. "It's been as big a surprise to me, Mike, I can tell you. I never realised that Lucy actually worked in the offices where they should hold the record of my complaint. I knew this lady as a student, back in Rome, when we were working on the Trinity and St Augustine."

We all sat on the apron of the café and reported on our morning's work.

Anthony had made his deposition to the police unaided and had handed over his document. Now he was looking depressed, despite the obvious lift the appearance of Lucy had given him.. "I suppose I should see it from their point of view", he said, "some clerical geezer comes in with a complaint which goes back more than thirty years. I always feel that they don't believe me, or if they do they despise me for being in a position to be abused, and they don't think it hurt me, and they think I'm doing this because I am trying to destroy someone's reputation out of spite, and, and… and so on."

"Anthony" I said, "what does it matter what you felt? They have the allegation. That always had to be the first step."

"No, Mike, you are right. They were better than I could have expected, in a way. I think the inspector I talked to must have had experience with allegations in the past. Having the Bishop here, it's not surprising, is it?"

Alexis chipped in. "They played the risk-assessment card on Anthony as one of the reasons why a prosecution might never happen."

"Meaning?"

"Well, if they fail to prosecute Peter Mobile, will that put other people in danger? I guess it is unlikely."

"Wrestling with young men?" I asked. I could tell them something, but I kept quiet. Anthony ignored it.

"But they promised to look for evidence, at least", he said. "So if we get that picture of the Pilgrims, it will help. Thank you Mike."

"Well", I admitted, "I can't say that my visit to Bishop Marcus Andrews was much of a success as far as the case against Peter Mobile is concerned. I really wonder why you ever thought it was worth while trying, Alexis. And I can't help saying I find your

251

chippiness very irritating. What's so bloody good about today, Alex?"

It was the wrong thing to say, not because of Alex, who stuck her tongue out at me, but because of Anthony.

"I really wish I had never done this", he said.

We had lunch and I tried to worm out of Alex what had happened to make her act as if the morning had been a triumph. Anthony was drinking too much and getting more and more angry.

"Where is that bastard this afternoon, did you say? Which one? Why His sanctimonious Right Reverend Bishop Marcus Andrews, of course. Playing golf? I'd like to see him and remind him what my face looks like. And that no matter what he says, he won't have ever forgotten that day that we all met here."

"Oh Uncle Anthony, don't ask for snubs" Alex begged him. "We've had enough for one day."

"I want to beard him" Anthony said. "Why can't I?"

Lucy surprised me.

"You know, Alexis, it's quite an idea to go and confront him. I'm not afraid to."

"I'd be afraid for what you might do, Anthony, that's all." I said. "You wouldn't use your hip-flask on him, would you?"

"Hey, that's confidential, Mike. Anyway, I don't carry a hip-flask any more."

Alex seemed excited at the prospect of more action.

"I think that could work" she said. "Seriously. That priest is going to know that there's something in his cupboard that needs to be admitted, because if he doesn't do it, he will be even more discredited. Let's do it."

"It's going too fast for me" I put in strongly. "Remember I know how bad you can be if you drink too much, Anthony. I won't approve it unless you just lay off the booze, Anthony, if you don't mind."

"My apologies to everyone" Anthony said with a winning humility. "I can see that if we can catch the Bishop at a moment of weakness he may acknowledge that we have met before. So let me calm down with a good plate of eels here, and Lucy and I will visit him at the golf club."

"Is it easy to find it?" I asked.

"They have no reason to suspect me back at the office. It won't be hard to find out."

We had an excellent lunch at the expense of *Sunday Seven* and discussed our progress. Alex said "You know, it really has to count as a good day for your case, Anthony, with Kenelm and the possibility of the picture."

"I'll let the police know that we have Kenelm as a witness on the way back from the golf course", Anthony said. "Though I doubt we will have recruited Marcus Andrews as a second witness about my complaint."

"Don't be so negative" said Lucy. There was real electricity between Anthony and Lucy, who kept looking at each other with quiet delight. But besides this new (and no doubt sinful ingredient in the venial league of Catholic celibate priestly sins) I felt the anguish that Anthony was experiencing. Alexis' cheery body-language annoyed me more and more. Though I couldn't see the benefit of Marcus Andrews cowering before the anger of another cleric, even one fortified with Dutch courage, I too wanted to see fear on that hard self-loving 'concerned' face, and watch his eyes swinging shiftily to left and right as Anthony signalled that pretending to forget was just another lie.

"You don't understand, Alex" I said.

"I'm sorry" she replied. "There have been developments and I'll tell you as soon as I can. But I could tell you this, at least. It doesn't prove anything, but I've been on to your old school, Anthony, and they have sent me a copy of the page in the Exeat Book for 21 April 1982 which shows that you went to this town with Father George on that very day."

"Why didn't you bloody well say so!" I said to Alexis. It was part of my sulk for the fiasco of my trying so stupidly to get information from someone like the Bishop who would never have given it just like that – an attempt made, I now felt, out of complete and maybe even passing infatuation with Alexis.

"Look", Anthony said. "Lucy and I will go to the golf club and the police station and do our bit with Marcus Andrews. There's no need for you to hang about, so we'll take the train back to London later. We want to catch up with each other's lives too, you know."

Anthony was looking calmer and just a little less pink-faced now. Maybe the meeting would be successful, particularly as Anthony had the evidence from the school to act as a reminder to the former Bishop's Secretary, now in the top position in the same diocese.

My mood was sullen as Alex and I went back to London. She wanted to cuddle up to me in the train, but I insisted I was preparing for the meeting with Peter Mobile. Did I really think he was going to admit his actions that night? I concentrated on nothing beyond what I was going to say to Peter Mobile at 8pm.

Alexis confided she was concerned for her uncle.

"He did drink a whole lot too much at the time he left the order and gave us all so much of granddad's money. He would stay with us sometimes and I had to give up my room and use the sofa. Mum couldn't trust him on it in case he was sick on the carpet in the living room. But he came round in the end. Honestly, Mike this is unusual. But I think Lucy is good for him, don't you?"

"On the evidence of today, I wouldn't be surprised if they got married" I said. "Are you playing Cupid with those Arrows of Innocence?"

At the terminus I gave Alexis the keys to my flat, so that we could have a post-Peter Mobile debriefing some time after 9.30pm She went off to a meeting, destination undisclosed (I suspected it was to report to Bill at *Sunday Seven*) and Anthony and I headed out for North London. Anthony was staying with the Lecces, mère et fille, and I went home. Despite my continuing feeling of failure, I found time to change the sheets on my bed.

The *Pietas* headquarters were buzzing when I arrived there at eight o'clock that evening. There were at least twenty young men and women using the common room, and another eight conducting a round table discussion in one of the three smaller salons. Some teenagers were playing table tennis in another big room.

I was directed up in the building to Peter Mobile's private flat. I knocked and heard him shout "Come in".

He left his desk and shook hands with me, the muscular grab that I recalled from my last abortive visit when he had been wearing a white track suit. The athletic gear was still in evidence, but now it was black and thinner in fabric than the last time. We exchanged queries about health, and I went straight into the facts of the case against him that we were building up.

"Father Anthony Mulherin has made a complaint today to the police that you assaulted him in a mountain refuge near Chamonix in 1979."

"I knew this was coming" Peter Mobile said. He looked grave. "I was advised to deny it, but I am going to talk about it to you because I believe you have enough goodness in your heart to hold back from what an accusation will release on me."

"There's nothing special about me, Monsignor Mobile. I think that the guilty should come to justice. I'm glad you don't deny it, because otherwise it would have been even worse for you. Let me remind you that you and I have history. Not just the wrestling incident, but the way you bundled me out of here when I said your possession of the picture of the naked boys was proof of your being homosexual."

I watched his blue eyes. There was a caution there that meant he was not going to rise to my baiting.

I went on.

"As it happens, I want to start by asking you about the Arrows of Innocence, because I've learnt a lot more about it."

"Go ahead."

"Well I know it was taken by Tom Benson, who died in 1979 in tragic circumstances near the refuge in the Alps, when you were there with the two other boys, Anthony Mulherin and Kenelm Bates."

"That is true. That is why the picture is dear to me, and I keep it as a reminder of my own mistakes and fallibility. I was responsible for that boy's death, Mike. I say it in the trust of a fellow member of those who want to serve the truth."

"You mean that you were in charge of him as a minor, and he fell to an accidental death?"

"More, more than that. I was a young man, you must remember that. I tried to seduce him, Mike."

"And you can tell me this, someone you hardly know?"

"I am telling you this in the freedom of Jesus Christ. If I had gone on to a life of evil, then I would not be free to talk like this. But I tell you because in the openness of Christ's compassion for the sinner, I can do this. I can do it and know that you will grieve as I have grieved for that boy, Tom Benson. I count on the strength of forgiveness, Christ's forgiveness. I count on your silence, too, the silence of compassion."

He continued, talking about the picture. "It was prophetic, the way that the archers held their arrows back ready to let fly. It has been my destiny, as that of all celibate priests, indeed of all chaste Christians, to remain ready to shoot my arrow, but forever restrained. To do this for Christ, and apply that strength to the work of his Church in *Pietas*."

"Well, that may be true or not" I answered. "I would like to remind you that when we wrestled back when Sarah Louise and I were 'married' and trying to save our marriage, you were the person who snapped back my underpants to look at my penis. What was that about?"

"I'll tell you, but you won't like it. The Church has a lot of trouble with homosexual inclination, you know. Don't smirk, I've faced it in the way that good Catholic priests do. We are eunuchs for Christ, we are not practising homosexuals, any more than good so-called straight priests are not practising heterosexuals."

"I know the theory, Monsignor, and I am quite convinced that most priests are heterosexual and very few are abusers. That's not the issue. It's not a general thing like does celibacy push men towards being gay. No, Father Peter, it's really quite simple. Never mind about what you did or didn't do to poor Tom Benson, the issue is that you assaulted Anthony Mulherin even before you went on to try to groom Tom Benson."

"What did Father Anthony Mulherin and Kenelm Bates tell you about me?" he asked. "What do they say?"

"Anthony says you tried to bugger him."

"Kenelm? Kenelm! What did he say?"

"He saw nothing . But he does know of a photo which you would find incriminating. The Pilgrims – you remember that?"

"I do. If Anthony puts this in the public domain, I shall end my career as Ordinary here. I suppose you think that that will destroy the Church, do you? Why did you come here, Mike?"

"I came to hear you admit what you had done, because I want to have the assurance that it is true in order to follow the accusation through to the bitter end. Which I now will do. But before I go, I'd like you to know that I regard you and your Church as the major cause of my split from Sarah Louise. Yes, I *am* bitter about it. What did you do to her? What were you telling her? Why couldn't I get her to agree to go to a marriage counsellor with me to sort it all out? God, you know she is a very intelligent woman, she was troubled but she could have found her way out of all that and we loved each other, until you came along with your solution."

"What are you talking about? I never claimed to be a counsellor." Peter Mobile was angry. "I did advise her, yes, and it was courageous advice entirely supporting your marriage. I told her she should submit to you sexually, which she knew was her sacred duty anyway, but more than that, I advised her that she *could* do it, through the grace of Christ."

"I see, she was supposed to let herself be raped, effectively, for the sake of Mother Church? That poor terrified woman, with God knows what hang-ups, boiled and battered with crazy advice from you as a last resort. You don't know what you are talking about, how could you speak to her about all this?"

Monsignor Peter Mobile was calm now in the face of my fury.

"I'm not impressed, Mike" he said dismissively. "Sarah Louise told me you were impotent."

For a moment I wanted to deny it to him, but the malice of what he had said must be ignored, that is what I felt, because I was deeply hurt.

"I hope you understand, Mike" Peter Mobile said as he got up to signal the end of our meeting, "My mission to serve Jesus Christ in his Church will not come to an end if what happened in the Alps comes into the open. I have carried the burden of those events all my life since then, especially the death of Tom. I was and I am a sinner but I have been redeemed."

"I understand all that" I said in reply. "It will make no difference to the outcome."

"Whatever you do Mike, I understand that my future is in the hands of Jesus Christ as well as your hands and the others' – whatever you do, I want you to remember one thing."

Peter looked at me with his striking blue eyes, leant towards me and spoke solemn words. I looked at him in disbelief. He was a chosen one; I could see it, someone who could walk through a battlefield with a rose in his hand. Just at that moment, before he continued speaking, I believed that telling the truth about him would change nothing. Then he spoke.

He said "Remember that God loves you more than you love yourself."

I turned my attention to getting home and welcoming Alex for the first time into my flat. I had cleaned it and removed all traces of Sarah Louise that afternoon, not that there were many souvenirs to show.

It was bus and foot homewards, and a feeling of anger and sadness that ran down my collarbone between my sore ribs. But despite the sadness, sharing grief with Alexis was what I needed to do.

I let myself in with my key, ringing the bell at the same time. Alex came running down the stairs towards me, and we were together again, consoling each other, united after a bitter battle with the world.

"I got Peter Mobile's confession, for what it is worth" I told her, "but not recoreded. He didn't pretend not to know about our investigation. It was a crazy meeting. That man has been a living saint, in his eyes at least. He didn't deny the assault on Anthony, or admit it, but he did own up to trying to seduce Tom Benson. He wanted to impress me that he was using his repentance to give back something bigger than he could achieve on his own. I can see how he deceives himself, but he showed some nasty malice to me, so it was silly, yes."

"It is *all* crap, Mike! He needs daily suffering, does he? The daily suffering he needs is from everyone knowing about how he hounded that poor boy to his death."

"He fooled us into thinking he is a good person, Alex, outstandingly good, don't you agree?"

She answered dismissively "He nearly did fool a lot of people. If building up a large organisation of people who try to live to the highest standards of ethics requires goodness, he has got it. And he's quite warm with it too. All right, all that maybe, but he has the complete obedience mindset of a fascist. I can't see him doing dirty tricks now, but he pulled off two very dirty tricks on my uncle. First the assault, then the denial."

"He told me something in there," I told Alex, "it wasn't true, but it had to do with breaking confidentiality about sex things. To do with Sarah Louise and me."

"Are you going to tell me?"

Could I tell her what he had said? I could.

"He betrayed me."

"I thought you said he told a lie?"

"Yes. It's about my trusting him. I thought he was a saint, you know that, I was desperate to get our marriage started with Sarah Louise by making love to her, and that man was supposed to be showing her and showing me the way."

Alex was comforting. "I know that, but how could this super old saint ever know anything about boy-girl love and sex?" She smiled gently.

"I was desperately wanting to believe that somehow God's grace could come in here and help me. My own little miracle – you know what I mean. And what I got was hugs, when we wrestled, and then his peeking at my dick. I was so frightened."

"Were you afraid of being gay?"

"No, I was afraid of being attacked or seduced or maybe even ridiculed. And then this lie, that I was impotent."

"But leaving aside the fact that you are quite obviously not impotent, Mister Stiffy, were you impotent with Sarah Louise?"

"Oh God, if you knew! I was camped outside her walls every night and day of our so-called marriage."

"Yes, but the Inspector wants to know was your battering ram strong enough to break down the walls?"

"I'll strangle you if you make any more silly remarks like that."

"I think you need to be clear in your head just why you are so upset by Peter Mobile. Just going back to the wrestling, do you think maybe it was a gay guy checking whether he turned you on?"

"Yes, could be, and when he saw he didn't excite me, he decided to hurt me when he got the chance."

"Could Sarah Louise have told Peter Mobile that you were impotent?"

"No, it would be a lie, but I suppose she might have done. You see, Peter Mobile had told her to submit to me, sexually, because it was God's will. She had got to get herself ready to …"

"Be raped?"

"Thank you for saying that, Alex. Yes, that was it exactly. This poor sad frightened woman, my wife to be, was supposed to lie back and do it for – I won't say do it for Jesus, but do it for the Catholic Church. Maybe not even that. Do it for *Pietas*."

"And you didn't?"

"And I could have, but I wouldn't."

"It would have been…?" Alex asked.

"Abuse. Violation. Rape. Her will to suffer it doesn't make it any less violent. I would never behave like that."

"But you think Sarah Louise could have called your refusal impotence?"

"In that lady's confused world, yes. But why does it rankle so much that Peter Mobile should call me impotent? Or claim that I was impotent with my would-be wife?"

"Because it's you, Mike, silly little boy, can't you see, *you* are your *willy*!"

"Leaving aside the obvious truth of that, why did he say that just now? Did he want to hurt me where it would hurt me most?"

"Yes. You will have ruined his life, soon, he knows that. The old saint is not so saintly as he makes out. He is malicious. From the male point of view, too, if a man fails to penetrate his wife, he is impotent. There's a sort of truth there, patriarchal wisdom, the male sword flourished but unused etcetera."

"What would the female take on all this be then?"

"Less drama. Sarah Louise had problems. With the help of good counselling you might have sorted them out in time."

"Which is what I told her. She wanted this magic bullet stuff from the holy men."

"But you fell for it too, didn't you Mike? You were attracted to the Peter Mobile holy shaman stuff, you said so yourself."

"Look, Alex, do you still want to marry me?"

"Yes" she replied, but it didn't sound as enthusiastic as I had hoped. I went on. "I have to admit that I have always been looking for a father figure with authority all my life. I thought someone with real authority was going to sort me out, and it might even be Jesus Christ and *Pietas*. But as soon as I get near to any authority figure I always rebel. I discover I've found another self-deceiving shit demanding my complete obedience and I won't submit."

Alexis was cool and a little coy. Eyebrows raised, she said "Danger signal. I'm the latest authority to assure you that you are all right. How long before you realise that I'm another lump of shit?"

She flinched as I shouted "It's all over! No, not with us, I've cracked it! My search is over, with *you*. I am attracted to men with authority, because of my awful father. I can admit, there is something gay in me, why not, it's my feminine side."

"There's a hell of a lot more of heterosexual in you, Mike."

"Lovely, lovely! So you can guess how much I suffered with Sarah Louise, can you?"

Alex nodded. "We'll destroy that arrogant bastard, we'll get him and the whole sorry crew of self-righteous deniers and we'll make them suffer for what they have done."

"Look, Alex, what he believes about me still upsets me, because I'm not *sure* he was lying. Why didn't Peter say that Sarah Louise had said I was a sex-maniac? From her point of view that might have been nearer to the truth."

"It wasn't true. Can't you see, Peter Mobile was trying to hurt you? He really didn't have to choose his words, almost anything he said would hurt you because it was breaking a confidence. If he told *you*, he could tell *anyone*. Maybe she *never* said anything like that."

"Maybe. But it's no comfort. That bastard raped me by looking at my cock."

Alex shook her head in disbelief. "If you could see your face! Come on, Mike, think of my poor uncle, think of all those thousands of boys and girls truly raped by those disgusting clerics. Think what rape means to any woman."

"Oh God, that's it" I said, suddenly realising the truth about all of these violent acts. "Alex, the slightest deviation from the respect of other people's bodies is a violation. What happened to me was nothing, I had it coming to me for being such a fool as to wrestle with that man. But it's all part of the same thing. We must stop these evil men. Even if it continues to destroy the Catholic Church."

"The abuse by priests has done the destruction work already" Alex countered. "Anyway, the abuse comes from a particular way of educating priests and revering them as holy, doesn't it? Did you get any more information from Kenelm about that?"

"Not much you can easily put in bullet-points. But yes, Alex, there is a weird view of sexuality in your Church."

"Hey!" Alex laughed, "Keep that up! Calling it my Church means that you have distanced yourself from it even more, and you need to do that."

Alex gave one of her 'I've been a naughty girl' smirks and said "It's my turn to tell you about my successes."

She was indeed rightly shamefaced about her activities on that Monday.

"Remember me asking you to take a walk through the office to the loo at the Bishop's Office? You were right about the espionage. I knew the layout of the office because of Lucy."

"Oh God!" I complained, less ready to get on my high horse than earlier on, but angry at what I suspected nevertheless. "You mean you want to break in and steal a file from the office? So I was supposed to help you do it?"

"Wait a minute! It was Bill's idea, not mine, and it's already been done. Not a file, I might say, but a whole filing cabinet. We just borrowed it for two hours and took it back. It was the one with all the dodgy information my client Lucy was never allowed to access. Although it was her job to put things right and see justice was done."

"I've got it, Alex, and I don't like it. I suspect that the man who came in just after I arrived to take away a filing cabinet was doing the job. Am I right?"

"Yes."

"Thank you. That was timed nicely, wasn't it? I get it. If he hadn't been able to take the filing cabinet out, you would still have a plan for a future burglary. Even if the burglary is off, we are still all accessories to a crime."

Alex made a little moue of Oliver Hardy foolishness, a 'silly-me' response to a deserved reproach.

"What happens with these files?" I asked. "You can't use them without admitting you have stolen them. You can't use them for your dismissal case either, can you?"

"Lucy went through them at lightning speed. The relevant ones about Peter Mobile and three other cases were taken out and the crucial ones were photocopied, and we did a sample of the rest. I was over with the *Sunday Seven* team, directing which ones to go for while Lucy did the first search. I've even read a few of them already. It was all done in less than two hours, and the filing cabinet was taken back. No one blinked an eyelid. The Bishop probably doesn't even know it happened, and may never find out until we get to court."

"It's just bloody nonsense as an argument" I replied. "The crime was so smooth and undetected that it's all right, innit? Pathetic, and you know it."

"Oh sure. Could I remind you that all the force of the law in Ireland was needed to get the files about abuse from the Irish bishops? And it took over two years?" Alex was angry at the way I had countered her defence and went into attack. "Let me tell you now what your father said to me on the phone in Rome."

"What has that got to do with it?"

"Well, maybe you aren't the number one beacon of whiteness, either."

"Alex, this is sheer nonsense. I don't like the way you behaved, but bringing my father into it is even further madness."

Alex looked me in the eye and said "Less attitude please, more logic. That's all I'm asking. What your dad said was 'Well I hope he treats you better than he did the last one'".

"The bastard, the bastard!" I shouted. "He knows nothing about it. I feel ashamed of him, Alex, what an awful thing to say. He's not coming to our wedding, I tell you."

"Listen", Alex whispered, stroking my stubbly cheek, "let's call it a draw shall we? We've done some dirty things, and there's no excuse, but we want to go on with all this, don't we?"

Alex smiled and reminded me "You knew it was going to be dirty. And your flirting with *Pietas* when you were married to Sarah Louise, fooling yourself that you were going to be a convert isn't exactly shining white, is it? Even if you fooled yourself, which I really doubt. It's going to get even dirtier, too, especially for poor old Anthony."

"Don't tell me you are having second thoughts too?" I asked.

"Yo!" Alex replied, "Didn't I see some champagne in your fridge? You know, I could live quite happily in this place when we get married. The view of London is fantastic."

"The public transport is awful" I said, going out to the fridge. We celebrated and talked abut the shadow of Sarah Louise in the flat, about my neglect of her and later on towards midnight we decided we had to move out. As we went over and over the recent history and our hopes for the future, I suddenly recalled Kenelm's envelope addressed to Alexis.

"I've got something for you from Kenelm" I explained. "Sorry, I forgot it. Wherever we live, I think he wants to be available as the architectural consultant." I handed the envelope to her.

"Oh these are up-market ideas" Alex exclaimed with delight. "So right! But what's this?" She screamed with excitement.

Suddenly, all the evidence we needed was in our hands. It was the black and white photo we knew as 'The Pilgrims' but had never yet seen. "Wow!" I shouted, but looking at the picture brought back that feeling of sadness below my throat and felt like the deepest of misery.

In the photo of that evening in 1979 in the Alpine refuge's room the four earnest faces of the naked young males were turned towards the camera. One of them, Tom the photographer, had been dead now for over thirty years. Only his face had a look of complete serenity and composure. Anthony, tall and square-shouldered, looked thoughtful, embarrassed, naked like all the others, but more vulnerable. Kenelm was the epitome of the charm he has never lost: he was the only one to be lightly touched by the events of that night. His insouciant posture said 'I'm here but I find it all a little bit funny, and I'll amuse you about it later on'. And lastly there was Peter Mobile, shorter than the boys by just a little, obviously older than them and stronger, and full of pride. Maybe it was the pride of his barrel-chested physique, perhaps a pride just at that moment in his leadership of these young men to a vocation to be, like him, a priest modelling himself on the selfless generosity of Christ.

I saw that, but the reader of *Sunday Seven* would see the work of the gay groomer discovered by a camera that does not lie.

Alex said "It makes me want to cry".

17

It was three thirty on the Tuesday morning when Alex woke me up and said she had to get back to her mother's.

"Do you think maybe we've been a bit too hasty?" she asked me.

As Alex gathered her clothes together and started to dress a private warning bell started to ring persistently in and below my lungs. She had a deeply traditional mother, I knew, but was she starting to backtrack on getting married? Or was she simply keeping up the pretence that we were not lovers by staying back at home with Mum?

An infallible instinct told me to stay by her side now until she got home. I wanted more than memories of a Roman romance, thank you – it had to be life together for Alex and Mike and nothing else. Maybe I had fulfilled my function, was that it?

I took Alex home. I kissed her goodbye right outside that same door where our romance had first begun.

As Alex turned her key in the door we both jumped with shock. The light came on and Alex's mother Letizia appeared in a fluffy green dressing gown. She looked disapproving, her mouth flexing downwards in disdain.

I was like a teenager, ready to hide, but Alex held my arm. "Mother, this is my fiancé, Mike" she said with complete self-composure.

I pulled myself up straight and extended my hand. Letizia, small, round, fiftyish and beautiful was flabbergasted, her mouth hanging open for a short, undignified moment. She had not expected to meet *me*.

Before she could speak Alex took the initiative and said "We've come home to get some of my clothes. From now on I will be living with Michael."

Letizia played it back with surprise but aplomb. I shared her astonishment, but not the distress that she concealed with perfect British phlegm. "I'm delighted to meet you, Michael" she said quite warmly as Alex scurried upstairs. "Would you like to help Alex pack? Come on in, and we'll have a cup of tea. You're invited to Sunday lunch, by the way." How much more unruffled could you be than that?

I was led into the living room, and a moment later I heard the clump of feet down the stairs as her brother Anthony came down in his pyjamas to join us.

"Hi Mike, I couldn't sleep" he said. "What's happening?"

"Alex is going to move over to live with me, and we've just come to get her clothes."

"At three thirty in the morning? Don't tell me – the exigencies of love! I don't think my sister will like this. What happened?"

"Alex's mother was lying in wait behind the door when I delivered Alex back after our... ...extended evening. When we were outside the door Alex had no intention of coming back with me. In fact, Anthony, the vibes I was getting were rather as if – well, it might all be over. I'm as amazed as you are."

"She's always had a will of her own, has Alex, and she was just waiting to win a fight with her mother up to now. Luckily for you, she just got one. She's contrarian, Mike, but what a gal you are going to be marrying!"

"You're telling me that Mum's appearance was a blessing for Mike Claver?"

"I am. If she hadn't been there, it might have gone another way. You never know! I think Letizia's being there made Alex's mind up, instantly. That Alexis! She's pretty speedy, isn't she? I'll smooth things out with her mum while I'm here for the next week. And I couldn't be more pleased about it. *And* I haven't told you yet about the Bishop on the golf green, have I?"

We were both roaring with laughter, now – the meeting with Marcus Andrews had obviously been successful.

Anthony looked so cheerful. "What happened?" I asked him.

"Well, we stalked him, Lucy and I, out at the golf club. He was actually on the eighth green, so we went out there to confront him. I claimed to have an important message from the Vatican, which is partly true."

"I'd have loved to be there, Anthony" I told him. "But only as a fly on the flag. Did he look like a startled rabbit?"

275

"Angry, too. I just went up to him and said 'Do you remember me, M'Lord?' He couldn't hold my eye, but looked away and said 'You have no business to be here. Go away or I'll call the Steward and the two of you will be seen off, maybe prosecuted for trespass.'"

I asked "What did you do next Anthony?"

"Lucy had warned me about standing there ranting, so I worked on the 'fear of fuss' platform. 'I've got proof here of our meeting when you were the Bishop's Secretary, and it is important for a case against Monsignor Peter Mobile. So could I briefly show you the evidence after you've finished your round, maybe in the Members' Bar?' I didn't give him time to say yes or no, Lucy's advice, so we scuttled back to the Clubhouse and waited."

"Did he ask you your name?"

"No, I think he knew me from your visit yesterday morning, Mike. The rest was anticlimax. He met us, tried to be genial, promised to be a witness if need be, and even said he was in favour of married priests."

"Do you trust him?"

"Absolutely not. He ignored Lucy completely, after warning her that she could not talk to him because of the legal case. But you know, if she hadn't been there it would have come out completely different. You were almost right, Mike – I could have socked him one whether or not I'd carried on drinking."

"What next?"

"As we left he became superior, so I was seething when we got our taxi back to the station. I'm afraid

I've been weeping again, Mike, but Lucy was a terrific comfort."

"What do you mean, 'became superior'?"

"That nasty little smirk was there when he said 'You know none of this can be a case in Canon Law'."

"What did he mean, Anthony?"

"Apparently there is a statute of limitation so that complaints from people over 30 are unacceptable. It took the edge off the feeling of success a bit, and makes me wonder what all that stuff in Rome about having a Socius was about. I'm going to find out what is going on. But anyway, I'll get these guys for what they did and the way they covered it up, one way or another, I'll get them."

He went on, recovering his smiling face.

"I'm applying for laicisation, Mike, a sort of de-priesting at an official level. I'm looking for a job, even before we nail old Mobile the abuser. Are you pleased about it Mike? Didn't we do well, thanks to your and Alexis' help?"

"It's gone so fast, hasn't it?" As I told him *our* news, Anthony's face lit up. "It's all over, Anthony" I told him. "Now we've got all the evidence you'll need for your case, even if they decide to fight it. Yes, Anthony, we've got the photo of the four of you naked in the refuge – the one you call 'The Pilgrims' – Kenelm gave it to us. *Plus* some ancient diocesan files. Amazing! One of the letters is about the complaint against Peter Mobile by one Anthony

Mulherin. So we could counter Marcus Andrews if he decided to play ignorant."

"Oh terrific, terrific!" Anthony was laughing and waving his arms in victory. "I feel so liberated, it's fantastic, so absolutely amazing!"

"I've not told it all. Peter Mobile confessed too!"

"What! No! Recorded?"

"No. But he seems to have given up on denying what happened. I know now that his *'I was a sinner but I strive to be a saint'* pose is ridiculous. But still, I think he will play it straight. Mind you, the guy needs to be pinned down. He admitted to hounding Tom to his death, but he never said a word about your accusation."

"I want him sent down" Anthony said.

In the kitchen Letizia was making noises as if the tea was close to delivery.

"Does your sister know about Peter Mobile?" I asked.

"Everything. I've told her the lot. Letizia is behind me. Actually she is not someone whom I'd ever have expected to hide behind the door to catch her daughter coming in late. But I've learnt it now, I think – what people say they *believe* and what they actually *do* can be very different. She couldn't help herself. She was worried about her daughter, as if she were still sixteen instead of over twenty-seven."

Thirty minutes later, after a lot of excited talk, Alex and I made our way back to my flat. My fiancée would be spending the next week picking up more and more of her belongings from her former home.

As we left the house mother and daughter hugged and cried a great deal. Setting off into the night, now brighter at the brown eastward horizon, I asked Alex whether her mother would come round to approval.

"Actually, Mike, she did say something which I think could be hopeful. As I was going she whispered to me 'Isn't his accent refined?'"

Next day, the Tuesday, Alex, Bill and I had lunch back at a familiar smart restaurant near Sloane Square.

"This is a special place for us Bill" Alex said. "It's where we met."

"Does it bring back sweet memories?" he asked. "Business please, business first."

I interposed "Just a minute my friend. We're having an engagement party before the summer exodus. Will you be our guest?"

"If you are still talking to me then, yes, I would be honoured. Business first. This is where the sticky stuff starts. Thank you first of all for the photo, Mike, that will be a clincher. We're checking out the copyright situation with the photographer's parents."

"God, I hope that you haven't used one of your idiot heavies to do that" Alex exclaimed. "I saw Tom's parents, and they are wonderful people. But they might well object to a picture of their poor dead son naked in your redtop rag. With all the hint of homosexual abuse. They need to be told about the whole thing and got on side or they'll be furious."

"OK, well why don't we use *you* to do it?" Bill asked. Alex agreed. Bill went on "What is the status of Father Mulherin's complaint with the police? Can we refer to it? Or is there a legal problem?"

"The law is not definite" Alex replied. "The identity of people who are abused is protected by law, but Father Anthony plans to sign a waiver. He wants the whole issue to be out in the open. Old abuse cases were supposed to be dead after six years, but because there was a death, even an accidental one, a public prosecution is possible. *Sunday Seven* will need a legal opinion on this, but probably you will be able to name names."

"You two are wonders" Bill said. "Now what about the status of any confession from Peter Mobile?"

"There is no confession as such. I didn't get a recording. Anthony thinks you won't need it", I told Bill. "It's more of a moral thing for Alex and me, you see. It makes it certain that Peter Mobile did something wrong. Anthony got something from Bishop Marcus Andrews, just his agreement that they did meet in 1982. Peter Mobile didn't admit to trying to abuse Anthony at my meeting with him, you know."

"I thought you had nailed him."

"Oh he mentioned Tom, and admitted he had driven him to his death, but that doesn't have any direct bearing on Anthony's allegations."

"But you know we'd be so much better off with a recording, wouldn't we?" Bill asked.

"We don't need it, once Peter Mobile has stopped denying he was guilty, Bill. Because the Roman Catholic practice in England is for abuser priests to plead guilty so that no witnesses are called. Much easier to keep all the details out of the papers."

"That's not justice, in some way. Well, Peter Mobile's face is going to be in the papers in connection with a photograph, long before he gets to prison. No, it's not justice. But now," Bill asked, "is that the business? You mentioned the other name on the letter to the Vatican, Bishop Andrews – is there any more about him and Anthony Mulherin? Are we going to be nailing him as well?"

Alex shook her head. "I don't think we can actually get him on the same ticket of covering up the abuse of Anthony Mulherin. There was a faint hope that Mobile had been moved out of the diocese because of further allegations of abuse, but we found no other cases involving him in the files. Peter claims to be a reformed character, and he would seem to be one. In fact most people regard him as a saint."

"With the exception of this person here" I said.

"I know" said Bill. "I always thought the wrestling business was a bit dodgy –he did make a pass at you, didn't he?"

"You know Bill, I don't want to talk about it." That word 'pass' is just one that is used to trivialise abuse, by men who grope or proposition others.

"I know personally now why people don't want to be identified in these cases of abuse" I explained. "Even a child will feel after the abuse that they were at fault for being naive. That's what you think, isn't it? I have only myself to blame? I can't explain it, Bill – but Alex knows. And I can tell you that the man is cruel."

"So he did make a pass at you, didn't he?" Bill teased. "Anyway, to get back to the Bishop – Marcus Andrews gets off?"

"Not if there is a civil case brought by Anthony for compensation for abuse" Alexis explained. "Then he will be called as a witness, and our possession of a letter about the meeting where Anthony complained will put pressure on him. Look – Marcus Andrews is not an abuser."

"But he was almost certainly complicit in this abuse case, like all those other Catholic bishops and their secretaries around the world" I said, rather loudly and strongly. "We don't believe you, those bishops said, we won't believe you, and if we have to accept all your evidence then we'll settle it by Canon Law – that was their response. Anyway, Alex may still nail him in the case she is supporting for constructive dismissal. Remember Lucy, the diocesan worker who was supposed to help people abused by priests? We wouldn't have found the right filing cabinet except for her. There were plenty of other letters in that filing cabinet you borrowed, you know."

"I really don't know what you are talking about" said Bill. "Surely that *is* all the business, isn't it?" We nodded. "Roll out the champagne!" he ordered the waiter, and we began to talk about Alex's' new, *real* personalised engagement ring, the one I had just bought her, and future wedding venues and dates.

At the end of a delightful meal Bill asked me to send in my invoice and expenses after we had got the story written. As I had suspected, that was the end of the assignment. Back to hard grafting at the PC, but now it was to be for my future wife and family and not just for me.

Sunday Seven's headline over my article that next Sunday was

DEAD TEEN LENSMAN'S FINAL PHOTO FOUND

Then there was the photo, 'The Arrows of Innocence'.

> *This picture is a collector's prize, the famous 'Arrows of Innocence' composed and taken by Tom Benson over thirty years ago.*
>
> *Prized by collectors of rare photographs, it also has a special place on the walls of the leader of the Catholic Pietas movement, Monsignor Peter Mobile, in his cell at their lavish headquarters in North London.*

It is called 'The Arrows of Innocence', and the Very Right Reverend Monsignor says that it 'represents mankind's highest spiritual aspirations.' The picture is used for teaching about sex by Pietas, who claim that it embodies the spirit of Catholic teaching. 'Readiness for sex, which is good, but only for its true target of conceiving children in marriage' was how one member described it.

'What about the nakedness?' I asked Monsignor Mobile when I saw the picture he so proudly displays in his room. He answered "It is called 'Innocence', and there's nothing else but innocence there".

Certainly Sunday Seven does not equate nakedness with impurity. Tom Benson's family were committed nudists, and his portfolio of pictures, now being valued for a possible auction, includes over thirty pictures of unclothed children of both sexes, as well as adult men and women.

A lot about Tom Benson's life followed, with a quote from his mother:

'He was such an outgoing loving boy. Everybody was surprised by his gifts of looking at the world and finding beauty.'

> *How then did Tom Benson meet his death, and why?*

Then there was my full report of the expedition to the Alps by the three teenage children with Peter Mobile, and the fall by Tom Benson and heroic attempt to rescue him by Peter Mobile. The local newspaper's report on the British inquest was quoted:

> *The Coroner praised the action of Father Peter Mobile in trying to pull teenager Tom Benson up from a crevice in which he was wedged in a tragic mountain accident in the French Alps in August this year.'*
>
> *"Father Mobile showed no concern for his own safety in scrambling down the rock face to bring the unconscious youth back to safety" the Coroner said. "Sadly, it was already too late to save Tom Benson's life."*
>
> *Does this newly discovered photo shed light on the tragedy?*

Then came the photo we knew as 'The Pilgrims'.

The genitals of the four young males in the Pilgrims photo were edited out, but it was clearer than clear that they were completely unclothed.

They were named:

> *Peter Mobile, Ordinary of Pietas in England, distinguished architect Kenelm Bates, Tom Benson, the dead photographer, and Father Anthony Mulherin, millionaire cleric.*

There was a last quotation from Tom's mother.

> *"I think it's right that the photo should be shown to the world. Tom was a proud nudist, and this is exactly how he would like to be remembered."*

> *Sunday Seven has not succeeded in getting any comment from Very Right Reverend Monsignor Mobile.*

My name as author was clearly visible, but there was no credit to Alexis Lecce: not even as a researcher.

I was almost shaking when we went into Letizia's home for Sunday lunch, fearful of Anthony's reaction as well as Letizia's. Letizia and Alexis Lecce had invited Anthony Mulherin, Lucy Peer and me.

I was right to be nervous. Letizia was extremely angry about the *Sunday Seven* story.

"It's so snide and weaselly" she complained, her face raised up in a pugnacious way even as I came through the front door. "This thing, Mr Claver!" She had the newspaper in one hand and the other hand was floating free, ready to hit me. Which would land on my head first? – why it was the rolled up paper, bashing the side of my head.

"Hold on Mum" Alex said, but Letizia stood her ground and went on, loud-voiced and accusatory. "It's about nothing!" she sneered. "It's a sort of clerical celebrity sex-scandal article, and what it has to do with justice I fail to see. Do you feel proud of what you have done, all of you, in making this scandal come out after all these years? And especially you Michael Claver in how you have written this?"

"Hold it, hold it Letizia" Anthony said without raising his voice. "I'm one of two who were abused and I'm pleased with it. It's a light brought to a very dark place, it's a blow against hypocrisy and it's something to make all the other abusers know that the truth will come out."

"It isn't justice" I said. "But Anthony and Tom Benson never had any justice done to them."

"We know one wrong doesn't justify another "Alexis interposed. "It was the best we could do in the timeframe, Mum, as far as getting the evidence goes. But Mike, what you put in the mouth of Tom's poor mother is downright stupid, given all the atmosphere of clerical abuse paranoia in the press. You didn't need to have that in there, did you? And she never said that, did she? She was proud of their nakedness?"

"Oh yes she did, Alexis, and she said it to you! And not as you are spinning it, either." I was getting angry: this wasn't fair. "You gave our report on your meeting, and I quoted it verbatim, as I did everything else. Don't forget, we both researched this story."

"Well, don't be surprised if Mrs Benson denies it later on" Alex shouted. "All the press will be down there by now, you know. I didn't do all this to have it hurt the one person in the world who was most damaged by Tom Benson's death."

"But this isn't logical, Alex. Read what I wrote, again."

I felt Anthony squeezing my arm, and looked towards him. He was signalling 'Calm. Calm.' "Let's hear what Lucy has to say" he suggested.

"My case has still to be heard, Letizia" Lucy said. "Maybe when it is you'll see that it *was* all fair even if Mike was a bit insensitive in what he reports that Mrs Benson said. After all, Bishop Marcus Andrews, who was my boss, wouldn't actually let me get to work on the files which were concerned with the cases about abusing priests. Including this one, as it happened. And he pushed me out to stop it ever happening. These clerics aren't after justice – they want to escape from justice."

"Come on Letizia" Anthony added to the argument. "Have you read the papers? The police in Belgium have just made a raid in Mechelen where they confiscated the computers at the diocese offices *and* the PC at the Cardinal's flat as well. They didn't wait to get permission, because that would have been a waste of time. The Bishop of Bruges has just resigned after admitting sexually abusing his nephew."

"But one wrong doesn't justify another" Letizia said, repeating what her daughter had said. "You're going to have to do something about this, you bunch of hypocrites."

Alexis picked up on it straight away. "We'll go down to see Mrs Benson at once." Turning to me she said "No need for you to come, Mike. Anthony and I will go."

Letizia was a little taken aback. "Have some lunch before you go, won't you?"

Alex made a move towards the table, but intercepted me and pushed me towards the hall and the front door. In a moment I was out on the pavement, as she shouted "Don't expect to see me again!"

I stood for a moment bemused, feeling I had been gashed and betrayed by my lover. Anthony came out quietly while I was still waiting there.

"Hey, women!" he said. "Maybe what they taught me in the monastery was right after all." He was behaving as if it would all pass over. I hoped he was right.

"Don't be seen to be on my side" I warned him, "Or they'll turn on you as well."

"Listen, I wanted to say that no matter what, come to Lucy's and my wedding next Friday week, will you?"

I signalled disbelief.

"Yes, we're getting married and I'm going to be a father a real one."

"Oh Anthony, I'm so pleased for you. But that is so fast – is this just a way of talking?"

"What do I know about these things, but we are going to try. It's our objective! We're making up for lost time and racing against the biological clock, ha! I'm sorry to sound so cock-a-hoop, Mike, but I'm sure Alex will come round back to you. So see you at the registry Office in the Kings Road at eleven-thirty precisely. Alexis and Letizia will be there. No references to God at the service, but you could be my best man, eh? I'm even planning a stag night on Thursday. Will you come?"

"Yes, of course!"

Letizia was at the door, and called "Anthony!"

"I'll ring you" I said.

Alexis managed to keep out of my flat until Tuesday, when she no longer had enough clothes back at her mother's.

"Did you get to talk to Mrs Benson?" I asked her.

"I did, but I don't want to talk about it. Ask Anthony."

She departed as crisply as she had arrived.

Anthony's stag night was graced by seventeen priestly chums in mufti, some of whom seemed to think they were daring in being there in a pub with a clerical renegade. To my unpractised eye they were rather a smart bunch, and they came from all over the world.

Anthony and I got together early, and he explained that by a lucky chance there was a patristics conference in Oxford on that very day, which had swollen the ranks of old friends attending the pub bash.

We were still talking out our glee at nailing the saintly abuser.

"You're happy now about Peter Mobile?" Anthony asked me.

"Happy?"

"That I wasn't making it up."

"I feel some of your hatred – no, I think that's the right name for it, Anthony – for that whited sepulchre. You remember what he said to you, which I can hardly bear to repeat?"

He made a mouth of disgust. "That? Oh yes. I heard exactly the same formula from him and Father David the school abuser: *'Remember – God loves you more than you love yourself'*. I don't really know when Peter Mobile said it, but it was when I heard it again from Father David that the disgust really kicked in. So you got the same phrase, did you Mike?"

"Yes, precisely. He used it on me, after our meeting. When I heard that, as a sort of special mantra he was giving me, I felt what you must have felt, Anthony. It's not just the abuse, it's the hypocrisy that is so disgusting."

"What about Mrs Benson?" I asked him. "How did it go?"

"Well, we admitted that you could have written it differently, or put it somewhere else in the article. Because of the context it seemed to suggest that nudism is really a perversion, which is exactly the opposite of what she wanted to tell the world. She was awfully angry, and I'm glad we went to see her. Couldn't you have written something different, Mike? You didn't need to mention her at all at that point in the article."

"If you knew" I replied "if you really knew what a battle I had with the editors at *Sunday Seven*. They're as big a bunch of anti-clerics as I am, or maybe worse now that I have met you and decided you're not *all* jobsworths and creeps. My piece was edited and edited down, and they took that bit out of context and – bingo! You know, I know, there was never anything there except simple goodness, but the stain of abuse has come off on Tom and his family, and made it look as if he was dodgy, like Peter Mobile."

"That's what has happened to the Church too" Anthony said, "As a result of all this abuse. Nail the abuser, that's my motto."

Before I left at the end of a merry evening hosted by *the millionaire cleric* (a tag Anthony did not like in the *Sunday Seven* article) Anthony asked me about his priestly friends "How many of my pals here do you think would like to see an end of the rule that priests must not marry? I'll tell you. From past research, the figure is usually over fifty per cent. Sometimes much more. It's over 75 percent for Austrian priests in 2010, for example. It's a tough life."

"And you are showing them the way, Anthony" I said.

"No way!" he answered. "I don't fool myself. I've got skills, but I also have money. They are not short of obedience, they're not into fornication or abuse or any of that, but they are short of money. Some of them could never get a job, you know, or at least we all think so."

That is nearly the end of this account of the sufferings of two young men abused by a priest, and the struggle of a much older priest to get justice.

I have reflected a lot about Peter Mobile's allegation that I was impotent, and that Sarah Louise had told him this. Why did he tell such a lie? Was it to probe whether I was really gay, and that was the cause of our marriage breakdown? Or was it that Sarah Louise had given him this version of events?

I couldn't think so. The whole problem had been too much desire on my part, and none on hers. If she had felt a need to paint things in lurid colours the easiest thing would have been to claim I was a husband rapist.

But you see, if she had indeed talked to Peter Mobile, that was the point at which I would draw the line and say 'It was not his business because it never anyone's

293

business except Sarah Louise's and mine.' Which was a defence that all the bishops clung on to in their dealing with the abusers.

Alex and I had unravelled the meaning of the Arrows of Innocence in ten frantic days, decided to marry and then had gone cold, and now we were to meet at the wedding of the whistle-blower who had set the whole thing going.

Anthony is the hero of our story. We hoped that because of his courage other clerics who had been abused might start to think about making public denouncements through their national legal systems, by-passing the ecclesiastical Canon Law system and merely photocopying their cases to the Vatican officials. Anthony's life had changed for ever for the better at that meeting in Rome when I sat with him and the Vatican Questor on a hot spring morning and he announced his decision to denounce Peter Mobile. He had a real reward from sticking to it despite the oath that he was forced to make to try to keep him silent.

What of Kenelm, who was so keen to oversee the decoration of what we had hoped would be Alexis' and my first marital home? Had he seen something that made him suspect that Peter Mobile had actually pushed Tom off the path?

"No, be sure, it *was* an accident" he said. "But the more I thought about it, the more I felt that the whole business of abuse in the Church was an accident waiting to happen, in the same way that Peter Mobile's running after Tom caused him to stumble and fall. We lay people have just not looked hard enough at what those priests were taught to believe. It was an accident that Peter and the three of us should all have been alone together in one room, you know? But the abuse was an accident waiting to happen. It is time to go for justice and transparency, and the possibility that we can have married priests. Don't you agree?"

We do.

Kenelm sent a special message for Lucy and Anthony's wedding, but he couldn't come. At the Kings Road Registry Office there were Alex and Letizia, a dozen friends of the bride and groom, thirty members of the Mulherin-related and Peer clans and me. Lucy was given away by her father and after the brief ceremony we went into a nearby hotel off the Kings Road and had a marvellous luncheon at the groom's expense.

I knew that negotiating contact with Alexis would be tricky, but to my delight she approached me as soon as she saw me and pushed herself into the seat next to me in the Registrar's. We held each other's hand. Outside, with her beautiful mouth erupting in gusts of laughter in sheer pleasure at being together again, Alex explained "It was the best way to manage things with my mother."

She has come back to me. Will we ever bring up our children as Catholics? It depends on her, but mostly it depends on what happens in the Catholic Church. One thing *is* sure: we will have a church wedding.

She led me to her mother. We looked at each other for a moment and then began talking at the same time.

"Has Alexis explained?" I asked her as she said "Alex has explained it all. This is not how it should have turned out, but we can thank the Monsignor for that. Anthony has done the right thing."

I wondered did she approve of his marrying Lucy as Alex chipped in "Letizia approves of Anthony's choice of wife, you know."

"I do indeed" Letizia confirmed. "But it is hard for both of them you know. Anthony's whole life has been the Church, and all his friends are scholars or high-up clerics, all over the world. This is a valid marriage, Anthony says, even in the eyes of the Church, but I know he feels some sadness about it."

"I think your brother has a lot of guts" I said. "He'll find a job to match his abilities I'm sure. But do you accept me as a suitor for your daughter's hand?"

"Yes I do, Mike. I forgive you for that awful article because I now realise it was the only way to get it all out into the open. But I do want my daughter to have a proper church wedding, Michael. Will you promise me that?"

"I do promise, Letizia, but you will know better than anyone that I can't answer for my fiancée."

Later I told Alex the sad news about Sarah Louise, my wife who never became my wife. She has entered a clinic for anorexia in Canada. But another way of looking at it is that she has a chance of tackling her troubles now, with the help of professionals in disorders which have everything to do with body self-image. How could someone like Peter Mobile think he had any expertise whatsoever in the area of marital love?

Alex said "Let's get the bad news out of the way, then. Lucy has abandoned her case for constructive dismissal against Bishop Marcus Andrews – it happened on Tuesday."

"I am sorry about that" I said. "How does Anthony feel?"

"He is reconciled to it, but his detestation of that particular cleric is as great as ever. But I told him, I couldn't ask Lucy to fight to the wire to show that the Bishop kept her from looking at the records of abuse, now could I? – not just for his sake."

"Maybe for the sake of others?" I asked her.

"Well, she did talk to Anthony about it, but she decided, as a good feminist, that she is entitled to a life which is not entirely dependent on Anthony, even if she is his wife."

"Is there a marriage settlement?" I asked.

"There's a contract, we're in the 21st century, Mike."

"Did you get a good out-of-court settlement with Bishop Marcus Andrews for Lucy?"

"You bet we did" she said.

My speech as best man included greetings from friends, and there was a large card from Kenelm Bates. I held it up and said "These wedding wishes come from Kenelm Bates and, in a way, from Tom Benson. This gives me a chance to tell anyone who doesn't know that Lucy and Anthony owe it to this photograph that they are here today as Mr and Mrs Mulherin. This study of young archers is called 'The Arrows of Innocence', and has since been published in a certain Sunday newspaper. You may not realise it, but Alexis was the person who re-introduced our wonderful bride and groom to each other. Yes, she was their Cupid, and used the very arrows we see in Tom Benson's photograph.'

"It was Anthony, in fact, who sent the picture on this card – don't worry, I'll send it round in a minute – to that well-known journal of romance, *Sunday Seven*.'

"What Kenelm Bates has done is find a second photo of the young archers which has never been seen before. It shows the scene *after the arrows have been fired.* I think we lost a great photographer when Tom died. Just look at the sheer disappointment, bafflement and despondency of the boy archers! Not to put too fine a point on it, the young archers weren't too good in their aim, and none of the arrows actually got anywhere near the target. Is there a lesson there?'

"The greeting to our bride and bridegroom from Kenelm and Tom is

> *'The bow work is beautiful.*
> *The firing is fun.*
> *Never stop trying'."*

As I conclude this story in the summer of 2010 we still await the visit of Pope Benedict to the United Kingdom. Is it any wonder that the country is so under-awed in expectation?

As I write, Catholic feminists like Alexis are not preparing welcome banners for the man who has just seemed to put sins of abuse on the same level as the 'sin' of supporting the ordination of women as priests.

We are near to the end of our story. Alex and I had been asked to find out how abuse had happened, and we had done that.

But the only point of finding it out is to make sure it never happens again.

The abuse in the chalet, the abuses all around the Church whether of a nephew by a bishop or of a whole bevy of orphans by clerics in institutions, all had happened because it was an accident waiting to happen. Men who have had no chance of having normal emotions, lonely young and old boys who have been set apart from ordinary life, pilgrims crossing an emotional desert in which they will never have to pay a bill or lie awake at night worrying about their children were surprised by sexual urges that had no place in their abnormal lives.

Anthony spoke out at last not for himself alone, but because he had lain in the dark and heard the suffering of another victim, and he had not turned on the light and halted him. Because of deference and fear he was left with a terrible guilt.

But he realised that standing by and washing his hands won't stop the abuse from happening again. Abuse which hurt children and those who loved them, and so hurt the whole world, will not be ended if the good Catholic laypeople do nothing.

Why has the Church been attacked again and again in this year of 2010 about this abuse? Because it has done nothing to deal with the pain it has caused in everyone's lives.

There will only be two ways for the Roman Church to go forward, as far as this atheist can see.

The most likely one is for the Church to decline and disappear in Europe and possibly worldwide as the old priests die off, so that it will just be a collection of hugely valuable real estate by 2040. As the priests disappear, Catholics will have lost the Mass they say is so important to them.

The other way will be for Pope Benedict to resign and admit that the model of unmarried, conservative priestly perfectionists owing unthinking allegiance to a non-fallible Pope has brought the Church to disgrace, collapse and death, while he was on the watch in

Rome. This is the admission of failure and repentance and opportunity to change that the world awaits.

It was before we sent off the bride and bridegroom on their honeymoon that Alex looked up excitedly from examining an incoming text.

"Oh tell Anthony and Lucy, Peter Mobile has resigned!"

Anthony's face was a study as I passed on the news, shaking his head from side to side in disbelief. We all embraced each other and Anthony wept a little, which was par for someone as emotional as he could be. But he whispered to me as he walked with Lucy towards the wedding car "I won't be happy until he comes to judgement in the Courts".

Like all of us, Peter Mobile is now going to have to wait on the decision of the Public Prosecutor with regard to Anthony Mulherin's allegations. Because of the fact of Tom Benson's death it is not so easy to dismiss his case after the decades-long delay.

If the official decision is to drop the case, Anthony will go straight on to a private prosecution. It is certain that it will not be contested.

Sacred sacred justice. Scared of nothing but fear itself.

Let justice be done.

END

FROM THE PUBLISHERS - ABOUT THE BOOK

The story and the people in it are entirely fictitious. There is no such position as 'Vatican Questor'. *Pietas* is a fictional entity.

The background of the clerical abuse scandals around the world and the debate about it are factual.

The two instances of abuse and denial of it in the book are based on the experience of the author and his friends.

Leo Cavanagh is a pseudonym employed to protect the identity of the abused.

OTHER BOOKS FROM 3SCORE PUBLISHING

Poems by June Osborne
Crisp celebrations of great paintings, especially Italian, ironic put-downs and a simple wonder at ordinary life, all in poetry that begs to be read aloud.

[ISBN 9780956402905, price £6.99]

Daisy walks across the Channel
by Peter Clifton For children from 8 to 80
An exciting 21st century adventure in which an English children's team tries to keep away from the lying Professor Fauvette-Graasmus's FOG TV News as they prove that Europe is more peaceful than it was in the 1940s – while walking for a week from Canterbury to Dunkirk to Brussels.

[ISBN 9780956402912, price £7.99]